Honey Watson

LESSONS IN
BIRDWATCHING

ANGRY
ROBOT

ANGRY ROBOT
An imprint of Watkins Media Ltd

Unit 11, Shepperton House
89 Shepperton Road
London N1 3DF
UK

angryrobotbooks.com
twitter.com/angryrobotbooks
Flesh of the Gods

An Angry Robot paperback original, 2023

Cover by Glen Wilkins
Edited by Paul Simpson and Robin Triggs
Set in Meridien

ISBN 978 1 91520 253 6
Ebook ISBN 978 1 91520 254 3

Printed and bound in the United Kingdom by TJ Books Ltd.

9 8 7 6 5 4 3 2 1

James

I

Fukuyama has defected. This does not matter. It is so insignificant that his enemy won't even know about it for months. He is just a man who has realized that he is being used, his requests for assistance ignored, his findings denied. A scientist lost in politics.

He had wanted to warn the others, show them the marks on his skin, describe the tremors in his mind. He knew he would sound mad and feared that he was.

He'd also considered, in a brief and humorless moment, whether he ought to pack his pillow. Does the resistance have decent mattresses? That is how he thinks of them, 'the resistance'. He is yet to find out exactly what they are resisting.

He only knows for certain that it has infected him. Whatever it is. Whatever it infects people for. A disease of the bone, a sickness of the mind. He is sure that he can hear it. As if it is talking to him, inhabiting him in a purposeful, deliberate way. A new facial tic, getting worse. He cannot tell whether its attention feels like punishment or love. He will damn well find out.

He stands now with his feet on either side of his suitcase, waiting. The city feels haunted. Electricity pulses through neon, unaffected by the mood.

The resistance, if that is what they are, have sent the foulest of them to collect him. She is instantly recognizable. The sight of her empties the streets. Curtains twitching, hands searching for each other in the dark, a squeeze to communicate their unspeakable fear. A desperation to fall asleep, as if rest could be an alibi.

She does not need the machete. Its handle bounces in her palm as she hits it against the bridge. A metallic echo. Don't hold theatrics against her, they don't let her out very often. She does not need the machete but she has brought it anyway because she really, really wants to use it. She watches the shadows, willing the others to try to stop her, give her an excuse to attack. They won't, which is a bad thing. She is running out of restraint.

He can smell the terror in his sweat and knows that she can, too. Her face half concealed in an orange strobe. A frenetic energy about him which she recognizes and does not like. His fingers clicking soundlessly at the end of a limp arm. Her eye focuses on it and he stops, had not known that he was doing it.

"Sorry."

He winces at the song of her laughter before it gets lost in the fog.

II

Achira sat on the windowsill of an octagonal pagoda. It was hastily made with concrete and steel, painted yellow. Barbs of twisting metal escaped its symmetry here and there; angular, without pattern. Accidental, uncorrected flaws. Achira used one of these to hang her shoes to dry. The slow, soft sound of the Crysthian Empire's official language staccatoed from the room in front of her. It is an alien tongue on this planet, but it is welcome nonetheless. Coveted, even, by its native inhabitants.

Achira was shouting, laughing. Enough of a smile in her voice to suggest humour, enough of an edge beside it to betray the effort of suppressed anger.

"This is not how we've been playing, Jasef." She held the corpse of a coffee mug to the light of their kitchen and the two men sitting beneath it. "And I say you lose this round."

"What are you talking about?" The man named Jasef responded.

"Jasef, don't be a git." The other made a pained beckoning motion to Achira as he interrupted. "You're gonna make the game boring if you're playing them rules."

"Exactly. It's supposed to be a break. Fun." She acquiesced to the gesture, came away from the drop which made him nervous, and took her seat at the table.

"You're not seriously blaming me for your inability to adapt to the native way of thinking?" Jasef.

"Oh, for fuck's sake." The larger man pressed his tongue to the vaporiser implant in his mouth, expelling a cloud of gently narcotic smoke. Even the most casual of observers would know that the smoker believes himself to be in charge.

Achira placed the shattered vessel in front of him. He excavated a handwritten note from the mug's remains with calloused, healing fingers.

Not Jasef, it read.

The game is disarmingly simple. Each of the five who inhabit this concrete hut will take it in turns to commit a micro-crime, leaving behind a note revealing the identity of the criminal when they do. A stolen shoe, a stained counter, a broken mug. All its discoverer has to do is find evidence other than the confession, than the mere fact of blame, to confirm its truth. A parody of the service they provide for the alien people whose planet this is.

"Jasef thinks," he said, faux conspiratorially, to Achira, "that he is the only one of us that understands the task that we perform every day. Imagine how horrible it must have been growing up with this kid. Think on him counting to three over and over again as loud as he possibly could and wondering why nobody wants him playing hopscotch."

"I do not see why, if you're so brilliantly fluent at Apechi thinking, it could possibly bother you when we use their rules to play a game based on the same system!"

"No, I know you don't, so listen instead of just doing the same fuck-annoying thing over and over." He took another drag. "It's a game, it's supposed to be fun, not frustrating and weird."

"Frustrating and weird. That's what the perspicacious Peter Pïat-Elementov will have to say of this planet upon his return?" A strange inflection pronounced on the surname. That is because surnames are unusual, a symptom of having descended from one of the champions of Crysth's most recent internal spat. In most situations, the name Pïat-Elementov would be impressive. Among these few however it is flamboyant and vain. A reminder, perhaps, that some may have had to work harder than others to be here. "You'll have a fleet of awards celebrating your contribution to the sciences. I envy you."

"Yeah, and I'll fly it straight into your fat head, you self-righteous cunt."

"Stop it, now," came the voice of a second woman with the unmistakable coastal accent of the imperial capital, "there'll be no cunts on a Tuesday. You're spoiling what would be an otherwise lovely evening of wishing we were somewhere else."

She emerged through the trapdoor which separated their kitchen from the rest of the tower. Peter relaxed as she rose, relinquishing authority, softening. Her expression was passive, always so, eternally jaded in a face of flat, toneless color which spoke of a complexion long and suddenly deprived of light, food, joy. A trait they all shared. She straightened herself from the floor and dropped a bamboo crate of bottles onto the table.

"How long you been listening?" Achira.

The newcomer smiled and turned to look through the window at the vibrant mist of Apechi night. It may have been the psychological effect of that drawl, the coastal accent associated so perfectly with the most beautiful part of the capital, but she always carried something of the sea with her. Nothing wild, nothing remarkable, just the kinetic effect of volume which inserts a certain peace into silences everywhere. That is one of the reasons she was elevated to the rank she now occupies. Another is that her name is Wilhelmina Ming. It's a meaningless surname, divorced from the culture it was taken from, chosen for covetous reasons by people who thought themselves masters of the new world. But she knows its power and so wears it in front of her like a shield. It cannot sneak up on her, it cannot be used against her. She hasn't answered to anything else since she was a teenager; she is always and only Ming.

"Any news where these came from?" Peter handed Jasef a bottle of the imported ale with a conciliatory nod.

She shrugged.

"Oh, you could have asked them for a news-paper," scolded Jasef. There is an odd pause in the middle of the portmanteau – he is not used to it. The panels which usually communicate news to the worlds various of Crysth have not been erected here despite a seemingly human population, Apech is not yet part of the empire. A burden lies heavy on the 'yet'.

"My meeting was..." she wiggled her fingers in a motion which indicated complication, tedium, "I hurried out."

"Ah. Sorry. How come you didn't take the train this morning?" asked Peter, pulling a chair out beside him.

She sat. "We didn't meet at the embassy."

There was a silence at this, a silence in which three pairs of eyes flicked at the black fingerprint which dirtied the maroon of Ming's lapel. Conspicuous in its apparent shabbiness, it made them strangely embarrassed to recall the identifying badges on their own formal uniforms – objects which brought them so much pride whenever out of the shadow of this lone, dirty mark. It outranks them by several orders of magnitude. They did not ask where she had been.

"Listen," began Peter, turning the ruined mug to face Ming, "Jasef has put the kibosh–"

"I have done nothing of the sort."

"Kibosh on this round of pagoda detective. Look," he offered her the note, which she read but did not take, "it isn't true! It was him."

Ming shook her head slightly as she took this in. "You know the rules."

"Ha!" Jasef.

"Yes, but it's not fun, is it? I don't want to bring that into the house with me." This is Achira. "If we do it like that in here too, I will lose my mind."

"Agreed." Peter, disappointed that Ming had not sided with him. "I like having some fucking proper logic up here."

"You are being Crysth-centric." Jasef.

"And? We are from Crysth, and they wish they were."

"We are really not supposed to think like that, P. That is sort of the whole point of us being here." Achira's tone was only a gentle scold. "But I know what you mean."

"You all know what I mean." A cloud of smoke eclipsed Peter's sulk. "We shouldn't have to police ourselves all the time. Not when it's just us."

Ming nudged him with her foot and smiled benevolently at Achira, who hated it. "Peter is right, but so is Jasef. There's no need to fight."

There's no need to fight. These are not friends. If they met before reaching this planet then it was only fleeting. A nod in the university's spiraling gardens, a shared bottle of wine at an end of semester party. They belong to different imperial factions and will serve different emperors; their distance is by design.

They are each very brilliant in their own way, though. All have been chosen from round after round of examinations, applications, psychological assessments, years of uncertain striving. Here they are at their worst, flung far afield and told simply to produce. To create a worthwhile piece of work alone. Return to the university empty-handed or return ready to make their case for entrance into the highest levels of civil service.

The exile is designed to break them. They know this.

A Crysthian observer might wonder if these few are serving their time in the monstrous, lonely grimness of Lon Apech because they have much more to prove than the rest of their cohorts. The others can be imagined whiling away their own exiles on planets closer to home, on planets with beaches and gardens and magic and beauty. One might suppose that these five are here because they were at the bottom of their class, or that they are contrarians, or that they are out of their goddamn minds.

"Yes. You're right. I am sorry for the remark, Peter." Jasef's apology happens only because it was Ming who suggested it.

"No." Ming, "Peter needs to be more careful with comments like that. You know they follow us; they are not the only ones being studied."

"Not here?" Jasef. "Surely?"

Ming shrugged and took a swig from her bottle.

"They do do shit like that don't they." Peter's voice was a whisper. "Speaking of which, has anybody seen Ar today?"

"What the hell do you mean 'speaking of which'?" Achira.

"No no no. I mean, just, Apechi don't like him, do they?"

Achira relaxed. "No, they certainly do not. They're not a particular fan of me, either." She looked up at Ming. "They like you, of course."

"It's my job to make them like me," All eyes to the fingerprint again. "I'll leave the ethics of it up to you."

Jasef and Peter shared a swift look of concern. Peter said, "Ar, where's Ar?"

"I'll go see." Achira.

Beneath their pagoda, the city sank and stretched in a seething web of painted concrete. Always burning, always growing, the artificial slab of its ground floor hammered into reality some distance above the earth. Here and there walkways leeched between architecture like metal vines. The blinding glow and steam of industrial labor burst through gaps in its impossible floor. Vents formed geysers of screaming waste which mixed into a constant fog. The refracted neon glow from giant proclamations of sales or comfort, brought here as gifts by imperial scouts fought for supremacy without the sun's arbitration. The star's low altitude forced it to cast only disorientating shadows against the turmoil of design which was so jealously lifted from the surface. Lon Apech was a capital modelled on capitals, a patchwork of empty monuments.

Achira's face reemerged above the waning iridescence of her uniform. "He's coming up for a drink."

"Nice. Hey, Ar." Peter pulled the beers towards him to detach one for their fifth and final member.

This is Ar. He is not like the others.

"Hello. Been writing?" asked Jasef, turning to watch Ar's unusually proportioned body unfold from the trapdoor.

Ar gave a half smile and tilted his head, *trying to*, the gesture said.

"Tough luck." Jasef.

"How's yours going?" Achira's question was directed towards Jasef, who did not have the sense to be humble.

"Excellently. Really excellently, in fact. The whole thing turned out serendipitously, my theories truly show their durability in a place like this. Especially since–"

"Good to hear," Achira said, "but let's not get into it, shall we? Ming's had a rough day too by the sound of it."

Ar looked sympathetically to Ming, whose maroon jacket matched the color of his shirt. Same faction. She just rolled her eyes, whatever.

They quarrel and laugh, form temporary conversational allegiances and make the odd, futile attempt at sign language in Ar's direction. He humours them, moving his hands in gestures which they pretend to understand. His pen and paper lie unused by his side. His difference makes them self-conscious, and they respond by patronizing him, reassuring him that they do consider him one of them. Sign language had been demoted from a requirement for entering the civil service to a higher-education elective within three years of the Muhr race's achievement of human status. There had been too many complaints from failing students.

That night, Peter fell asleep with his head on Ming's thigh. She lay still, watching his ceiling and waiting for the purring breaths of deep sleep to rumble through his chest before she moved him away. Outside, the tortured screams of a thousand caged birds were punctuated by laughter. She listened for a long time before shutting herself into her empty room.

A few hundred years before this montage of humanity would come to occupy their pagoda, the Red faction of Crysth's government had concluded the centuries long Data War with waves of destruction which ruptured the empire into four symbiotic sections, each of them with its own imperial figurehead: Red, Military, Green, Ethicist. It works.

All forms of private transport had been forbidden since the war. As a result, none of the planets under Crysth's control could be reached by individuals not affiliated with or permitted by the transport ministry – a sprawling and irretraceable sector which had come to dominate the flow not only of people but of information over long distances. All of it strictly centralized. Nobody who knows how the systems work is allowed out of the central palaces unwatched. They are mutilated as reward for their skill, fitted with a prosthetic jaw which allows them to communicate directly with the machines they command.

The force of the law extends to the ground of each planet in Crysth's protective, possessive grasp. Old ships, jets, cars – all collected and repurposed into metals for the development of railways and giant dirigibles to be distributed unfairly across Crysthian territories. Illegal vessels favoured by smugglers and the rich are still hunted with almost casual joy by Military captains in open space. Apech, having been discovered a mere forty years earlier, was not officially part of the empire. Nonetheless, its leaders had immediately fought each other for the right to obey Crysth's laws.

This was unusual. Their fawning brought distrust. The fact that they appeared but did not behave human doubled it. There's a magic in the air here, and Crysth has a certain paranoia regarding the strange, the unnatural, the unexpected. Space exploration will do that to you.

And so the only train on Apech, a gift from the empire, sped towards the city's central station with a clutch of Crysthian cargo. They wore their formal uniforms, representing each of the four imperial factions between them. Two maroon Reds with a midnight-blue Military sitting between them. A sage lined with gold uniform for the Green opposite them, and a pearl-clad Ethicist by the window.

Graduate rings from every university but the highest gleamed on their fingers. They were not looking at each other.

The machine coughed billows of thick white smoke produced by burning oil as it went, a native addition to its sleek design which did nothing but mirror the images of trains in pre-rupture Crysth. Its quaint bile disappeared into the city's fog as quickly as it spilled. The untamed demon which possessed the metal pulled it miserably along the track.

"Do you think it will be a long one?" Achira's fingers pulled at the silver-pink threads which complicated the white of her Ethicist's suit into a shade called pearl. The sentence was a question without the inflection of one, her voice too pained to rise.

"It shouldn't be. Pretty clear cut, really fast. The accused is guilty. Actually guilty, yeah. A *tama*," Ming turned to the other woman as she sighed, "but I'm going to have to call a commoner witness"

"Oh, fuck me," Peter.

"Can't avoid it." Ming flipped open the binder on her lap. "If we're all extremely nice to him, he might make it out of there alive. They are following our lead, after all."

"Pfft." Achira. "Don't say that. This is their design, not ours."

"Has the poor twat had anything to do with them before?"
Peter.

Ming shook her head, eliciting a hissing intake of breath in
response. It never went well when the aristocracy and their
subjects mixed. For the latter, of course.

"Will the ambassador or any of the embassy staff be along?"
Jasef, forcedly casual.

Ming looked up at him. "I doubt it." A warning not to pry.

The train stopped after travelling a negligible distance, its
machinations only necessary because of the bizarre topography
of the city's pedestrian routes; it would have taken them over
an hour to travel the same distance by foot. Rain moistened
their faces when they disembarked, a warm rain so fine that
it was difficult to tell whether it was just the whirling fog
congealing on their skin. Maybe it was. They all felt that it
should be raining.

At the very center of the city, the triangle prow of Apech's
court leered towards them through the mist. Modelled after a
photograph of a galleon long sunk on Earth's northern shores,
the Vasa's concrete crust glittered with industrial perspiration,
shimmering with colored light from the neon baubles arranged
around the square. Palaces and towers faced it, each as much a
hollow copy as the last, their interiors designed by minds who
had never seen a Crysthian home to serve as the residences of
the planet's aristocracy. They were already onboard. Waiting.

Beside the ship stands one of the few structures in the city
which is not fashioned after Earth. A suggestion of a man,
stories high. Peering eyeless onto the Vasa's deck. His features
are only vague, dreamlike. A different face from every angle,
all of them formed from the memory of Farön Kis. poised to
chase or to strike. A threat, a reminder of who and what had
won Apech's civil war.

The statue's distorted physiognomy is also a reminder that
the people who grew up on this planet see the world differently.
Something afflicts them, shows them intrusions in time. It lets

them play with it too. There is a volatility to their being that the Crysthian natives lack. It is this which brought Crysth here, on its endless search for unnatural things to destroy or to claim.

But the Vasa. It is huge, masts extending sixty meters high and equally as long, all of it formed from thick, glutinous concrete which gave it the appearance of a ship petrified, melted, impossible. No sails. Its masts are beacon of Apechi legislature and executioner's weapon both. Symbol united with function, an aesthetic inversion of the hollow palaces in their shadow. They are thick with justice, teeming with death. The steel rods point insult to the sky's eternal dusk with spiked tips, the three of them crowded even from this distance with figures at their base – human figures impaled and dead and dying and rotted. Here and there, clothing, the suggestion of flesh still clings to grey bone.

Lon Apech loves violence. It's kind of its thing.

Today, as always, the hull was mobbed by a crowd of locals. Too important not to attend a court date, too lowly to dare touch the ship. They are a theatre troop costume box ensemble of people; copying Crysthian styles but with no idea as to the time or context of the fashions they mirror. A nurse's uniform, a baseball helmet, spurred heels, suits of armor. A mysterious fondness for beads. They cheered and called in natively idiosyncracized Crysthian, thrilled to see the corporeal representatives of their integration into the empire arrive.

Ming led the way, always so – her cultivated apathy slashing a break in the crowd which the others, even Peter with his size and the deep blue garb of Military strength, were unable to mirror.

Here, on the haphazard strata of the capital's artificial ground, fog hemming the crowd around the ship, one could forget what sinks beneath it. Crysth's envoy barely sees the others, the born-doomed at work below. Lon Apech is a strange vacuum, hauntingly empty and yet filled with intangible things: light, mist, sound, cruelty. A population still recovering from the decimation of civil war.

"You're here, my friends!" Perfect Crysthian from someone who has spoken this language his whole life but has never been to the place of its origin. Always slightly odd. The words came to them the moment they were all stood upon the reeking deck.

Ming and Ar were the only ones able to keep their faces neutral.

"Distan, how are you?" Ming clasped his hand.

"Hello, hello, please, come up." His eyes met hers, something was unsaid. He nodded. She moved away.

Miré Distan invited the rest of them further onto the Vasa with a wave of his arm which he may have imagined was mayoral. He's stocky, heavily scarred.

"Peter, Jasef," he shook their hands in turn, smiled at the final two without extending a limb, "welcome."

And with that, most of the aristocrats were mingling with the Crysthians, outnumbering them six to one and gabbling with jolly enthusiasm, trying not to jostle each other with eagerness to be close to Crysth. Ar was noticeably alarmed, his big eyes always flashing for signs of violence whenever someone approached, keeping close to Jasef whose much smaller frame did less to conceal Ar than did his simpering politeness. Peter was mostly ignoring the attention around him, looking instead to two figures who had not yet moved. A man and a woman, leaning against the door to the galleon's interior.

Ming had gone directly to them. She had both of her hands between the woman's, who was talking to her in fast, low excitement. There was a possessiveness in the hands, she twisted the rings on Ming's fingers as confidently and comfortably as if they were on her own. The shade of her gown was like the maroon of Ming's uniform. As like as she could get, in fact. But Peter's attention was focused on

the man, who had not moved, who was still leaning quietly
against the ship's concrete. He behaves as if it is his. It is.

"Hello, Peter." The words sent a rush of embarrassed anger
around Peter's head. He had not heard them, just seen them
formed through the leaning man's mouth.

Peter saw the mouth move into a smile, the eyes look at
Ming, then back to himself. There is meaning in this. Or that is
how it feels. The woman gave a wave of delight when she saw
that Peter had noticed them. Ming nodded her goodbye.

Peter felt trapped. He could not ignore these two, and nor
could he control himself well enough to have a truly civil
conversation with them. But he had no choice but to try, and
so he defaulted to obedience. He marched, actually marched,
towards the couple before giving them a swift salute.

"Your majesties." He turned his wince into a game smile as
they laughed.

"Majesties, today, are we?" crooned Zara Ustra, wearing a
pair of spectacles on top of her head. Peter knew these to be
passed between the gentry as a token honoring whoever was
to preside over the court that day. Apechi people had no idea
what spectacles were really for, they just recognized them as
belonging to images of Earth's revered. It is easy to tell from
the way they blink when they wear them that the treated
glass does something quite unpleasant to their already strange
vision.

Peter smiled and exhaled a little laugh in turn, raising his
finger to indicate the spectacles. "You're in charge today, your
majesty." This was said with a smile, almost flirtatious. He can't
help himself.

She gave a giggle of delight and touched the other man's
arm. "I am! Isn't it amazing?"

Up close, you could see how much younger she was than
him, how much she adored him. Peter was foolish enough to
feel sorry for her.

"She is." The man spoke, revealing grey teeth in an otherwise carefully kept face and putting a strange emphasis on the first word. "How are you, comrade?" It is impossible that he does not know how much this annoys Peter.

Peter offered his hand. "Well, yeah, really well. Yourself?"

Xar Kis closed his eyes and inhaled deeply before replying, in a whisper, "Bored."

This word had the effect of knocking Peter's thoughts clean out of his mind. He tried to cover the evidence of his brief ego death by proffering his hand to Ustra instead, who shook it around between both of her own.

"We should," Kis' voice was still a whisper, not a whisper of secrecy or quiet, just as if he could not quite be bothered to raise his voice, "find something else to do with the five of you. I think we've already learned everything we could out of this little exercise."

Ustra pouted. "I think it's fun."

Kis was not looking at her, had not taken his eyes from Peter's. "Do you?"

"Erm. I think that enjoyment is beyond the purpose of the day's proceedings."

The planet's ruler laughed, once, a rising bark of ill-humored glee which sent his eyes flashing.

"What's funny?" Zara Ustra swatted Kis' chest with the back of her hand, which he caught and held to him.

"Words that mean nothing."

Peter wished he could hit him. More so, he wished he didn't know that he'd lose the fight.

Crysth does not know what these people are, quite yet, but they do know that for all the technological pruning and pumping that has been carried out in Peter's body, this older man can pick it apart. A symptom of the affliction. This is a reason, along with many more, that the empire is holding Apech at arm's length.

"That one's always very attentive, isn't she?" said Kis, after a while.

"You what?" Peter turned and realized that Kis had meant Achira. "Oh, I, yeah. She's, er, you know," he had no idea what to say, "into justice. The Ethicists, it's what they do."

The lines on Kis' face deepened as he lifted them into a grin. "Then let us not disappoint her. Shall we lead the way?"

III

The ship's interior is a copy of a drawing of a Crysthian courtroom. Squashed, elongated, not quite pentagonal as Crysth's official spaces are supposed to be, but recognisable nonetheless. A long, continuous bench spirals downward to a central platform where sit the judge and the accused, ostensibly equal before the law. Zara Ustra tapped her heels happily beneath her.

Opposite Zara sat the *tama*. A woman with a broken mind. The word means cursed, ruined, sacrosanct. They are the last physical evidence of whatever it was that had brought the Crysthian scouting party's magical compass shuddering towards Apech decades ago. It used to be that Apechi lost half their children to it – a creeping ailment which leaves a prepubescent either with altered vision or an altered intellect. Now it claims fewer and fewer as the magic weakens or dies. But it isn't gone, and Crysth is naturally suspicious of anything unnatural; a result of having spent centuries encountering the horrors of the unknown universe. They will not allow Apech into their fold until they know what it is. Was.

Apechi treat the *tama* as toys, empty vessels. To be shunned rather than mourned, hated rather than pitied. The one in the center of the courtroom is utterly doomed and has no way of understanding why. She whistles.

Peter was desperate to disentangle himself from the company of Xar Kis but couldn't catch Ming's eye in time. She sat behind the aristocrat, and Peter settled unhappily next to her while she leaned forwards, whispering into Xar's ear. The others joined one by one.

"Look who's here," Jasef murmured, indicating a man in a grey three-piece suit on the other side of the room.

"Shit. At least we won't be bored." Peter.

"Bored?" Achira, from Jasef's other side. "There's someone's life at stake here."

"Is there, technically?" Jasef. "It's not as if she might... you know. Survive."

Ar lowered himself to Ming's right. He is almost unwelcome here. His visible inhumanity insults the Apechi court and will do so for as long as he is Crysthian while they are not.

Ustra stood on the bench and clapped her hands together before trilling, "Where's Niko?" and waving at the woman who answered. "Amazing! Come start."

The one named Keh Niko adjusted her tartan beret with an air of self-importance before joining Ustra on the lowest platform. The room watched her circle the *tama*, standing oblivious in her shackles. It was a performatively anticipatory silence. Niko grinned at Ustra, nodded. "It's the same one."

A round of what sounded like applause, directed at Ming. They know they should make the noise but not the mechanics of making it. They snap their fingers, tap their arms and feet. None of the Crysthians have corrected this, out of terror of social awkwardness.

"Well done, Ming!" called Ustra. "Now will you come tell us what she did?" As Ustra spoke, she played with a silver spike which hung from a fine chain around her neck. It's a railway spike, a talisman of her grandmother's leading presence when Crysth installed the train.

Ming said, "Certainly. At least I can begin. I will need some help making it all the way to the end."

Another theatrical noise from the crowd, a hum of playful expectation. This is a social gathering.

A man in a black dress began to raise his hand. "Is the end now?"

"No, the end's when the accused is executed." Another.

"She is executed, though." Someone else.

"No she's not, she's right there."

The other looked at the *tama*, puzzled but acquiescing. "I suppose... so. But it's only a matter of waiting."

"By that logic we're all dead and it's only a matter of waiting." Ustra, delighted that they were already playing. Younger Apechi, and those closest to the embassy, are better at thinking about time in the same way as Crysth's envoy. "It's the waiting that's important."

Achira's pen flurried across her notebook as she recorded the disagreement. She is looking for clues about how their visions affect their perception, not because she has to but because she wants to.

"Are we dead?" asked Miré Distan, turning to the Crysthians.

"Not yet." Ming.

There was some contented agreement from the crowd. Not dead.

"The end," Ming began again, "is right here. Now. What you decide to do after now is the next part."

Ustra wrinkled her nose. "But Keh Niko said that—"

"I saw that one dead." Niko interrupted, pointing at the *tama*. "Up there." Pointing at the ceiling.

"Yes but that has not, as of this moment, happened," assured Ming. "It still might not. That's why we call them the accused rather than the executed. See?"

"Yes. Well, but it has happened somewhere." Someone else.

They agreed before Ming said, "That somewhere doesn't necessarily have to be here."

Mass confusion, in which Kis turned to Ming with a smirk. "Stop teasing them."

Ustra raised her voice over the collective bewilderment to say, "Amazing! We all agree that everything has happened somewhere. We just work out what was here."

"Keh Niko," called the grey-suited man, "may I ask how you know how the thing you saw did happen 'here'? Where exactly is 'here'? You know sometimes these things don't quite happen."

The man's voice had inspired everyone to glance in failed surreptitiousness at Xar Kis, who gave a tiny nod to Niko before she answered: "Erm."

"Don't look at Xar!" Ustra complained. Beating the railway spike against her hand with every syllable she added, "I'm in charge."

"Sorry Zara. Erm. It was upstairs."

"See?" Ustra waved the spike at the grey-suited man in gratified accusation. "Upstairs."

He did not respond.

"And it was definitely her," said Niko again, gaining confidence in the man's silence.

"Amazing! So it's settled. Ming, tell us what she did." Ustra.

Achira raised her hand. "Would the gentleman care to explain what he means by saying that sometimes things don't quite happen?"

"No!" Ustra sang, grinning. "He wouldn't."

Before Achira tried to insist Ming said, "Do you all want to know what the *tama* did?"

A round of not-applause.

"So." Ming flipped open her folder with a conclusive snap. "I knew from Niko's description that the accused had to work within a metalwork cylinder." *Tama* can be directed to perform simple, repetitive tasks. They have identifying uniforms, but they get tattered and torn and decorated with whatever appeals to their ruined minds until the display offends someone enough to fix it. The one in the Vasa's center wore a beige jumpsuit with scraps of shining metal pushed into the fabric. The pieces must have caught the skin a little, but she did not seem to mind. She shook them from time to time, admiring the light. "And luckily for me there are only a handful of these which are staffed by *tama*. I took photographs of all of those matching the description," – ancient instant cameras were one of the few devices which had been approved for use on Apech – "and returned them to Niko."

"She was easy to spot," confirmed Niko. "Look at all the dazzle on her." It was clear from her tone that she did not approve of the dazzle.

Remarkably, the *tama* seemed to understand this. She looked down at her sleeves. She seemed self-conscious.

"But what did she do?" said someone in the crowd.

"Well." Ming snapped her folder shut again, disgusting the other Crysthians just a little by playing into the drama. "For that I need my witness." She raised her voice. "Taer Agan?"

Heads turned in the direction of her outstretched hand. A man lingering on the topmost bench, as near the exit as he could politely get. He's dressed in pink, extremely new and clean. Absolutely terrified.

"Thank, er, yes," he warbled.

"Come down here." Ustra. "Join me." This is a taunt.

Agan clearly dared neither to disobey nor to stand too near the woman who spent all her time beside Xar Kis. He dawdled awkwardly by the *tama*.

Peter leaned forward to watch him. Agan lacked the physical self-control of the aristocrats, either from fear or lack of learning it. He moved with an occasional twitch, a sudden lurch. A nervousness around the hands and eyes. Evidence, perhaps, of not quite being able to tell what's real.

"Ming, remind us, where are witnesses supposed to stand when you do this on Crysth?" Ustra.

"Achira is the expert," Ming responded. "Where exactly should this particular type of witness stand?"

"Where he is is fine." Achira cursed herself as she realized she had missed an opportunity to let this poor man go back up where he was more comfortable. Most of the bullshit she tells them is bullshit crafted to make life on Apech slightly less awful, but it never works.

Ustra said something under her breath which was likely to be *amazing* before beginning again. "So? What have you got to say."

The dawdler peered at Xar, who had turned around to talk to Ming again. Something about getting a radio working across the city. The ambassador had been resisting this, until she realized that the Apechi may not even suspect that she could monitor it.

"Stop looking at him!" Ustra. "Speak up."

"I. I help your Ming." He pointed to her. "To find what the *tama* done wrong."

"We know." Ustra aimed her spike at him. "She said that already."

Achira cleared her throat. "In the Crysthian court system, that might count as intimidation. You have to be nice to him."

"I am being lovely!"

Ming applied a gentle pressure to Xar's arm which stopped him from intervening.

"Of course you are, I'm just providing a helpful reminder not to point spiky things at anyone." Achira.

"Anyone?" Ustra repeated, incredulous. The building they were in was, essentially, a spiky thing to point at everyone.

Ming covered her face with her folder.

"I think what our guest is saying," the grey-suited man, "is that we do not need to threaten anybody with harm. Or indeed carry out harm at all."

"Exactly." Agreed Achira.

"I fear our guests are being somewhat too spirited with us, today," Xar said. "Peter's uniform is enough to tell us that the threat of harm is a necessary part of imperial cohesion."

Peter looked down at the treacherous deep blue of the Military faction. "Uhh."

"I'm afraid so," agreed Ming.

"Amazing! Now you," the spike returned to face Agan, "say stuff."

He made a sort of cosmic horror noise before saying, "She takes things."

"What things?"

Ming decided to interject. Not to spare Agan the torment of his position, but because she was getting bored. "Agan is the foreman of the factory she works in. He showed me to her dormitory. The shards you can see on her clothing are part of a much larger stockpile. She has been hoarding tools, sheet metal, this manner of thing. She is a thief."

The crowd took up the word. Thief. This was exciting, this was an actual crime. There was a word for it.

"Achira," called the grey-suited man, across the room. "If I may ask – do Crysthian courts execute those found guilty of theft? I don't believe they do."

"But we do," Kis.

"I was under the impression that the point of this exercise was to familiarize ourselves with a new system."

"The point of this exercise is to dispense justice."

"And the justice dispensed – should that be an execution, for theft? Achira?"

Achira's heart leapt. She shook her head.

Pandemonium.

"That's not strictly true," corrected Jasef, "we assess crime on a case-by-case rather than categorical basis."

"Jasef you absolute twat." Peter, not quite under his breath but drowned to alien ears by the relief Jasef's proclamation had stirred.

"Case-by-case!" Ustra.

"And it strikes me," added Kis, in a low voice which silenced the room, "that here we have two."

"Two?" She took off the spectacles.

"Yes." he hissed, looking straight at the grey-suited man. "One *tama* guilty of theft, and one foreman guilty of neglect. We'll deal with that later, I imagine."

Agan quivered in his spotless new boots.

"Amazing!"

Ming emerged from the hull into the swirling, dancing darkness of Apechi midday almost half an hour later than her peers. She searched the deck, found Achira's shining pearl suit and started towards it. The other woman's face was turned towards the grey-suited man, yearning to speak to him but knowing that it would cause more trouble than her satisfaction was worth. The locals made her research hard enough for her as it was. They were sick of her interest in the *tama*, bored by her questions and diabolically yawnsome at her responses to their own. Apechi consensus seemed to be that the Ethicist faction were up to no good. She was sidelined and ignored, but not as much as Ar, who was still stuck to Jasef's side as the latter chattered away at the crowd. Peter watched for Ming.

"What did they want down there?" he asked, shuffling along the lumpy concrete ledge to make space for her beside him.

Ming rubbed her thumb over the mirrored sword on his lapel and tilted it to her face, "Oh, you know. Miscellaneous." She sat, raised her voice; "Do it."

"What?" replied Peter, but Ming was looking at Achira.

Achira turned. "Do what?"

"Talk to Rama. He's a contrarian too, you'd get along. I've worked with him before."

"Rama. Is that his name? Grey suit? What do you mean contrarian?"

"Ed Rama. You saw. He lives a few minutes north of the

embassy, in a rust-red building that looks like a fort. It's worth seeing." She hoped the inevitable rejection at the end of this journey would be enough to end Achira's curiosity. "Gets on Kis' nerves just for the sport of it."

"Why's he after doing that for?" whispered Peter, excitedly conspiratorial.

But they were distracted from Ming's answer by a chorus of laughter – movement on deck, the crowd suddenly thrilled that it was time to enjoy justice rather than just perform it. One seized the opportunity of this distraction to start snapping the fingers of one of the impaled corpses. Rotten flesh moved on its arms as he twisted the bones this way and that, spattering the more decomposed dead below with new vitality. The Crysthians froze, barely breathing, sickened, ashamed, trapped.

Zara Ustra waited in the middle of the deck, grinning broadly. The victim was not worthy of being brought up through the entrance to the courtroom. She was dragged, by the same chains which had tethered her in the hull, underneath – briefly sending her last screams to the sympathetic floors below – and over the side of the ship. When she emerged she was covered in new, rancorous welts. She fell into a shapeless, moaning heap on the deck.

Miré Distan stalked towards the base of the mast, losing some of his flamboyant composure to the excitement of the day's real purpose. Xar Kis followed him, his hands clasped behind his back. Their behavior would give anyone the impression that the former was, in fact, the commander among equals. And then something in the cold, almost irradiated irrevocability of Kis' personality would swarm to light in the distant authority of his bearing – the way he walked as if nothing could ever get in his way.

"Miré, the wheel!" He began to turn the ship's wheel at Ustra's command, glancing at Ming to make sure that she had noticed that it was he who had the honor.

It turned, with a groan of rust against concrete, it turned. The new chain which Ustra had attached to the woman's hands began to tauten, lifting her up with a deafening grinding of metal churning out into the fog. Her feet, her toes left the deck and the crowd lashed out, cheering at her dangling, screaming body as she ascended like a spirit into the sky. One of the younger was lauded with yells and laughter as he leapt into the air, hanging onto the *tama's* foot to dislocate her shoulders as she rose. Swinging unnaturally now, her screams were sickeningly garbled as if something liquid had broken inside her. In steady lurches, three feet at a time with each turn of the wheel, she was hefted to the top of the pointed mast.

Ming was the only Crysthian still watching her rise. The others looked around at their hosts, perhaps with hatred, perhaps wondering how they were going to forgive themselves.

An expert in preserving tortured life waited at the acme of the Vasa's tallest mast. She had perfected the art of piercing a body without silencing the screams which came from it, without extinguishing the life inside. She was a shadow in the dark, a mohawk and a long flowing tunic in the fog. Could mistake her for a hipster on Crysth. She would manoeuvre the unmoving mast, or rather, manoeuvre the struggling body around the mast, through skin and past organs and intestines and bone to leave a wound that would bleed, fester, rot. No joy in a guillotine.

Nobody saw the moments in which the mast was burrowed through the *tama's* torso – the executioner was hidden from view behind her lookout. The anticipation of concealment made the cry from the waiting courtiers even more furious with the relief of sadistic yearning when the body slid, impaled, down the pole. She slithered jerkily downwards, retching with pain and aiding her own terrible descent with mad wrenching of her arms and attempts to pull herself back up.

Achira glanced over the galleon's side to see the excitement of those who had come simply to watch. Each of them looked around for their own legitimate distraction. All, except Ming – who still stared unflinchingly at the body in its throes.

IV

The train was waiting for them when they finally made their exit. Jasef and Peter had already moved through an argument into silence. The former had delayed their departure by staying to talk to the person whose vision he was currently investigating. "Unconnected to this case, apparently," he had said, as if this information was what his colleagues had been waiting for, rather than to flee the reeking death and shame in the Vasa's shadow.

Lon Apech's central throng had begun to thin, too. The commoners of Apech were retreating; curious but unwilling to be anywhere near the Vasa when Xar Kis made his descent.

The man's father had been a master of the war, formidable and commanding, adored and feared as the unifier of Apech's disparate peoples. His father drew crowds. His father had a plan: Priest murderer, altar smasher, pyre builder, architect. Xar had one too – but he believed himself born for it. None of the striving and speechmaking which had made his father who he was: just certainty. Utter, complete faith in himself and his right. It made him unpredictable but for his fondness for the girl Zara Ustra. Those who remained in the square as the Crysthians departed were those secure enough in his service not to irritate him with their gaze. Some of them went out of their way to bow to Ming, only Ming.

At the limits of the square's tight fog, the mottled shapes of central palace buildings suggested themselves with odd refractions of light. The bases of looming columns, statues draped in cloth. Mist roved among them, rolling glimpses of neon and spurting vents around the corners of visibility. Concealing and revealing. A damp, living veil. To the north, the late sun began to fight its pathetic battle against the city's towering ground level. Pinpricks of gold shocking their way through gaps in the lifted floor. It was the largest open space in the city, hemmed in on all sides by the mansions of the planet's most feared.

The incongruity of the locomotive was strangely comforting after the Vasa. Shining, precise, smooth metal winding through the hollow city.

The train was inconsistent in speed, accelerating to a running pace to travel straight between mock pyramids and cathedrals, slowing to crawl around smaller, higher pagodas and tree houses perched on oaks of steel. As they slowed, Achira heard Peter mutter, "They think this place is a fucking joke."

She followed his gaze.

Outside, a group of Crysthians disturbed the city's jumbling architectural emptiness with their presence, their administrative uniforms marking them out as some of the temps who lived and worked within the embassy. They were painting what looked like a tiny amphitheatre brightest, nauseating pink.

"For gods' sake," she said, "it's not even funny."

"Is it supposed to be a joke?" asked Jasef.

"I'm sure it is," answered Achira. "Children, they are."

She was only half wrong, it was a sort of distraction; a task not unlike their own which satisfied the Apechi desire to monitor Crysthian behavior. Lon Apech's natives had no real understanding of the pictures, books, histories they had been given. They would get things so nearly right, but so terribly wrong. As if to mock this – and, yes, really to mock this – the Crysthian envoys which worked temporarily for the embassy had taken it upon themselves, in their quest to *spread the benefits of the Empire's progress scientific, moral, and aesthetic,* to paint Lon Apech's copies of the old Earth's buildings in absurd colors. Luckily, these strangely sad creations were barely visible against the city's constant darkness. Projected light detoured through fog into long shadows over every street.

"They are not stationed here long enough. It shouldn't be allowed, I plan to write a paper about it upon my return," agreed Jasef. "It's all well and good to have temps on the established colonies, but these part-timers do us a disgrace here."

An awkward, introspective silence followed.

Their sense of unhappy similarity to the embassy temps, people who would not be allowed anywhere near the palaces of government back home, was deepened by a certain awareness of how much more useful they were to Apech than themselves. The students are all too well brought up and too rigidly schooled in the art of neodemocratic politics to outright believe themselves superior to the embassy staff, but they do feel that this is a backwards sort of arrangement. The temps make constant interviews with the locals, help put up structures, go on excursions to the remaining forests – which, granted, Ar is often invited to join on account of the nature of his ecological research – and in so doing uncover much more about the hidden past of Apech than the students who outrank them ever could. The students are watched much more closely. Kept in the company of the aristocracy so that the vernacular Crysthian of people like the foreman at the trial cannot offend their imperial ears. It had been a mistake to allow Apech to know what the embassy's internal hierarchies were made of. The difference was so great that Achira was sometimes forced to conduct interviews secondhand, visiting embassy staff whose unabashed delight at withholding information from an Ethicist caused her as much trouble as anything else in the city.

Ar waved a hand in the air, using the opportunity of their silence to indicate that he wanted to speak.

"What's up?" Peter folded his hands between crossed legs.

Ar pointed to Achira, *did you,* then to her eyes, *see,* he paused for a second, cut-throat gesture, pointed to his arms.

Achira ran her tongue over her lips. "Did I see…?"

Ar smiled ruefully with his tiny mouth and took out a notebook: *Did you see the executioner's arms?*

"What say?" asked Jasef.

"Did I see the executioner's arms."

"What arms?"

"She has arms, Peter." Jasef.

"Yeah, obviously she has arms I mean what about 'em don't I, I know you know I did."

"Stop." Ming. "Achira and Ar are talking, you are being rude."

"Honestly Ar, I try not to look up there."

Ar nodded. He wrote and handed the paper to Achira, who read it aloud: "She is burned. Badly scarred. Left side of face gone. No eye."

"Yeah, I noticed that. I'd torch the evil shit too if I had half a chance."

"Peter, shut up." Achira this time. "What about her arms?" Ar released his notebook again for her to read. "Tribal scars, looks like. Ordered, regular, purposeful. All down her arms."

"No?" Jasef tilted his head curiously. "How old is she?"

Ar shrugged, gestured at his face, *no face.*

"I wonder what that's about?" mused Jasef. "Perhaps I shall ask the ambassador if an interview could be set up between ourselves."

Peter fixed him with a gaze of utter disgust, "If you can sit in a room and be peaceful with that murdering, torturing cunt I will personally break—"

"P." Ming, quietly warning tone. "We are all involved in this. Remember. Jasef, drop that idea. They don't let her out very often. Only for the executions, and even that's a mistake. She's a liability."

Jasef's brow wrinkled in confusion before he asked, "Who is 'they'?"

"Never you mind."

Solemnity settled over the carriage once more.

"Anyway," said Achira, watching the side of Ming's face, "I doubt she'd tell you anything even if you could get the interview. You know how they are."

"Speaking of how they are, what was that with your Ed Rama? We haven't spoken about that yet."

"Nothing more than court squabbling." Ming.

"There's only room for one boss and Rama does not like it." Peter.

"But he was so…" Achira began, opening and closing her fingers in silent quest for the word. "Different. He has been before. Different, I mean."

"I did suggest you speak to him, didn't I. Like I said, he's just contrarian. Might have something interesting to offer about the *tama*, though."

This was a peace offering, and Achira understood it as such. It was also, Ming believed, a lie.

The train picked up speed through a district of large, waterless fountains peppered with aviaries. The trapped birds made Ar deeply unhappy. He had rescued one as a stand-in for the rest.

They mounted their pagoda, their sanctuary. Its entrance hall – at the top of a long, spiral staircase – was decorated with minimalist posters whose symbolic plainness was designed to generate imperial solidarity. Four kites of the thrones. Black hand of the ambassador. A cadet's chevron. A general's star before the intersecting lines of their troops.

The first two floors housed their bedrooms, cramped affairs

which made them pine for the apartments back on the capital planet. The third was occupied only with the kitchen and their writing desks, where they would conduct the research projects which were their primary purpose on the planet. Their precious papers, the jewel of their exile which would serve as application for their careers beyond the confines of the university system, lay heaped around the room. Jasef climbed straight to this topmost floor and flipped open his notebook, full of photographs of the most impressive Apechi attempts to recreate Earth's architecture. His project, *Apechi Assimilation; a Master-Peace,* was already half written. The others had to beg him not to allow the natives to read it, suggesting that it would endanger those whose topics were less sympathetic to them if the tradition caught on.

Ming followed, herself wondering whether it was worth tipping Achira off about the photograph she had left with the *tama*. The Ethicist had been working on their behavioral patterns, trying to find some logic in their fascinatingly unpredictable, unlikely minds without arousing the suspicion of the planet's aristocracy. Unable to consistently do so, she was engaging in a thorough assault on existing species evaluation discourse while using the *tama* as an example of its failure. Her application to the rank of judge, Ming thought, was all but approved.

"Ming?" She did not start at Peter's unexpected voice behind her but turned slowly to face him. He had tears in his eyes.

She lifted his left hand and kissed it. It annoyed her that he came to her when he felt unhappy. Or happy, or anything for that matter. But this is what she had to do, while she waited to go back to the coast.

"Are you working today?" she asked.

"No," a whisper, "I can't."

"And I don't want to."

He looked at her through the mist of his unexpected, delayed despair, watching her eyes search his own, fall to his chest, to her own reflection on his lapel. She moved her thumb over his palm as she thought, seeming to him already so much like the commander she would be. That impression was not solely born of his adoration for her; the ambassadors really did look alike. You would not mistake them for relatives, but they all had a certain disarming plainness about them, severed by an unusual quirk in structure which drew the eye, made the onlooker think about their face rather than their words. In Ming, this was a cupid perfection of the upper lip arching somehow unprettily above a dimpled chin.

She looked back to his face, saw a tear fall, kissed him.

He sniffled a little.

She tutted and, soothingly, said: "Do you want some drugs?"

He managed a sad nod.

"'Chira!" Ming yelled, dropping his hand suddenly.

"What!"

"Must you all?" Jasef lifted one of the flat speakers of his headphones from his face and frowned at them. Another retro device.

"Must we what?" Peter bristled, forgetting his temporary lapse in composure.

"Shouting!"

"I supposed you would be heading back out, Jas." Ming began to rummage in their refrigerator, which had been brutalized in its journey between planets, for wine, vodka, whatever.

Jasef sniffed. "Yes. But I still don't see why there needs to be all this noise all the time. Oh my, you are not all going to start drinking now, are you?"

Achira's face popped up in the refrigerator-shaped trapdoor. "I said what."

"When?" Ming.

"Just now!"

"Then why are you telling us?" Ming shook a bottle at Achira's temporarily disembodied head, which rolled its eyes. "Cubes?"

"Oh thank goodness. Coming right up." Achira grinned and ducked out of sight.

"You are all shameless." Jasef looped a polaroid camera around his neck, making himself look like an ad for forgotten technology. "If I come back and find you all dead then I shan't be shocked."

"Better dead than be listening on you mate." Peter raised a bottle of rancid pre-mixed spirit to Jasef's retreating back and blew a ring of smoke around his head. A mane of defiance against propriety.

Ming quietly disliked both of them as she settled into her usual seat at the table.

"Look," Achira held three red cubes, "but we better eat first, or they'll send us sick."

Peter nodded *fair-enough* and started rifling through their cupboards for non-feathered sources of food. The idea of cutting meat made his stomach turn.

Almost an hour later, Achira finally unwrapped three of the single-use cubic stamps. The cubes contained a narcotic substance which was effective as a hallucinogenic mood elevator to almost every race under the empire's giant wing. They each took one, thrust it hard against the wrist of their other hand, and waited. Peter and Achira clinked their glasses together and began chattering in happy anticipation of the cube's amber, knowing that Ming preferred to stay quiet while it came. Ming stared at the tiny slit it had made in the skin of her right wrist and poked it on either side. The wound opened to reveal a perfect oval of scarlet under her skin, but did not bleed. She allowed her mind to wander on the subject of coagulants until she could convince her eyes that she could see the drug frothing among her veins. She looked up and smiled at her ersatz friends, whom she had forgotten that she despised.

Peter said, "Hey – you know that fucking weird shit with Kis and Rama? Reckon they're having a duel right now or something? I'd love to see that." He swiped his arm like a sword in the air as he spoke. "I bet they fight like, fucking, praying mantis wizards. I bet they fuck like it too."

"Want to find out?" Ming.

Peter made a noise of disgust.

"Not even Zara?"

"Ming," Achira grimaced, "don't be revolting."

Ming winked. "You can't pretend she isn't beautiful."

"She's maybe twenty years old."

"So were we once."

Peter, sensing an argument and working distraction, said; "Okay fuck partner kill: Xar Kis, Zara Ustra, and... the executioner."

"Oh gods. Foul." Achira appeared to think about it nevertheless. "I think you have a moral obligation to kill Kis–"

"The executioner." Interrupted Ming. "Kill the executioner."

"You really hate her don't you." Peter.

"Do you not? She's a pestilence."

"Well, I'm partnering with Zara. I could fix her," he replied.

"Yeah but then you have to fuck Kis or the executioner."

"If you partner Kis, you get his house." Ming. "And the rest of the planet."

"But you'd also be legally tied to Xar Kis. Don't do that."

"Who are you fucking then, him or the executioner?" Achira.

Peter pouted in thought. "I guess... well fuck. I guess the executioner. Cause that means I get to kill him don't it."

"You wouldn't be able to." Ming.

"It's a game! What about you, 'Chira?"

"Same as you. Kill Kis, partner Zara, fuck the executioner." She shuddered. "Ew."

They laughed, their eyes roving around the room's corners – watching them melt and bend and swim in the haze of their affected imaginations.

"I had a weird dream," Achira. "I had this," she cupped

her left breast, "bit of cotton sticking out of my skin here. I pulled it... and it brought out a cactus. It was all covered with blood and pus. Dreams hurt, I think. You know everyone says dreams don't hurt?"

"Dreams hurt." Ming.

"That's not even weird." Peter. "I think that's like, representing your soul or something. Cacti are nice. You know what I dreamt once?"

"What?"

"There was this church, like an old Earth thing, with a big spire. But it wasn't made of stone. Well it was, but like the stone was under a layer of crocodiles. They were all dangling from the outside, sleeping like bats."

"Cool." Ming.

"Nah, nah," answered Peter, speeding up, "because every now and then one of them would snap in its sleep and then there'd be a wave of snappy crocodiles." He waited, there was no response. "They had human hands."

"Ugh," Achira, "with scales or people skin?"

"Scales."

"Yeah, that's nasty," agreed Achira. "Don't like hands at all."

"Hands." Ming concurred.

"Hey. Hey. Do you want to be looking at something fuck off nasty what I've found in my room?" Peter lifted a conspiratorial eyebrow and looked from woman to woman.

"How fuck off nasty are we talking?" Achira stood to wrestle three more bottles from one of their diminished crates.

"The fuckiest, most off you've ever seen." He did not wait for a response. "Come on!"

"Oh dear," Said Achira, handing Ming a bottle as they followed him.

He was sitting on his bed, drink on the floor, book in his hands. Ming felt her heart skip when she saw what it was.

"Wh– why do you have this? Where did you find this?" The two women sat on either side of him, Ming trying to bring herself to sobriety as she stared at the cover. "Why didn't you tell me?"

"What is it?" Achira.

"Found it yesterday but wanted to wait 'til after the trial to show you, cause it's so horrible. You ready?"

"This shouldn't be here." Ming, but in a tone which made it clear that she wasn't quite protesting.

Peter flipped over the cover. Achira screamed, "Absolutely not oh my gods what! Ew. Put it back!"

Ming laughed and put her hand out to prevent Peter from hiding the image. "Wow."

"Fucking grotesque, right?"

"How are you both sitting looking at that, oh no."

"This really should be at the embassy, this is our business, I need to take it."

"Fucking have it mate, it's foul. Was in the bottom of that desk drawer under a load of spare linens. Your science guy Fukuyama must've left it, right?"

"Right."

Achira braced herself to look. Her drugged vision swam over the page. She fought it, wrestled the image into the naked human figure it was. "This is what happens to *tama*, isn't it?"

Ming nodded and turned the page. "Yes. Either because of the magic or because they live in such filth." She lowered her voice, said something she ought not, "Caralla thinks it's the filth, but Fukuyama thought it was the magic."

"No way." Achira.

"Cool." Peter.

"Shh." Ming. "I didn't just say that."

Her finger meandered over the photographs, each of them showing a body or body part with the same disfigurement. Short black spines erupting from the skin, little shards of bone arranged in clusters around joints. Bruising and bleeding the flesh around them.

"I don't know how you can look. Doesn't it remind you how... miserable it all is." Achira. "The poor *tama*."

"We're working on it." Ming.

"Are you?"

She waved her hand dismissively. "Yeah."

Peter placed the book on the floor and put his arm around Achira. "See? The embassy have it under control." He kissed her.

"Hey. Hey did you lure us down here on purpose? With *that*? Peter," she complained, but didn't stop him.

"I'm scandalous."

They entwined themselves together, becoming a mess of limbs as the drug's euphoria disconnected them from the world. Confused, primal pleasure as they explored each other, deepening confusion as they closed their eyes and forgot whose neck that was, whose tongue.

Ming's hand sought the floor, found the book, and flipped it open.

V

Ming stood at a concrete spaceport on the eastern side of Lon Apech. Watching as the same ship which had brought her less than a year earlier docked inelegantly before them.

The ship looked like a deep sea jellyfish – bright and bulbous, with flashing lights along its side as deterrents to the predators of space.

Aristocrats strode to the edge of the platform, arranging themselves in a line to be introduced to the newest arrival from Crysth.

Peter Pïat-Elementov descended behind the pilot and began to shake hands while very unsubtly trying to process the selection of thespian ensembles which belonged to their owners. A man in a black toga, another with a huge crown. A dinosaur costume, which he could not bring himself to look away from. The outfits get progressively tamer every year as they realize that this is not the Crysthian norm.

"What," exhaled the maroon-suited woman who stood to Ming's side, "is a Military kid doing here?"

"I have no idea." Ming. "I miss Fukuyama already."

"Hm-hm. Well, working on something urgent like a disease does mean one has to get whipped off quite quickly," said Jasef, as if he knew. "I wonder if this one will be able to fill us in on the news from Hecubah."

"Shall we go over?" Her name is Els, this woman who has been and gone.

"I'd really rather not." Ming.

The four of them hung back in a distinctive clump sharing understanding, conciliatory and frankly embarrassed looks with the metal-jawed pilots, who themselves had not moved away from the ship – as if fearing that any second one of the locals might need to be outrun.

"It was easy – once we figured out how to – well, no, I mean, almost everybody died, it wasn't easy but once the Ethicists had figured out how to get them to talk to us it was easy." That same night, the newcomer was already as settled into the pagoda's octagonal kitchen as if he'd been there for years.

"Almost everybody died – and you're telling us it was easy?" Jasef's natural respect for a Military uniform had already soured into horror at their bombastic fifth member.

"Yeah, yeah no it was tragic and all that but once the pearls figured it out it was so simple." Peter laughed, disproportionately tipsy – a side effect of the journey. "We were going about it the wrong way. They were only fighting us cos we hadn't said nothing to them what was interesting!"

"What was the death toll? Why so many?" Jasef, deeply concerned for his nameless and faceless comrades-in-arms about whom he had only just learned.

"Well, if I had an army of fucking necromancers I'd want a few corpses lying around too." He paused to laugh, pumped smoke out of something in his mouth. "You know about the necromancers? No? Well, they're fucking appalling. The people they were bringing back don't even know they're dead – can't understand that time has gone on, all that. Just repeat themselves. So they can't control them, really, so they need neuromancers to–"

"You're talking about the different factions on Hecubah forming allegiances? Impossible." Jasef.

"Oh, they were always allied! The Greens got it mad wrong, no offence."

"How could our intel be that wrong?"

Ming managed not to roll her eyes at the word 'intel'. Els and Ar did not.

"We forgot they're just people is what it is." Peter paused for a drink. "We thought they couldn't stand the thought of... er... interdependency because it was all about how... how fucking strong the factions were alone. If you were looking at Crysth you might assume the blues and the pearls don't get along, wouldn't you? Like it's obvious Military and the Reds are pals but that doesn't mean we don't tend to get closer to the Ethicists on the ground, right? What we were missing is that this wasn't like it was a competition between them. They was on magic's side, not the planet, not each other, it's about the magic. That was it, that's how we got them."

"Peter, for goodness sake, tell us about the necromancers!" whined Els.

"Oh, gods." He paused for solemnity. "You can't imagine. They sacrificed the weakest of them, turned them into nasty berserker footsoldiers – which would be totally fine, machine gun, lasers, unholy shitstorm, you know what we can do, well we couldn't not there anyway but anyway yeah – but they were already fucking dead by the time we were even trying to shoot them. See, the necromancers, even the good ones, they can resurrect but they can't, you know, control."

"So, the necromancer brings a corpse to life and the neuromancer points it in the right direction?" Els' mind slotted imagined drivers into imagined cadaver vehicles and delighted at the nefarious picture.

"Backwards. You can't control a dead mind. It just carries on doing whatever it was doing. Like you can't really bring the dead back to life, just a pretend life, doing the life thing but not living. So, the neuromancers fill these kids with the most murderous fury you could possibly imagine, like I say mad berserkers, and then slit their throats. Push the body forward and the necro to the right has turned your pal into a single-purpose genocidal zombie before he hits the ground."

"Fuck me. But, still, surely you can just firebomb them? They're still flesh…"

"No, we couldn't firebomb shit. We couldn't even shoot, actually." There's a pause, here, while he gathers his thoughts, looks at them all in turn to draw them in to the colossus of his next reveal. "There was a deity down there." Gasps from the others, Ar's knuckles touch the table in excitement. Goosebumps rise. This is the empire's boogeyman. "Yeah. Yeah."

"You saw it?" A whisper drawn from Els' throat.

The soldier shook his head. "The only reason I'm alive is that I never got sent down from base."

A moment of silence for the imagined fallen. The invocation of their common enemy has made their deaths more real.

Ar touched the table in front of himself, nodded encouragement to continue the story.

"Yeah. So." It is immediate, this man's ability to gather himself and change gears. "Few of the fucks had made some allegiance with a deity of what we decided to call magnetism." Don't be fooled by these words: deity, demon, technomancer, magic. Crysth's decisionmakers do not believe in that kind of thing. "They didn't even know it was a god, just thought it was like, a mine of magic. You've heard the stories, you know, it's – you know – pretty much fucking impossible to figure out what any sort of deity is actually after. But these lot had, like…" He sipped his drink as he sought a word, "monks? They thought they were wizards. Could fling our own bullets back at us, crush ships like cans. We didn't expect the planet to be natural, it had attracted the scouts' compass, but that lurking fucker took us by surprise." They all nodded enthusiastically to demonstrate their loathing. "Honestly, if it hadn't been for the pearls, we would have all been fucking killed."

"So, how did the Ethicists get the better of them, in the end?" Jasef.

"They didn't... Not really. It was the magic thing. All they cared about was the magic and they didn't give a fuck about Crysth because they didn't think we had any of our own. They were just going to rip us to motherfucking pieces until we stopped coming and never think about us again.

"Anyway, someone in pearl had the idea to argue that Crysth was magic. Some Green sounding bullshit, like we're a magic binding a part of the universe together and getting bigger and bigger. Well, they loved it. Yeah, I think the more open-minded ones saw it as a way to find new, new magics. Like they'd never seen a laser before, you know?" He hiccupped. "Got them to kill the fucking god for us as well, part of the bargain."

"How?" asked Els, looking first to Ming for silent permission to ask.

Peter sneered. "The evil fucking thing was taking more from them than it was giving, obviously. The poor fuckers didn't live long. We told them we know what it is and that we know how to kill it. They turned on it without a second thought. Much easier than usual. It was making people die in a really, er, visibly horrible way." All of them wanted to know but none would dream of asking. "So they torched the monks, flattened the ground, rolled out the red carpet for a black hand with a team of deimancers and they nuked the fucker." The others followed his lead as he lifted his glass to murderous theism. Ming nodded slightly as he made an extra tip of his drink to her, and to the black fingerprint on her lapel.

"Literally nuked?" asked Els.

"Oh, nah. We got it in the same way we got..." He made sucking noises with his mouth while he sought an example these non-Military might recognize. "Do you know about the water deity which made it actually onto Crysth, into the capital?" The Reds nodded, so Peter turned just to Jasef with the rest of his explanation. "Okay so, this thing had managed to follow a shipping crew by, er, manifesting on board and helping them. They kept it to themselves because they were scared, and it seemed harmless, so the fucker ended up on a port in Crysth."

"Right where Ming's from!" exploded Els, excited.

"Oh shit, of course," The Ming family residence has its own instantly recognizable skyline along the coast. "You must have been a kid, right? Do you remember? Do you want to finish telling?"

Ming smiled but shook her head.

"Alright, cool. Erm, right so people start to think someone's up to tricks. Stuff missing, huge piles of fish turning up in living rooms because that's what it thinks we want. But then there were beached whales and sharks all over the place... and..." he looked nervously at Ming, "no one you knew, I hope?" She shook her head again. "Oh, thank fuck. Anyway, so the deimancers got called in and they all went apoplectic furious the moment they were near the place. They could tell that this thing was mega powerful and really particularly good at trying to communicate with people. But its problem was–"

"The same thing that makes them good communicators tends to make them especially reliant upon faith." Jasef finished the sentence, to Peter's mild annoyance. It isn't true, the faith thing. It's a simplification, like the word deity itself, designed to cauterize enquiry. Crysth renders certain things falsely arcane in order to cut them off from prying minds – keep them in the realm of what they call the unnatural. Technomancers, deimancers. A false separation between science and fantasy which keeps the latter firmly under state control.

"Yep," he agreed. "So it was psychological. Show it for the monster it was, deal with anybody who it clung to. Relatively easy victory in comparison with the weirdness of it. Exact same thing on Hecubah, but even better because the, er, monks weren't particularly liked or happy anyway. Not at all like the ones with physical sources that we have to destroy, those are fucked."

"Who were you working with when you were there, anyway?" Els.

Peter grinned; he had wanted this question. "General Avon Stal."

Noises of disbelief and awe came from his audience's mouths; Ar knocked his knuckle on the table in respect.

"What is she like?" whispered Jasef, leaning forward.

Peter took a sip. A dramatic pause. "Awesome."

They all laughed with excitement. The Stals are perhaps the most famous, or most revered, of the families. And Avon is perhaps the most famous or most revered of the Stals. They have all seen her image, falsely young and eerily beautiful, pasted all over the capital. She is practically level with the Military Emperor himself.

"Go on, tell us about her," urged Els.

"She's just so wicked." He shook his head, lowered his voice. "When she talks about the Emperor, she just calls his majesty 'Vard'."

"What does she say about his majesty?" asked Jasef, stunned.

"Well like, she's been at that rank for so long that I don't think she would, er, you know, it wouldn't occur to her to talk about his majesty like he were anything special – as daft as that sounds." There was an amazed silence. A member of the Ethicist faction would scoff at this – they are essentially anarchistic despite having an official Emperor of their own. "She fights like a fucking blizzard."

"Really?" Jasef again, overeager. "Does she still have long hair?"

"Careful little guy, think I'll have to knock you for one if you're getting hard for the boss."

Jasef began spluttering in embarrassed outrage as the others laughed, Els decided to save him.

"So, you're going back to work with her? You're her man?" She nudged him under the table, grinning.

"I hope so." He smiled, winking at her and shifting his posture to tense his arms against his shirt. "Depends whether or not I survive this place."

"What are you going to do for your project here? Not much going on for a bruise."

Peter winked at the cheeky familiarity of the word 'bruise'. "Yeah, takes the piss a bit, doesn't it? I'll probably just get the embassy's blue to fight me, see if we can figure out, er, you know, how the locals won that civil war of theirs while we're at it."

"So, your time on Hecubah doesn't count?" Els.

"Nope. But I can still get back to be Avon's captain when it's over, so whatever eh? She liked me, asked to keep me personally." He looked at Ming when he said this. "Anyways, I didn't get much of a briefing about Apech, what with the sudden turn about. What's going on over here? It's weird that I've never seen any of you in any of the combat buildings, because people behave like the locals are fucking lunatics."

"They are," laughed Els, the others joined in half-heartedly.

"Ha! Like, how? What's with, you know… so… they can see the future?"

Too many seconds, silence. Ming decided to break the tension. "We don't know. And we don't know what they think they look like, either, so don't ask. Try not to ask them anything, actually."

"Huh? I was told that they hire us, part time, as like, detectives? Somebody tells us they've seen a crime and we have to stop it before it happens?"

"Er… sure." Els. She herself was here at the ambassador's request, testing rocks and drilling. Whether the famously weird ambassador to Apech would help establish her a career back home based on these labors was entirely unstipulated –

but this is what was usually expected. A project, a glowing recommendation followed by graduation and application to some top-secret endeavor.

"That sure didn't sound very sure." Peter showed them his teeth as if it were a smile.

Ming watched this expression with rising curiosity. She had met Avon several times, and so had been trying to figure out why the general had chosen him. His rank meant that he had to be much cleverer than he behaved, which she supposed was even more useful because he didn't appear like he was actively trying to conceal it. She imagined that his promotion would be swift but brief; he would distract attention from real power, obscure Avon with his earnestness. Ming decided that he would be hers, in that moment, for as long as he was here. She might have done something about him much faster had she paid more attention to the man than to Avon's desire for him.

Els was still smiling. "Well we don't really prevent the crimes from happening, we find the perpetrators."

"Oh! Well, that's... that's fine, right?" He did not know why getting to play police chase for two years was such a cause for concern. "I guess it's like... irresponsible for them to let the crime happen if they know it will? But I've seen this stuff before, like have you read that novel by–"

"No," interrupted Ming, "It's that they do not care. They just want to watch us put things in order, and behave formally."

Peter tried to work out what she had said.

"That is to say," Jasef cleared his throat, "that Apechi have what we suppose are, erm, visions of future events, and we have to, ahem, participate in making them happen. They want to study our thinking."

Peter looked back to Els, who he had decided was only the second most sensible in the room but a lot less frightening than the first. "Help me out here, mate?"

"Er... well it's just like what Jasef said. They see a

vision and we make sure that it happens. Last week the ambassador sent me to this woman who had seen two men being executed for the murder of a metalworker down in the floors below."

Peter shook his head, "I knew there was a death penalty. What's that like?"

Ming shot Els a warning look which she understood to mean that *we will deal with that later*.

"So," she continued, ignoring him, "I didn't know who had been killed, or was going to be killed, and if you ask for more information they won't give it. I had to find a cylinder where somebody had been murdered, or at least disappeared, and then figure out who was… most likely to be responsible. Took photographs of them all, and the woman who saw them being executed picked them out from the photos."

"I'm struggling a bit… you're meaning to be telling me that we find people to be killed without any proof that they've done something wrong?"

"More or less," Ming answered.

The newest student on Apech did not speak again. Clearly unconvinced but as likely to question a black fingerprint as he was to jump out of the window. This will change.

"You'll get used to it. It's really a, er, learn by doing kind of thing." Els.

"But hang on, how do we know they can see the future?" probed Peter. "Who's telling you it?"

"Well…" Els drew breath through her teeth. "We're not sure. Sometimes they… when you're speaking to them sometimes you might notice them respond to something you didn't say or didn't do. Or haven't done yet. It is very important that you ignore this. They do not like it when you point it out. And the ambassador has that in hand. Just some left over magic from before our arrival. Or similar."

"Understood." He lifted his drink to his lips as if swearing an oath of belief with the sip. He hadn't liked the reference to the embassy – that isn't his business. "Just about the courts then... you're telling me you make it happen? The executions, the arrests?"

"One always makes the future happen." Jasef.

"Can we not be philosophical for a bit of a minute though?"

"We don't really talk about it." Els. "You're supposed to be watching and listening but not really, just... I don't know, it's abstract."

"Abstract?!"

"Peter." Ming's voice. "We do not know a lot about these people, or this planet. What we do know is that they do not like being told that they are different to us. It is not your place to investigate this. It is mine." She waved her hand in a way which indicated vagueness as well as finality. She decided to excuse herself to the bathroom, give them a moment without her.

"Alright." said Peter, after the trapdoor was closed. "Why are you all here then? You three chose this place on purpose. Are you a set of absolute raving nutjobs?"

Els shoulders drooped in a polite laugh. "Well I'm here because the ambassador requested someone who knew about rocks to do a raw materials survey, find out if there's anything useful here, and I got the short straw. But it's kinda cool, it's not like choosing to be shipped to New Gholl and spending two years talking to natives who have practically rehearsed answers to whatever weak anthropological pursuit people go down with. We could do some really valuable work here."

"And I am here because it's so new, there's a lot of opportunity for a Green viewing this much infrastructure being constructed so quickly, especially when they're so happy to study–"

"Yeah, but, if it's so big why aren't there even more people here? You couldn't move for motherfuckers everywhere else I've been." He smiled more genuinely as the insult landed. "And here there's just... you lot."

"It's because it's horrible here, Peter." Els. "Do us the courtesy of admitting that you have noticed."

Jasef sniffed and leaned in. "Don't you see that this is rather another benefit? We have the freedom to really make a difference here."

He really should have worked out that this assumption was false by now, despite having only been in place for a couple of months.

"Cool." Peter shrugged the conversation away. "There was a redhead at the port who was kinda sexy. The one in the black dress."

"Oh yeah, she knows. But wait until you see Zara Ustra." Els.

"Who's that?"

"The bossman's girl," she answered. "They weren't at the port earlier, dunno why."

"There's a bossman? Wasn't told about a bossman."

"Oh, deffo. Not formally like, but there totally is." Els took too large a swig from her beaker and started to cough. "Xar Kis. He's scary as all hell, too."

"Super cool." Peter grinned, eyes wide with the prospect of meeting an alien monarch – someone powerful, but someone whose power could not possibly hurt him.

VI

"Fuck! Fuck!"

The sound of Peter's voice outside. Achira jumped up and stuck her head out of the kitchen window, scanning for him but seeing nothing. Huge metallic clanging beneath them told them that he was already running back up the staircase.

"What now?" Jasef slammed his pencil down and swiveled to watch the hole in the floor.

Ming, who had been opening a can of chickpeas by the counter, began to wash her hands.

"You okay?" called Achira, more for something to say than anything else. They heard his breathing as he reached the very top of the staircase.

"Get the fuck down here right now! All you!"

He commenced his leaping descent.

Jasef reached the ground first. The others heard him retching outside as they gathered, uncertain, at the bottom of the staircase. Peter was leaning against the inside wall of the pagoda, staring at them, unblinking, a look of disbelief on his face. He shook his head but made a movement with his hand as if to urge them to go outside.

They did. They saw it.

A corpse was half hanging, half plastered against the outside wall of the pagoda. Its, his, shoeless feet were crushed against

53

the concrete a foot above the ground, as if they had been hit repeatedly with a blunt object. His left shoulder was pierced by one of the larger sections of twisted steel which spewed irregularly out of the structure, another held his hand straight above his head. The right arm had received the same treatment as his feet – most of it had run, glutinous and awful, down to the floor. His head lolled onto his naked chest.

Achira cried out and sobbed in low, gasping shock. Ar vomited and immediately retreated behind Jasef, who was bent double away from the building. Ming backed into the shelter of the pagoda – hiding her expression from the others.

"Who is it?" she asked, loudly, when she had controlled her voice.

Peter merely shook his head. He was trained in combat, trained to kill and to be harmed and to heal and to see damage done to dying bodies, but this horrified him in its deliberate ritualism.

Ming strode outside and over to Achira who, expecting a hug of comfort, burrowed herself into Ming's shoulder. Ming pushed her gently away and gestured to the others, gathering them into a huddle. Achira watched in quiet acquiescence, grateful that somebody was taking charge.

"Ar. Is there anybody still here that you can see? Any more bodies anywhere?"

He shook his head.

"Keep looking. Don't turn back to us. Keep looking around. Jasef? Jasef. Jasef!"

He removed the palm cupped over his brow.

"When did you come back?"

"I… seven? You were still in the kitchen…"

"And he was not there?"

"No. I don't think so… I don't know… No…"

"That's not good enough, Jasef. Was he? Did you see them?"

"I don't know!"

"Right. Ar, anybody? Okay. Peter, come outside."

"Why?"

"I just… I don't know, I want to be able to see everybody so we can think. Come outside."

"Come inside."

"We can think in the kitchen, Ming?" Jasef had a pleading tone.

"No. Look. I need to know who he is, so somebody is going to have to lift his head."

"No!" Peter. "We all need to wait inside until he's gone." This sentence will keep him up at night when he remembers it.

"Gone?! He's not going anywhere, he is a dead man. He is practically mush. Peter, he is *not* going anywhere." Ming looked around and realized that nobody was going to touch the body. Fuck, she thought, why have they done this to me today. "Peter just get outside so I can think. Now."

"For gods' sake. For gods' sake." Achira, muttering.

They had all seen a corpse before. Basic medical training demanded countless minor surgeries on cadavers of all species back when they were still undergraduates at the first and most densely populated academy, before their cohort started being weeded – or removing themselves – out into the civilian workforce. It was not the body that bothered them so much. It was the distinct, frankly obvious, notion that it had been left *for* them. Given to them. It felt as if acknowledging it was to accept a threat, that their response was a test. That they were cursed by it. Rarely did it feel to them like they were really here, like they were really loose from the university's austere halls – unshadowed, unprotected. Freedom can be as mortifying as it is liberating, but for these whose lives have been spent in affirmation and success, the notion that real harm might come to them comes only lethargically; too late, too vague.

Ming said no more but steeled herself to move back toward the body.

"What, *what*, are you doing?" hissed Jasef.

Ming pulled off her shoe, then her sock, and slipped it onto her hand. She turned back to her companions and mouthed it like a puppet. She looked uncomfortable, apologetic, as she did so.

"You're going to... sock chew it?" Peter.

"No!" she answered. They were all whispering.

"Put your blasted shoe back on!" Jasef, with rising panic, as if the corpse had contracted some bare-foot disease which had caused them to spontaneously paste themselves against the nearest surface.

"Ming what the fuck are you doing?" Peter was whining unnaturally in his lowered voice, yearning to move towards her, to protect her, but too afraid of the contaminated omen to move his legs. This will haunt him, too.

She turned to look at the sock, wondering to herself whether it was a good idea to do it in front of them.

"Ming!" Jasef.

"She's gone mental," came Peter's courageous diagnosis.

"For fuck's sake!" Ming, still whispering, "I'm going to use the sock hand," she opened and closed the puppet mouth again, "to lift his head. I don't want to get blood on me."

"Oh, shit, sorry. I thought you'd gone mental. Good idea."

She scowled at Peter and turned back to face the body.

"Fuck's sake," she muttered to herself again as she sidled towards the mess.

She was much shorter than the body but not so short as to be able to see its face without putting her own against its stomach. She bet they'd done that on purpose. Smiled grimly, extended her arm, gingerly pushed on the forehead. Not hard enough. Pushed again, harder, making a swiping motion to wipe as much blood as possible onto the sock as she did. Recoiled her arm in the same moment so the head would bounce up and all the way back down again. It did so, with a crack. She repeated the action twice before supporting his head fully. It weighed heavy against her palm.

Ming backed away from it, still watching, as if afraid to turn her back to him, or as if afraid to turn her face to them. She took off the bloodied sock, carefully, inside out, still watching the corpse, and held it between her fingers.

"Well?" Jasef, once she was back within whispering distance.

"Agan. It's Taer Agan. The foreman... from yesterday."

They all murmured agreement, almost relief.

"Yeah, you don't need to be an Apechi to have gone predicted that one."

"Oh, shut up," hissed Achira.

"Indeed. But it is still curious and alarming that they have chosen to give you the corpse, comrade." Jasef turned to Ming as he said this.

"Give me the corpse? Do not you comrade me, it is on our *house*, Jasef."

"But he was screwed at your trial." Peter.

"It was not me who was on trial."

"Really?" Achira did not need to complete the thought.

"No. What are we going to do with the body? This is a 'we' problem. We should not leave it here. It will look like we're bothered."

They all stood. Watched the body.

Peter spoke first. "I'm pretty fucking bothered."

"We could... not do anything?" Jasef.

"Don't be daft, we're not having some poor murdered bastard rotting next to our front door for the rest of the year." Peter. "Remember all those," – his voice cut off, as if he had stopped himself from saying something in poor taste – "people who were hanging from the tree outside Distan's place? They left them there for months."

"Don't say his name." Jasef. "This has got... them... written all over it."

"But why have 'they'," – meaning Miré Distan and Xar Kis – "done it at us? They never do it at us." Achira.

"You're right," agreed Ming. "I'm going to have to do something." This last almost to herself.

"You were on your way to the embassy anyway, P." Achira.

"Oh yeah, *ambassador ambassador somebody's been brutally murdered!* I'd be handed a clip round the ear and given three days bedrest for stating the bleeding fucking obvious. We are in Lon Apech."

Ming smiled briefly. "I think 'Chira's right. I'll come, too."

"Don't leave us here with him outside!" Achira.

"Well I for one propose that we all go." Jasef.

"No, if we all turned up, they would think we were being hysterical." Ming.

"There is a dead man pasted to our house." Achira.

"Yes, and like I say this is worth mentioning but… we can all guess what has happened here, and I think we need to remain calm." She defaulted to some buzzwords. "We have been trained not to respond in this way to intercultural miscommunications."

That one didn't land.

"Look, they probably put him here to reassure us that they're maintaining the status quo. You know how they are." This is not true. They have put him there because they think it is funny. Ming knows this. "You three go back upstairs. Pete and I will go to the embassy. I had to be in anyway, for a new assignment. We'll just… mention it."

"Please don't leave us alone with him," whispered Achira, still reluctant to turn around.

"There are three of you. Plus, he's really quite dead."

"Yeah, it's not like he's going to come crawling up the walls is it?" Peter had relaxed now he knew he was leaving, was already beginning to compare his earlier terror to his general self-perception and recoiling at the result.

Achira shuddered. "Do not say that. Why didn't we hear anything?"

"Because, my dear, you three were off your rockers on those godsforsaken cube things!"

"Well why didn't you hear anything then o sagacious one?

Fuck off." Peter resisted the urge to knock Jasef off his feet as he said this.

"For your information, I was listening to my albums to drown out the noise of you three doing... stuff!"

"Stop arguing. Go upstairs. Peter, come on. Ar ... keep an eye out, please?"

"An eye out for what?" Achira.

"We don't know, do we. Just stuff." Peter.

"I'm scared." Jasef.

"We know. We all are." Ming scrutinized her sock. "Take the sock."

"No!" yelled Achira.

"Take my damn sock!"

"You take your damn sock!"

"Take her fucking sock!" agreed Peter.

"No!"

"Achira just take the sock." Jasef.

"Oh yeah why don't you take the sock you prick?" Peter.

"She did not ask me to take the sock."

Ar extended two long, bluish fingers and made a pinching motion at the offending item.

"Thank you, Ar. Just... put it on the floor at the bottom of the stairs. I'll deal with it when I get back."

"Why?! In the house?!" Achira.

"Be instructed." Ming.

"We can't leave it out here all bloody, everyone will know we socked the man." Peter.

"There is nobody!" Achira.

Ar took the sock and held it at full length from his body.

"Right," Peter had regained himself completely now, "none of you lot take any action 'til we're back from that lot. Alright?"

Jasef nodded stoically and applied allegedly reassuring pressure to Achira's shoulder, moving her back to the door in front of him.

Ming waited until the others were back inside before turning to Peter. "Is the train coming?"

"No," he said, wretchedly. "I thought I'd walk... s'why I gone and left so early."

"Right. Great. Well, come on."

They set off through the topographically disturbing walkways of Lon Apech in silence. It was an empty morning, barren but for birdsong and the rusted groans of the suspended streets which came at them eerily through the fog. Signs suggesting *sales, happy hour, girls girls girls* and kicking their pink high heels eternally into the air adopted a newly foreboding significance. What had to Peter seemed random before now suggested some arcane linguistics in neon, birdcages, and cement. Something spelled out in the architecture itself, invisible to him but obvious to those who wrote it. For once, he knew himself alien. Agan's body was a message that he was too foreign to read.

Fog menaced them as they clambered along the bridges, treacherous with polluted dew. Above and below, movement stirred the city's nocturnal peace. Doors welded into the sides of concrete towers heaved open with the mosquito whine of rust. The wheezing clamor of sub-fauxterranean vents added a moaning aggression to the sound. The city, if that was an appropriate word for this hasty ensemble of stolen ideas, had no districts of which to speak; it was bifurcated horizontally into Lon Apech and the underneath. The latter was excluded from the psychological construct of capital city. Always under, never in, the addresses of the cylinders which housed their production related in low esteem to whichever monument roared above them.

The city becomes gigantic towards its center. Pyramids replace steeples and bold metal trees soar into the translucent sky with the pride of Apechi adoration. The concrete peace is shattered by castles, bridges, and nonsense statues which leer gargoylian out of the mist. Laocoon wrestles eternally under the shadow of a willow with chainmail vines, the pride of Ushakov stands useless atop an empty fountain. An advertisement for washing powder hangs from a hunter's taut bow. Something about their erratic ensemble might have breathed life into them, made them exuberant, surreal, playful. But Lon Apech forbade it. There was no joviality, irony or excitement in the solemn construction of these icons to its future; or the future it thought that it held.

Just over an hour after they had left their cursed pagoda, no time at all for the anxious, they arrived within sight of the Crysthian Embassy. Tall and sinister, only its wood-tiled roof visible within the gates which housed it. A metal jungle, literally, vines and broad-leafed bushes recreated in bronze and steel. It sparkled in the city's artificial light, the technicolor fog shifting shadows around it. The aquatic misdirection of light inserted huge volume beneath the tangled and inert branches, suggesting movement, suggesting something unlikely, predatory, prowling in the bronze and feasting on whatever fruits unliving trees could produce. The whole compound was a verbatim, if metallurgically undead, copy of the Muhr Embassy on Crysth. It was beautiful there, where grass grew, and trees breathed, and birds flew unhunted among the entwined bark of its artfully neglected overgrowth. It made sense, there. A patch of home sewn into the imperial quilt of the capital planet.

Two guards stood at the front gate. Two Apechi commoners with crossbows which did not work. They saluted, staring unashamedly at whatever strangeness their haunted eyes could see. The path through the dead forest towards an elevator shaft.

Peter looked expectantly at Ming when they reached the elevator. She did not move. She smirked and bounced her eyebrows in a gesture which said, you do it.

Surprised and delighted by her playfulness this close to the embassy, Peter pressed the call button. It flashed scarlet protest at his touch, then sputtered into the fuzzing activity of radio life as a voice came, "Who?"

"Me." Peter's pre-emptively annoyed response.

"Ha!" barked the radio. "What's the password?"

Peter looked at Ming, "You see how he behaves at me?" He pressed the button again. "Not today, Alessi. Let me in."

"Password," asserted the crackling, curt speech. "Or fuck off."

"Cunt," whispered Peter, looking to Ming who still didn't move. "Is it... swordfish?"

"Nah-ah."

"How about Crysth? Is it Crysth?" Peter folded his arms. He is reveling in this, letting the administrator embarrass himself for as long as he can.

"Wrong again!"

"Let me in, you absolute git."

"Incorrect."

Peter clicked his tongue, smiled at Ming again, and began in a sing-song voice which she laughed at behind him: "Cephalopod, windmill, wave, hurricane, banshee, clairvoyance, the moon, poison, altercation, disease–"

"Wrong. All wrong."

Ming reached out, extended her arm to place the back of her hand by the radio's call button. Its light turned green. The elevator began to descend.

There was a pause.

"Is Ming with you?" asked the radio voice, a shade panicky. "Has she, er, have you been there the whole time, ma'am?"

"Yep," barked Peter, dripping with satisfaction as the elevator doors slid open. "How d'you like me now, you twat?"

The Crysthian ambassador to Apech watched the two students over her steepled fingers. Her office, which hung precariously over the steel gardens below, was a deep shade of blue illuminated by hooded candles which gave it a transitory darkness, not unlike and yet jarringly dissimilar in its organic meandering to the flashing glare outside. The ambassador's quietly furious personality showed in the room's austerity. No letter from the Red emperor hanging in its gilded frame, no photographs of handshakes past, no plant whispering for Crysth's lost sun in the curling of its leaves. She watched the students, two souvenirs of a planet decades gone from her, and frowned. This is Gris Caralla.

"To what do I owe the privilege of a double event?" She said this to both of them, and not particularly unpleasantly, but Ming knew her master well enough to understand that she was being rebuked.

"We both need new assignments, ambassador, if there are any," Ming replied, innocently, but the ambassador knew her understudy just as well to understand that something was wrong.

The two women were looking only at each other, communicating a desire to be left alone, and something new. A sort of mutual suspicion, lurking under the sculpted indifference of the ambassadorial class. Perhaps it was a good thing that Peter was there, after all. There's an argument waiting to happen.

"I have something... odd." Gris' prosthetic fingers parted, caressed the surface of her desk as she sought whatever it was. "But still nothing for you, Peter."

Peter seemed to be relieved but licked his lips in a nervous gesture before speaking; "We have something odd too, ambassador."

Her hands stopped their motion, returned to their steeple.

Ming sighed inwardly at Peter's diplomatic inutility before saying, "There was a dead Apechi commoner pasted to our tower, this morning."

Caralla smiled humorlessly. "Pasted?"

"Yeah, like he'd been mushed against the wall with a big pestle." Peter mimed the action with a clenched fist against his palm as he spoke.

"Well. Be grateful that nobody pestled you, Peter." Her fingers parted again, returned to the desk, to an envelope. That was that, then.

The soldier scoffed with annoyance while Ming resisted the urge to look at him.

"This came from Ech Kon–"

"Oh no." Peter. "No way."

The ambassador did not look away from the envelope. "Excuse me?"

"It's awful out there, ambassador. Don't send her out there." He has forgotten himself. It's hard to remember to be afraid of a uniform when you spend your evenings inside one of its wearers. Worse, when you think you're in love.

Ming closed her eyes. "It isn't summer. Ech Kon should be near empty."

"Yes," whispered Gris Caralla, opening the envelope. "And yet." She raised her voice again. "You don't like the coast, Peter?"

"I do not, ambassador." There was something particularly disturbing about the Apechi attempt at a vacation resort. "It's creepy."

Caralla smiled, genuine pleasure. "Isn't it? Ming always enjoys herself there, though. I suppose it's pleasant for a Ming to get back to the ocean. Isn't that right?"

Ming's breath caught. Guilt swarmed her mind and rendered her temporarily speechless. Ming does prefer Ech Kon, but she really hopes that the ambassador does not know why.

"Yes, I enjoy myself when I have occasion to go."

Caralla looked at her. "I know."

Shit.

"What I do not know," continued the ambassador, "is who sent us this letter. Or how it got here, in fact."

"Huh?" Peter all but stood up. "Locals got into the embassy?"

Caralla smiled again. "Calm down, soldier. A *tama* gave it to an administrator who was out," – she wiggled her black fingers

in a gesture which Peter had believed idiosyncratic to Ming –
"doing their thing."

"What?" both Ming and Peter, together.

"Indeed," mused the ambassador, looking up at her
apprentice once more. "Any ideas?"

"No." Ming, pokerfaced.

"I see." Caralla unfurled the letter, started to read, "Madam
Ambassador. One of your ships has been stolen from the docks.
Do something about it. Van Agir."

"What?!" Just Peter this time.

"Indeed. Naturally, it sounds like this Van Agir – who
nobody has heard of, by the way – is referring to one of the
vessels gifted by my emperor." The possessive means that she
is indicating the Red emperor, Rhododendron. A man whose
skin is shattered with a pattern of glowing steel, and who sits
at the zenith of the Red faction with his twin in his shadow.
The possessive is particularly interesting here; Rhododendron's
parentage is supposed to be a mystery – but his appearance
gives him away as a likely Caralla.

Gris Caralla scrutinised the letter. "The handwriting is good."

"We're sure none of the aristocrats are out there right now?"
Ming.

Caralla closed the letter. "No. We aren't. I have not asked,
and nor will I."

Ming nodded.

"So…" Peter seemed to be getting excited. "Persons
unknown have allegedly stolen a Crysthian ship? And an
Apechi informer has asked for Crysthian assistance?"

"It would seem that way, Peter. I can think of nothing else to
which this could refer, although it seems less a request than a
demand." The ambassador swept her prosthetic hand through
her hair in a gesture designed to distract the viewer, but which
had become habit. "You seem happy about it."

"Not at all, ambassador. But, well, permission to make a
suggestion?"

"I fear you will make it anyway."

He does not process this. "May I and some of the blues go with her? It seems dangerous, you know, all the way out there–"

"Yes. But not immediately. This may be a hoax. Or an experiment. It would embarrass us to show full force for some prank."

Ming nodded again. "I'll make sure of it and report back."

"Yes, you will," she agreed. "That being–"

There was a knock at the door, loud, agitated. Caralla frowned, pressed her prosthetic fingertips against her desk in a rhythm known only to her. The door opened.

"Gris–" An older man in a blue Military uniform practically fell into the room, righting himself and pausing when he saw the two students. This is Agnes. He has as many rings on his fingers as do Peter and Ming.

"Agnes?" Caralla stood. Ming and Peter followed suit.

Agnes took the two students in, his expression worried, shocked. He seemed to make a decision, spoke: "Zara Ustra has been killed."

VII

Ming walked beside her master. The broad blue backs of Peter and Agnes hurried in front of them. A pair of soldiers, a pair of diplomats. Ming touched the black fingerprint, Caralla's lost fingerprint, on her lapel. She was almost certain that the woman whose position she was training to occupy had found out about her activities in Ech Kon. And yet she was sending her back there anyway. Did Caralla just not care? *She doesn't, but not for the reasons Ming can guess.* A dozen out of fifty or so embassy guards and administrators trotted around them, joined as they went by harangued looking Apechi commoners who, doubtless, had also heard the news.

"Ming," said Gris Caralla, tired. "You need to tell me now if you know something that I don't."

A pause, eyebrows knotted, unknotted. "I don't know what you mean, Ambassador." *Amazingly, this is true.*

Ming hung back as the old woman pulled herself onto a chain bridge which connected the platform in front of the embassy to another, allowing a rare glimpse to the subterranean levels below; the towering silo-shaped bronze workshops descending to a soft, formerly fertile ground littered with shards of discarded metal, bodies, oil. Obscured by fog and light. The bridge swayed as they walked, single file.

"Ambassador?"

Caralla turned her face slightly to the left to indicate that she was listening.

"I really don't know what you mean."

The ambassador to Apech stopped. Ming turned and squared her palm to those behind – move back. They did, retreating away from the two Reds now standing alone over the ravine, the distance between them and the men in front growing wider as they carried on ahead.

Caralla turned, fixed her understudy with that blank, apathetic gaze which was as much a trademark of their occupation as the black hands themselves. The prosthetics are matte, textured with a reptile topography, ostentatiously wrong.

"I need a cigarette," she said, turning to see how far Agnes and Peter had gone. They were visible only as shapes, now, standing on the platform at the other side of the bridge. Watching. Both women raised a hand to ward off concern.

Her rings clicked together as she reached for the cigarette case in her inside pocket. She offered one to Ming, who took it despite not sharing Caralla's weird habit. This was as much a performance as a conversation, the lights at the end of their cigarettes guiding the audience's eyes to their isolation. They could remain in silence, just two bodies adding smoke to the fog, and their onlookers would invent whatever top-secret administrations or decisions their imaginations desired of their empire.

That is what the black hand means; a Crysth away from Crysth, a Red beacon guiding the flow of empire to and from the host planet. The ambassadorial is the most populous of the highest ranked classes but respected no less because of it; a natural ally to the Military blues and a source of distaste for the Ethicists whose anarchistic routes raised suspicion in all those who wielded control. The task of the black hand was to negotiate with generals and businesslike Greens on behalf of whatever they deemed fit for the planet to which they were assigned. The black hand was sovereign on the colony until the moment that a Military general had occasion to arrive, carrying on their invisible, intangible negotiations just one rung beneath the Red emperor's steward. The presence of such an old ambassador as Gris Caralla on such a horrible planet as Apech was highly unusual. They often spared themselves to lands of silk and luxury in their latter years, or else remained on Crysth itself as one of Rhododendron's advisors whether he liked it or not.

"Why did you come with Peter, this morning?"

Ming took a long drag, exhaled. "The dead man has upset them. The one on our pagoda. I needed to be seen to be doing something about it.

"But I had something else to tell you, obviously. It's this business with Kis and Rama. They had one of their," she did the hand wave, "things. One of their non-arguments. Everybody saw. It was, very unexpected."

The ambassador nodded.

"Something has happened?"

Caralla looked to her with an uncharacteristic expression of annoyance, "Clearly. That letter... I also received one similar from Ed Rama."

Ming's face replied a question mark.

"He says that 'friends of his' were attacked in Ech Kon by persons yet unknown. I had intended to ignore him, but now I suspect that Kis went after him without my knowing – which is uncharacteristic of him. And now this."

"If Rama's friends were attacked in Ech Kon then it wasn't on Xar's orders. I will make sure of course, but it wasn't him."

Caralla let out a long breath which was almost a whistle. "If Ustra has been killed in retaliation against an attack that was not truly Kis' doing..."

"Right. Gods I hope not. I'll see what happened in Ech Kon, and hopefully Kis will be able to tell us something here."

Caralla's black fingers raised to her white hairline, cupped her face. "I have no idea how he will react to this."

"Badly."

"Indeed."

The ambassador flicked her cigarette over the side of the bridge, obliged herself another.

"Unless it was him," Gris added, probingly. "Giving himself an excuse to attack Rama in the open."

"You mean who killed Ustra? No," answered Ming. "No."

Caralla snorted out of her nose, disbelief. "You know him better than I, I'm sure."

Ming almost gloated before she caught herself, changed the subject. "Rama has a lot more sympathizers than before. I could tell at the trial."

"I know."

A long pause. Birdsong, the ringing of hammers.

"Has it anything to do with us?"

Caralla looked at her student again. "I doubt it."

"But someone..." started Ming. "This person at Ech Kon, I mean. It occurs to me that this would be a very good way for someone to lure ourselves and our Military away from Lon Apech. It's what I would do if I were Rama. Then he only has Kis to contend with."

"Yes."

"Should we tell them about it?"

"Kis and Distan? No. Find out what it is first."

Ming's tongue darted out to wet her lips. She will tell them anyway.

"We cannot," continued Caralla, "be seen to get involved with local in-fighting. The stakes are too low, here."

Ming knew that this was true, for the empire. But she had her own stakes. It did not occur to her that Caralla had hers, too.

"So," Ming risked a bluff, "there still may be real trouble in Ech Kon. I should take Peter with me, just in case."

"No. This is all a perfect opportunity for him to make a mess; I want him where Agnes can see him. You've got your gauntlet anyway."

Ming tried not to show relief, tried to replace it with feigned nervousness. She did not want to be accompanied to Ech Kon. "I do."

"So, here and now. Shall we tell Kis that I'll give him Military for a while? It might distract him from Ustra's death at least," suggested the ambassador, which would be emotionally rancid were she not speaking about Apech's leader.

Ming shook her head. "Leave him to me. I don't know exactly how he'll behave."

Caralla flicked her half-finished cigarette over the bridge. Peter and Agnes helped them down from the steps at the other side, the former's eyes filled with respect and wonder at whatever script his patriotism had supplied.

This is how it looks beneath the floor.

There's the earth, the dirt, the rust that lays there. It isn't a cruel planet. It has fertile soil. It likes to rain and soak you. It is home to red trees that creak and sway and drink and house nests in their branches. They grow tall, oblivious to gentle winds. An ocean laps at its shores, unexplored, untouched by analytical eyes. Its predators go about their benevolent slaughter in darkness.

It is not that Apechi are evil, or that the planet is harsh. It would be better to say that they are haunted, just like this beautiful soil which festers, now, robbed of light and coated with decaying metal. They have lifted their city from the earth because they want to remove themselves from the thing which poisons it, poisons them.

It doesn't work like that.

From the earth come the cylinders. Great tubes of copper-hued metal which pump into the sky, massive structures which would be impressive alone were it not for the slab of city level zero which they support. It shames them, shocking feat of engineering that they are, hides them and makes them small.

The cylinders spiral upwards. *Tama* sit here, day after day, hammering and tinkering and crooning to each other in the senseless noises which they love.

Now one of those cylinders is filled by a throng of bodies. Some of them relieved, some excited, some scared out of their wits. In the center of the hollow space dangles what remains of Zara Ustra. Her noose is chain, a grapplehook suspended from the central light fixture. She is mesmerizingly dead. Too still in her flowing velvet skirts to have ever been so animated an object as she was. It is clear that whoever has done this to her enjoyed it.

The cylinder hums, creaks, whispers. There is writing on the wall. It looks like blood but who could be so predictably macabre. Theatrics, again.

"This is fucking insane," hissed Peter, standing just behind Ming on a platform far beneath the corpse. "Who do you reckon it was?"

Ming waved him away, turning purposefully to her mentor. Scanning the room. Already she has realized that they should not have come here.

"Where is he?" whispered Caralla.

"To your right, and up." This was Agnes' voice.

Their heads scanned right, upwards. There he was. Sitting on the side of one of the platforms which sprouted plantlike from the cylinder's internal wall. His feet dangled over the edge. His hands were clasped in his lap as he stared at his lover's broken face. His immobility filled the place as much as the corpse.

"And Distan?" Ming, looking back to the body.

"On his way." Peter, quietly, knowing he had annoyed her. "To the left."

Caralla said something to her head of security, who responded with a nod to Peter that had the three of them melt into the background, leaving Ming to speak with Distan.

He was livid. Rage sprawled over his face, veins throbbing in his scar-mottled forehead and chin, jaw clamped shut and nostrils curled. Ming grabbed his forearm, hard, whispered hurried and furious assurances of retribution into his ear.

"Zara," he spat, "they went for Zara. Why would they go for Zara?"

Ming tightened her grip on his arm as if to control him as she looked back up to the body. "She would be the easiest, wouldn't she? Cowards." The last word whispered so that Caralla could not hear.

"We'll rip them to pieces." Growling, Distan looked to his master. "He hasn't given the order yet."

"Has he said anything at all?" Ming relaxed her voice, rolling it into a level volume now she was certain that Distan's anger was not laced with the unpredictability of grief. "How did you find her?"

"Foreman, this morning."

"Agan?"

"Who?"

"The – never mind. I need to speak to you both; I'm being sent to–" Ming looked up to Caralla again, who was approaching, and dropped Distan's arm. "What has Kis said?"

"Nothing."

The ambassador nodded. "Did you arrive together?"

"No, the – the foreman went straight to him. I didn't come until someone else came for me later."

"Where's the foreman?" This is Ming.

Distan gestured to somewhere behind his chest with his thumb.

"I trust justice will be swift?" Caralla.

"I think," began Distan, looked back to Xar Kis, "I think he's waiting for them to claim responsibility."

"You expect them to?" Caralla, surprised.

He pointed at the dead woman. "That looks like war to me. Why hide?"

A noise of loud disbelief from Peter drew their attention towards the cylinder's entrance. "What are you doing here?"

Jasef, Ar, and Achira were emerging through the portal, their formal jackets unusual over daywear even with the matching imperial colours. They had dressed quickly. Peter and Agnes hurried over to them, beating several Apechi who were rushing over to stake their claim on Crysthian attention.

Ming's focus wandered in the interruption, surveying the cylinder's occupants. No Rama, but she did find some of those who had seemed inclined in his favour the previous day. An act of war. Perhaps not. He would have warned his people, brought them to him, kept them safe. When her attention returned, she found Caralla and Distan talking in hushed, quiet tones. She took half a step back, testing whether or not they would ask her to stay, and then backed away completely when they did not react.

"Agnes," she said. "Can you get everyone out?"

But Agnes was not listening; Peter and Jasef were already squabbling, to the rapt attention of the nearest Apechi aristocrats. Ming clenched her jaw and pushed through to the two of them.

"Gentlemen," she said, "stop that now. Achira, hey. Who came to get you? Is Agan still there?"

"Um…" Jasef looked around until he spotted an Apechi woman in a blue fascinator. "That lady over there came to the pagoda, saying we ought to come see." Ming looked the indicated woman in the face, recognised her as a friend of Rama, returned her nod of greeting. "Yes, Agan is still there." Jasef gasped. "Are the cases connected?"

"There are no cases, Jasef. Agnes, I think everybody but Military should leave." Agnes nodded, to Jasef's spluttering horror.

"We were brought by an Apechi–" Achira, only to be cut off by Agnes' move to usher her outside.

"Peter." Ming. "Get all the embassy staff that have come out as well. Straight back to the embassy." She was much more anxious than she sounded – her suspicion that they had been brought here for the satisfaction of the culprits had solidified into certainty.

He busied himself away to round up the administrators. Ming looked up at Kis. He had not moved. He was sitting directly in front, she saw now, of a line of glistening, red letters. Alien letters.

Unbelievable, she thought, and started walking up to Xar Kis.

"What are we going to do about this?" asked Peter the moment the cylinder door had closed behind the last unnecessary Crysthian.

Agnes shook his head. "Wait for Gris." Then a ponderous tone, reluctant to speak but not able to help himself, "I don't think we'll do anything."

"What?" Peter snapped, "Why?"

Agnes tapped the black hand, which marked him as an ambassador's chief of staff, on his lapel. "We would not generally get involved with local conflict unless... we can directly prove that it impacts Crysth's interests..."

"Crysth's interests? On what plane of fucking reality does Crysth not support a regime change if the incumbents are murdering, slaving cocksuckers?"

"Keep your voice down. Are you suggesting that this is a coup? Are you suggesting we support an alien coup? How," he looked at Peter more seriously, "how do you know the people who did this are... what are you talking about?"

"Isn't it obvious? We saw him yesterday, that dude with the suit. Forgot his name. Rama. He was being all... I don't know. It was a whole thing."

Agnes shook his head. "You are jumping to ridiculous conclusions. Don't think about it, this isn't our business, this isn't our–"

"What do you mean!" hissed Peter. "They're obviously fighting, we can make these people's lives so much better if we just–"

"No!" Agnes touched his face in exasperation. "Stop this, you need to stop this."

"I will not, sir!" Peter was raising his voice. "How can you ask me to?"

"Not now. For goodness sake, lad, shut up."

"Agnes, sir." Peter lowered his tone and looked at his mentor squarely. "Grey-suit guy was one hundred percent trying to save a fucking *tama*."

"You do not know that this," answered Agnes, raising his eyebrows to indicate the corpse, "was anything to do with him."

"It's obvious!"

"Well... yes alright it is but shut up about it."

"How can you be talking like this!"

He said this last loudly enough that Caralla had turned to look at them, Distan watching beside her. She excused herself from his company before walking over to join them. She said nothing when she arrived, just watched Peter, waiting for an explanation.

"Ambassador, I, this feels like a real opportunity... is this going to be a fight, ambassador?"

Her eyes remained fixed on his.

"I mean to say, that," he did a desperate little wobbling motion with his hands, "there could be a regime change, we should support–"

"We will support Lon Apech and its rulers against acts of domestic terrorism."

"Domestic terrorism? Have you been to the Vasa, have you seen what they–"

"I have offered the service of my Military cohort to Miré Distan. We support the incumbents, it's policy."

"No."

The stare resumed.

"No." Peter shrugged. "It's not right."

Agnes watched the younger man, admiring him but knowing both the emotion and the resistance were useless. "Peter, this-"

"No."

On the other side of the cylinder, Ming nodded to the sound of Xar Kis' voice.

"What do you think you're doing?" snapped Agnes. "How dare you refuse an order?"

"I am not part of her Military cohort, sir. Not officially."

"What do you think this is?"

"A waste of time, sir."

Agnes looked at him properly, now. He was jealous and hated to realise it. This big, confident man with the manner and bearing of a halberd, this man who was only a visitor in the drenched misery of Lon Apech and who would return to a place at a Military general's side, was also brave.

"We obey the black hand," was what he said.

Peter looked to think about this.

"You obey the black hand," he answered. "I obey Crysth."

Agnes watched him leave and, shortly afterwards, watched Ming follow.

The manic architecture of Lon Apech did nothing to help Ming's mood as she followed Peter, half jogging to match his stride. She didn't bother calling to him, he would pretend he hadn't heard. Ming cursed him as she slipped and scrambled on fog-moistened bridges.

She lost sight of him disappearing through a steel arch. She knew where he was going.

It was their favourite haunt; she, Peter, and Els. They had come here to drink, to forget the rest of the city and to fuck, back when they were still bothering to hide it from the others. A cross-shaped church, hollow but for a staircase which gently ascended its bell tower to a flattened and sheltered attic space above. Their bodies replaced the bell, their voices gave sound to the clockface carved into the tower's concrete wall.

But what was spectacular about this space was not so much the illusion of separation or safety which the tower provided, but the gravestones which populated its yard. The Apechi hands which built this copy of some forgotten place of worship hadn't known what the stones they saw erected within its walls might mean. Significance was not something that would even occur to them to ask, and so in their naivety they had created something beautiful. The thick, metal and concrete floor of Lon Apech had been shattered, perforated and peeled to create rectangular gaps through to the sub-levels – windows to the cylinders, watched over by the metal which had been torn from them, teased into a semblance of a gravestone at their heads. From atop the tower at a certain time of day, the low sun shone upwards through these, turning them into dozens of windows of pure, beaming gold. The upward-streaming rays caught and bounced around the fog, throwing rectangular spotlight glares onto the church and its neighboring buildings, cutting into the erratic neon dominance of the city's usual light. It felt to the trio in these moments as if they were the sole occupants of a world turned upside down – spirit things living beyond the human world, unharmed and harmless. It was as if all they had to do to go back home was crawl into one of those empty, not-even graves, to be met with the familiar touch of grass and sun, rather than gravity sucking them to destruction on the rusting soil far below.

Ming rested there, beneath the archway which created the

entrance through the church's high wall, regaining both her breath and her composure. It was too late for the sun to work its beautiful magic, and so here was just a space. Her eyes climbed the tower. She could barely make its windows out in the fog. She wondered if he could see her, or if he too was looking at the space where he knew she would be, seeing only fog, thinking the same thoughts.

She started up the path to the church's open door.

"Peter." Her voice rang hollow up into the tower, estranged from her. "Where are you?"

"Up here," he called, eventually, "in the tower."

She ascended.

He was lying on his stomach, face in his hands, studying a chess board they had marked onto the floor in chalk. There were blankets, pillows and bedclothes strewn about the place, pilfered in a protracted theft from the embassy's storage room.

"Peter."

"I'm going to move my bishop, come watch."

She stepped over to him, stood with her feet on either side of his waist and lowered to sit on his back. Her ringed fingers moved up his spine in a gesture of comfort, affection, until she brushed his hair from the back of his neck to kiss it. She placed her chin on his shoulder, watched. Her expression said nothing.

He licked his thumb, rubbed out the queen's bishop, redrew it to the right of his knight's pawn.

"You always do that."

He nudged her head with his. "I like to get them all out there, know what I'm dealing with."

"You like," she nudged him back, "to cause trouble."

She felt him move, pushed herself onto her knees to swap her weight while he rolled over to face her. She changed her expression.

"I'm not helping Kis." he said, folding his arms behind his head.

Ming smiled lovingly, itching to touch the weapon around her wrist to his side, to shock him, to watch his muscles spasm and writhe, pull him into her as he died. She bent to kiss him. "Don't worry about him." She licked his lip, felt him smile. "Worry about not pissing off Gris Caralla."

"Why?"

"You know why."

He sighed and took her hands in his. "You know this is... I don't know. A waste of fucking time. It doesn't need to be."

"What do you mean?"

"Well... I'm only here until I can get back to Avon, you're only here until you can replace Gris for a bit and get a transfer somewhere you can be a proper ambassador. It's just... shit, isn't it?"

Ming laughed, raised his hand to her mouth to kiss his palm. "It could be much worse. When aiming for the highest office, expect years of tedium."

He nodded. "But seriously... fucking hell. It's not just about us, is it? If that grey-suit dude and Kis are fighting... I mean for fuck's sake; doesn't that mean we've got a chance to make this place better?"

"You mean by supporting Rama?"

"Yeah, Rama. Get him in charge, turn this place into less of a fucking nightmare. We're supposed to be government aren't we. It would be fine if we were like, ornithologists or something. We could just see what's rattling around in those cages and mind our business. But we're not so, this is our business."

"Peter."

"Peter what?"

She looked at him squarely, raised her right hand to the fingerprint on her lapel. "There are things you do not know."

He swallowed. "Like? Can you tell me anything?"

"You just need to know that Gris Caralla's plans are more important than whatever this is. Obey her."

"I don't trust her." He said this defiantly. A confession, an insult.

"Then you do not trust me."

"No!" He held her arms. "I just don't... get her. Why has she been here for so long? Why would anybody want to be here?"

"She has her reasons."

"What reasons? Why is she helping these fucking monsters?"

"Peter." She closed her eyes, affecting restraint, let out a little laugh. "If we cannot trust the black hand, we cannot trust Crysth."

He sat upright, catching her as she fell backwards. "I'm sorry, but no. I can't... she's just a person."

Ming's voice hardened. "Peter, if Gris is just a person, then so is Avon. Would you disobey her?"

His face emptied of expression, caught off guard. He thought for a long time. "Yes."

Ming laughed. He was not expecting it. He joined in, wrapping his arms around her and kissing her neck as he did.

"What would Els say," she said, "if she heard you."

He grinned. "You'd both be having me walk the plank, a regular old Red gang-up on this poor Military bruise." He resumed kissing her neck, longer, deeper. "I wonder where she is."

Ming shrugged, ran her fingers through his hair, thinking of Ech Kon, longing to leave. "Somewhere better than here."

His hands moved over her, under her clothes. "Will Agnes be yours, when Caralla's gone?"

"Afraid so." She leaned back.

He watched her face, moving his fingers. "What about me instead?"

She took a deep breath, closed her eyes, raised her face to the vaulted ceiling. "You belong to Avon."

"I want to belong to you."

"I know."

That night Peter flew into a miserable rage as Ming packed for the coast. He begged her not to leave, to wait until the morning at least, not to leave him to deal with Agnes and Caralla alone. He knew she couldn't help; he knew he was pathetic. This only made it worse. He pleaded all the way up to the train's closing doors.

VIII

The banana chips had disappeared. That was how Achira knew that Peter had not opted to starve, to sulk himself to death after embarrassing himself so spectacularly. She had left cups of tea outside his room to no avail. Big stupid idiot, to get so worked up over a woman like Ming. It was because he was Military, Achira thought, and she had that fingerprint on her lapel. He couldn't help himself but worship her.

It had been two days since Ustra's death and the embassy was getting annoyed. The blues had been sent off to Kis and Distan to do blue things, and Peter's absence among them was incredibly conspicuous. He was being absurd. Worse, he was being absurd while being right, which made rightness seem absurd.

She hit her knuckles against his door. "Peter."

Silence.

"Peter." Her voice was hard, annoyed.

"Yeah?" His voice bored, sleepy.

"Will you come out and talk to us?"

Jasef and Ar's worried faces appeared at the trapdoor.

"What about?"

"Come out. I feel like I'm doing a hostage negotiation here."

There was a stirring from the other side of the door, the other two men disappeared back into the kitchen.

The handle turned, Achira took a step back, the door opened. She realized that she had been expecting him to look bedraggled, like some Victorian convalescing from a bout of whatever dreadful thing ailed the feloniously romantic, but he was just Peter.

"Yeah?" he asked.

"Come upstairs? We're dying to talk about this business with Ustra and Caralla."

Peter shrugged and followed her up into the kitchen.

Ar and Jasef were sitting at the table, forcedly casual enough to seem like they'd just committed some obscene war crime by the fridge.

"Hello chap," said Jasef. "Do you want a cup of tea? Coffee? Whisky?"

"Wowza," said Peter, clambering out of the entrance, "is that Jasef offering me spirits before midday? You must be really fucking glad to see me. I'll put the kettle on – anybody after anything?"

"I'll have a tea if you're making one," said Achira.

"Roger."

He commenced a clattering and banging of cups.

"So…" began Jasef, "we've been thinking about what you said the other day–"

"Shouted," added Achira.

"About what you shouted the other day," Jasef shot Achira a dark look, "and we… well. I have something to show you."

"Alright."

Battering of spoons.

"It's really quite something," added Jasef.

"I," said Peter, "am making Achira and I a cup of tea."

"You are making," corrected Jasef, mirroring Peter's tone of voice, "a racket."

Achira threw her hands up in a gesture of *what the fuck* at Jasef, who shrugged, mouthed, *he is*.

"I can go back downstairs if you want, mate," Peter shot back.

Ar put his hand up to his face. The tiny pink parrot on his shoulder nibbled at it cheerfully.

"Am I not saying that I'm excited to show you something? There's no need to be so... damned... difficult about it."

"I'm just trying to make two fucking cups of tea, you're the one giving me shit for doing it git boy."

"Stop calling me 'git boy', it doesn't even make any sense you are so–"

"Git boy," said Peter, raising his voice and turning to point, "git boy, git–"

"Shut up!" Achira moaned, standing up and snatching the cups out of Peter's hands. "Sit down, let me do this. For gods' sake."

Peter turned to find Jasef glaring at him, and Ar doing the same.

"Oh come on," he said, taking a seat next to Achira's vacant one. "I'm just playing."

Ar's pencil scratched. *Stop annoying each other. What have you been doing for past two days?*

"Lounging about reading shit novels and feeling the fuck sorry for myself." Peter grinned.

Why sorry the fuck for self?

"Mate, come on. A couple of months ago I had two girlfriends and a job pratting about doing karate, now I'm down two girls and up one appointment to avenge a genocidal alien fuckface instead."

Ar laughed soundlessly, lifted the parrot, and offered it to Peter, who took it gingerly on his index finger.

"Girlfriend?" said Achira in disbelief, placing a cup of tea down in front of him and sitting by his side.

"You know what I mean." He rubbed his thumb over the parrot's head and addressed it softly, "Cheep cheep."

"She's coming back, isn't she?" asked Jasef, a little worry in his voice.

"Of course she is," Achira answered. "She's a black hand, or she will be, there'll be nothing happening over there that she doesn't know how to boss around."

Ar nodded.

"Don't worry about her. It's all this, all this we need to talk about." Achira. "Jasef, can you show him?"

"Of course." He extended a hand.

Jasef's index and middle fingers released what Peter's thumb and forefinger took. The former sat, self-satisfied, evidently excited for the latter's reaction.

"What's this?" Peter's tone had none of the disbelief or excitement which had been expected by its audience.

"What do you think it is?!" exploded Jasef, almost standing up in frustration. "Look!"

"Bitch, all I see is a picture of Xar Kis and his dead fucking child bride. How the fuck did you take this without anybody seeing?"

"Look at the wall you stupid oaf of a man!"

"The writing," urged Achira, "there is literally writing on the wall. And Zara Ustra was an adult woman, don't belittle her."

"What? Where? And she was a torturing lunatic is what she was."

Ar extended his pencil, tapped the tip on the first of the dripping, angular letters.

"What?"

"It's writing, that on the wall right there behind Kis." Frustration entered Achira's voice.

"Is it?"

"Yes!" Jasef.

"How do you know?"

"What? Do you not even recognise Apechi script when you see it?"

"Why would he?" interrupted Achira, before an argument could begin, "He was preparing to be sent to Hecubah."

Jasef scowled.

"So?" asked Peter, looking around at them all. "What does it say?"

Silence, Jasef beginning to look excited again.

"Go on you sly bastard, tell me."

"Well... we do not know very much Apechi. You know how it was, when the scouts arrived, they wanted to learn Crysthian more than the other way around. This, however, is an important word."

"And," added Achira, "what's extra exciting is that we, you know, we weren't sure that Kis and his ilk would even know how to write in Apechi script. They're raised with the Crysthian alphabet, aren't they?"

"But what does it say?"

Jasef leaned in. "*Crysthian*. Kind of."

"Huh?"

Achira put her hand over her eyes. "Jasef don't start. Listen, this isn't a word that means something as simple as 'Crysthian' or 'Apechi' – in fact," Ar's pencil began to move. She stopped speaking, started to read aloud from the pad he handed her. "No, it's simpler than those words. It is visceral, a slur, a gut reaction to a perceived difference between us and them.

"Exactly." Achira handed back the pad and looked to the other two to see that they had understood. "This is a really, really big deal Peter."

"I don't... why would they write an anti-Crysth slur on the wall when they've killed Ustra?"

Ar was shaking his head, writing again. The pad ended up in Jasef's palm; "Slur was too reductive. It describes not ourselves but what they perceive us to be. Pronounced like 'Parak'. It means still, uncomplicated. Straightforward. Linear. So, it tells us more about what they see missing from us than about us. More about them. Makes sense, doesn't it? Restless, unstill." Jasef handed the paper back. "Well put, Ar. Well put."

"Still… uncomplicated," Peter repeated, looking down at the image. "I don't understand."

"This all…" Achira started, stopped to think. "It means a lot of things at the same time. Firstly, it means that Apechi language is still being used, transferred, and understood. Writing is not a casual skill in any language, one does not pick it up incidentally. They must be teaching it to their children, which we of course don't know because we never see any."

"We know that," said Peter, "the non, you know, non-aristocrats, whatever you want to call them, they still speak it."

"Yes," cut in Jasef, "but we didn't know about reading. Whoever wrote this clearly had an aristocratic audience in mind." He raised his eyebrows and nodded to the image, Kis' blank expression staring forever at the dead face beyond the frame. "So they would not use a language Kis or Distan could not read."

"Right, so they're still using Apechi script, but secretly?"

"It's better not to guess at that. 'Secretly' is a loaded word, and they have a different… I don't know, cultural attitude to revealing things than we do." Achira.

"Damn right they do, fucking batshit attitude."

"So," continued Achira, before Jasef became enraged, "we can't assume that they speak and read Apechi in secret, just that they do speak and read Apechi. Do you get it?"

"Yeah. They're doing it, they're not telling us about it, but that doesn't necessarily mean they're hiding it from us."

"Exactly." Jasef. "And you should apply that same logic to everything you think about them."

"Jasef, they tell us they can see the future and then refuse to acknowledge the fact that they say they can see the future, you daft motherfucker how is that–"

"Shush, shush. Yes. There are a lot of things about this people that we do not yet understand, and that it is why it is so exciting to be here."

"So that's it – they still speak Apechi?"

"No that isn't *it*. Were you not listening to what Ar just told us?" Jasef.

Peter lifted his lip at Jasef and turned to Ar. "Help me out mate?"

Ar nodded, began to write, handed it directly to Peter this time. "Shall I read aloud? Alright. Not only does this tell us that they are still reading and writing Apechi, it tells us that they still perceive a difference between us and them. And that this is a point of contention. This thing happening between Kis and Rama is something to do with Crysth." Peter stared, frowning. "I thought... but we know that, right?"

Achira shrugged, Ar raised his hands and signed, *We don't know*.

"We don't know," said Jasef. "Truly, we have no idea, do we?"

"Why does everybody know what's going on but me?"

"Because you've been hiding in your room for the past two days while we think about what to do!"

"You could've told me! You usually just fucking... go along with this shit, don't you? How am I supposed to know you're up here thinking about it for once?"

This time Achira was offended too. "Peter. We do what we came here to do. We listen, we watch, we write. We have our futures riding on this, you don't. You are a Pïat-Elementov. You play soldiers with Agnes and wait to go home to an already glitzy post with Avon Stal of all people. We have to be careful."

Peter rounded his shoulders, suitably cowed. "I'm sorry. I don't mean it. I got worked up."

"Anyway," continued Achira, softening her voice, "as we have said, this is extremely complicated, and quite a big deal. It... kinda changes things."

"What do you mean?"

Achira licked her lips, looked to the others. "Well..."

"I have already said, for the record, that we should take this to Caralla." Jasef.

"She knows, Jasef," cut in Achira, "we've been through this. Peter, don't listen to him, she absolutely knows."

"Wait, knows what?"

"What the fucking," Achira paused, took a deep breath through her nose. "What the writing says. If Gris Caralla cannot read Apechi script better than we can and doesn't know what that word says, then I will literally eat that parrot."

Peter grinned and ruffled the pink feathers. "Hear that mate? But Caralla won't let us get involved, she says it's not our business, we can't pick sides. All that nonsense."

Jasef pouted at Achira, but nodded for her to continue. "She says it is not our business that an alien aristocrat has been murdered and a word which can mean 'Crysthian' written in her blood."

"Yeah, alright when you put it like that it really sounds like it's our business. Can you just... straight up tell me what conclusions you've come to?"

"We, alright. We agree with you that it would be the moral thing to do to support Rama if indeed he is fighting Kis for the," she clicked her fingers, searching for a word, "throne or, you know, being in charge, supremacy, but we don't think that's what's happening."

Ar frowned, signed *so so*.

"Yes," added Achira, "no, it would be better to say that we don't think that's *all* that is happening. Right, Ar? We're pretty sure, I mean – it says it right there, and they wanted us to see it, didn't they? We think it's about us."

"What? What have we done?"

"No!" Jasef drummed his fingers on the side of the table in an expulsion of frustrated energy. "We mean bigger us, people." Ar noted the use of the word 'people' in this context with some interest. "The fight has something to do with Crysth. It is our business."

Peter leaned over the table to hand back the parrot to Ar,

put his empty hands together beneath his chin. "What are we saying?"

"We don't know." Achira.

We do know, signed Ar, *but we don't like it.*

"What was that?" asked Peter.

Ar picked up his pen, *we don't like it.*

"Let me... you think that Caralla is purposefully ignoring something that might," he blinked slowly, "hurt us, or something?"

"Sort of." Achira, leaning back, "We think that she trusts Kis to put down whatever it is but... he couldn't even protect his partner, or whatever she was."

Peter started to shake his head, slowly, side to side. "She has all the facts that we have, but you also have to assume she has some more. If you don't trust the black hand, you don't trust Crysth."

"What?" spluttered Achira. "That sounds like something a Red would say – no offense Ar. Are you kidding me?"

Jasef looked pained, grumbled a little, spoke, "Well... I'm..."

"Look," interrupted Achira, splaying her bare fingers across the table in front of her, "Gris Caralla is a black hand. I respect that. However-"

"'Chira, you're a pearl. You're basically a professional insurrectionist." Peter was smiling as he spoke, Achira mirrored it back to him.

"Exactly. So I know a need to insurrect when I see one."

Quiet. Peter looking to Achira, to Ar. Jasef looking at the table.

"This isn't..." Jasef, hesitant, still looking at the table. "Insurrection. This is an acknowledgement of the fact of the... the need to investigate the situation on our own terms."

"That is the Greenest sentence I have ever heard in my life." Peter, obviously.

"For gods' sake." Achira snapped, slapping her palms against the table and returning them to the splayed position. "Let's just talk like people who don't live together for a minute, shall we? Let me be clear; Gris Caralla is a black hand. She's the Crysthian ambassador, and for that I have a world of respect and admiration. However," – Ar smiled; it did not perturb her – "she is old. She is old and she is unusual. We all know this. What other ambassador have you heard of who would keep the same crappy position for so long? What is it, eight years? Eight. Years. And she's had Agnes for five, so even her chief of staff quit. She has been here alone, more or less, for all that time, the only one of us here for so long. And that's what she is, only one of us."

"I see what you're saying," answered Peter, after having waited until he knew she was certainly done speaking, "you think that she's lost it."

Ar held his hands up again in the *so-so* motion again.

"Well, Ar's a Red. He agrees." Jasef.

Ar nodded, wrote, paused, wrote. They watched in silence.

Ar handed the pad to Jasef, who read "The black hand is not infallible. We have all heard stories of our own faction leaders making poor decisions. But we are not proposing a challenge, we are simply going to make sure we agree that a challenge does not need to arise." Jasef nodded aggressively as he spoke all of this, added "Absolutely."

Silence again.

"Do you see what we mean?" urged Jasef, "We agree with you, we do think that," he lowered his voice, "Xar Kis can be a bit of a sadist. I mean… we all know how that body got downstairs don't we. You don't need to say it, just nod. And we all know that this Rama character seems more inclined to being pleasant… and that Caralla probably has information that we are not privy to. We just… want to make sure."

"How?" Peter, quietly now, thinking of Ming, feeling excitement and hope rise treacherously in his chest.

"Don't you remember?" Achira's voice was soft, coy even. "Ming told us how. She told me to do it, in fact."

"What?" The mention of her name was as a break in an internal barrier which he had not known was there, allowing him finally to set back into his anger and indignance, his need to act, "What are you talking about?"

"At the trial, at the Vasa. She told me to go and speak to Ed Rama."

IX

Something has happened here. There are ruins of it in the air.

Fourteen hours of feverish longing. The train's straight rails slicing through monotonous miles of empty fucking Apech. Nowhere for enemies of progress to hide. Mountains yawn over the horizon here and there. A small pale moon, followed hours later by its brother. Indistinguishable, never sharing the same sky. Longing, intolerable need to be back by the ocean. The sun. Rain pelting itself suicidally against the train's windows as the brakes begin to tease it into a halt. Morning, but she had not slept.

Ming arrived at the only other Crysth-like settlement on Apech, the ocean resort of Ech Kon. Something has happened here. There are ruins of it in the air.

It is etched on their faces, too. A handful of people she has never had occasion to speak to before, nervous and tense, kinetic with the jittering movement that characterizes Apechi commoners who have not learned to control it, waiting for her beside the train.

They're odd here, anyway, in this town populated by those who either choose or are chosen not to inhabit the capital. Older, generally, with quiet self-preservation pulling them away from the melting cruelty of Lon Apech. Wearing plain robes, looking almost like *tama* but for their neatness. No

To where?" She started folding the letter back into her jacket, swift, certain movements.

"Over there."

Ming did not look where she pointed.

A woman standing to the first woman's left put her hand on the extended wrist, spoke. "We'll take you to him."

She continued to watch them.

"The man who wrote the letter." Added the woman, "We'll take you to him."

It crossed Ming's mind that it might be a good idea to interrogate these people, this nervous crowd who would give away the answers with their faces, but her training told her to wait.

She nodded, lifted her suitcase with its precious cargo, waved her hand to indicate she was ready. Followed.

Ech Kon loitered around them, bronze and oddly beautiful in its carapace weirdness. The buildings here were spiral in shape, gold brown metal combed into the air and growing rust. They were the only copies of Crysthian architecture on Apech that might pass for the real thing in darkness; copies of a fashion of shell-inspired towers which dotted pretty shores. Here they varied a little too wildly in size to be taken for normal. That, and the fact that they stood out too strange against the sandy shell which crunched underfoot, adding the voice of crushed rock to the metal groaning and the ocean's rhythmic pull. There was a pagoda, too, smaller than the one in the capital but built in the same vein for the habitation of Crysthian guests. The ocean came into view, folding itself forever against the long and shallow coast. Desire twitched at her.

There were more *tama* here than in Lon Apech, and they were more easily seen. In motion, the distinction between them was astounding. Apechi were hyperfocused, fast, unpredictable in their movements. The *tama* wandered as if they could only dream. Here and there they'd loiter, humming tuneless songs, congregating around the aviaries which stand stinking and cacophonous. There is no malice in their voyeurism as they watch the birds flutter around, no surprise but all wonder when they are collected and killed. They share handfuls of wild dates. Rain falls on them.

Ming's eyes found the docks, found the ships. Three of them, one missing. Oh dear. Scanned leftwards, saw the decorative lighthouse which served as her home away from home pointing squat over the horizon. She watched it for a long time, longing, thinking.

The beach narrowed as it curved south, giving way to larger boulders and eventually to a sloping cliff paved by a path of compacted sand. The architecture changed here, too; the spirals replaced by terraces poking out of the cliff face like rows of jagged, narrow teeth. This was where the town's residents lived, with a view over the cove and into the low green bush at the town's outer limit.

The woman who had initially spoken to Ming turned around to check that she was still following, gave a thin-lipped smile. That was the first time she had done this throughout their journey, so Ming supposed that they were getting close. The rows of houses began to open and thin until there was only one remaining, much further back, set almost directly into the cliff and angled in such a way that anyone inside would only be able to see out to the ocean. As they neared, Ming realized that the windows in all six of the houses which connected to form the row were fake, just gouges in stone.

She had never really bothered to come up here before, too in love with the lighthouse, but there was something melancholic about it – salt spray on stone. Wet grey cobbled together with ill-poured concrete and ill-standing roofs. She had always found the earth, the stone, the ocean and the horizon restful, liberating, but up here it felt even more oppressive than Lon Apech. It lacked the capital's madness, the fascination in its lights. She imagined the capital without all the smoke and fog from the pumpings of the cylinders below and realized that it, too, would seem like this flimsy shell of a place were it not for the hallucinogenic light.

"Well?" she asked, standing now behind the crowd, which had parted down the middle in a gesture to let her pass through to the door beyond.

"We aren't let in."

Ming took one step forward, stopped. "Who is let in?"

"Just him."

Another step forwards. "Who?"

Ming knew the effect this would have on them. Apechi did not like erratic movement; what she was doing now might even upset someone like Kis or Ustra who had been around Crysthians long enough to know not to expect violence. But

now their embarrassment was her tool, to push them to give
something away of what lay waiting for her in that house. She
could not be sure that she could enter safely, but she could
not walk away without losing her control. She asked again,
"Who."

The answer was a whine. Long, metallic, wheezing in its
excruciating volume. The crowd had felt it coming, had turned
their heads and stepped back towards her. They were afraid of
whoever was in there, more afraid of him than they were of
her. Fascinating.

The door of the furthest house was opening inwards. Slowly,
so slow it could have been for dramatic effect were it not for the
sound of its screaming hinges. She stalked through the crowd,
impulsively, quickly, to meet whoever was on the other side.

He had emerged too.

She stopped, too abruptly. He had won the greeting section
of diplomacy, then.

He was so old. Grey-brown hair braided out of his eyes,
skin hanging loose around his bare arms recalling a once-
powerful body. He reminded her of Xar Kis; he had the same
languid confidence, the same stature if derelict with age. They
watched each other. His face blank, her dimpled chin raised in
unantagonistic curiosity.

"*So,*" he said, and the word stunned her, almost shifted her
expression into shock because he had spoken in a language
which she understood but had only ever heard on tape; "*this is
what they think.*"

She stared.

"*Do you understand me?*"

She nodded.

"*I thought* [something in Apechi, tone suggesting
confirmation]. *Does* [something, suggesting negative] *boy know
you can?*"

"Forgive me," she said, opting for formality and speaking
in Crysthian, not trusting her mouth to make alien sounds, "I

do not know what you were referring to then. I have not had much occasion to practice your native language."

His expression turned cruel, and she realized that she had never seen an Apechi so old. Did he speak Crysthian?

"Have you not," he said, switching languages, his rolling accent heavy on the words.

He turned and walked back inside. She followed.

It was emptily black inside, heavy with gloom and a smell of sour, salt-washed rust.

"Shouldn't you be finding a lost ship?" he asked, gruff and impatient, moving away from her.

She placed her suitcase on the ground to her right, not wanting to let it go. "I was told I would be speaking with the person who requested our assistance."

"Our?" His voice was distant now, and his footsteps had changed tone – he was ascending, "There is one of you."

"You wanted more?"

Silence but for the footsteps, and a change in their pace as if he had come to a landing. She could see that there was a source of light above. Twin stretches of pale sun at the very top of the space, what she saw now was a sort of narrow hallway occupying the largest possible dimensions upwards and onwards, with only a gently sloping ladder to the furthest end. It was a high ladder, climbing three stories. She began to ascend.

She heard metal cry as somebody closed the door.

Fuck, she thought, Gris will be so fucking annoyed if I die. She smiled.

And the world seemed to change.

The moment her eyes reached the higher floor the world had changed. She could not understand what she was looking at. She pulled herself up until she could step over the ladder's head.

Daylight, coming in through parallel covered slits down the length of the roof, and colour. So much colour it felt loud, even though the room was silent but for the gentle footsteps of the old man. It looked like somebody had taken all the posters, the uniforms, the banners and symbols of Crysth and crushed them together into a violent rainbow monotony. It was oppressive, awful, stunning.

She stepped forwards into it, trying to discontinue this crescendo of uninterrupted vibrancy with her understanding, to piece it apart, find it, know it. Feathers. What? They're birds.

She touched one, amazed. Now she had found the thread the puzzle unravelled, it was all birds. Taxidermy birds arranged on plinths and tables and chairs and rocks and whatever space there was to find. But they were wrong. A parrot with four wings, a tiny, long-tailed sparrow with a row of beaks all the way down its spine. All of them, she saw as she wove her way through, following him through the space, were perverted, desecrated in some way by the bodies of another.

He wound his way through until he reached a workbench; a thick steel desk topped with a variety of tools which she did not care to identify. He sat beside it, a gnarled hand reached out to take a set of magnifying goggles from the surface.

"Do you find them beautiful, sad? Pitiful?" he asked, nastily, bending himself over a tiny orange budgerigar.

She suppressed laughter as she drew up alongside him, although she did not know why she wanted to laugh. "It's an interesting aesthetic."

He snorted. "An interesting aesthetic."

She thought, decided, continued in the same friendly tone, "I have never met an Apechi with such an artistic hobby."

"A hobby!" He started, banging a fist on the table and launching into the apoplectic fury which she had expected. "What nonsense word is this you aim at me? You [*something, probably a curse*]-" He stopped abruptly after the Apechi word had left his mouth and removed his goggles to swivel around and look at her. "*You know*. You offend me on purpose, do you?"

"Not at all." She said, opting for a tone of stupidity, "Not at all."

He ignored her after that, gritting his teeth and returning to the material of his occupation. She used the opportunity of his distraction to inspect the animals more closely and, as she did, the seed of understanding settled somewhere in her mind, somewhere yet ungraspable, but there. From uncanny to absurd, eagles with a mane of canary heads, herons with wings sliced from sparrows. She reached out to fondle a webbed foot which sprang from the gizzard of some flightless thing.

"Are they art?"

He laughed, without joy, and answered. "They do not contain their purpose within themselves, although I doubt you have enough understanding to have meant that in your question."

She had not. "So, what is their purpose?"

He looked at her now but did not remove his goggles, giving her the feeling of being scrutinized as an object for treatment. "Deconstruction. Reconstruction."

She did not understand so she did not react. "Do you find them beautiful?"

"That is irrelevant."

"You asked me the same thing."

"That is because you are irrelevant," he snapped, selecting a wing from the assortment on his desk. "Find that ship."

"Tell me about it."

"You are in no position to make demands."

"Describe my position as you see it."

"Does Kis' son know you are here?"

"Xar has no children."

"Xar is Kis' son."

She smiled in a condescending way, just to annoy him. "Forgive me for being more up to date."

They watched each other, and in the silence she noticed that he moved like a Crysthian. He was steady, relaxed. He had none of the darting motions or misdirected glances which characterised whatever was wrong with Apech. He could tell that she was appraising him.

"I have been maintaining order in Ech Kon. Kis' son should be grateful for that. I do not have the time to be chasing fools around on the open ocean. It's your fault they have the ships in the first place. Bring them back."

"What puts you in a position to maintain order, and who are 'they'?"

He switched to Apechi, said, "*I will answer you when all of those ships are back on shore.*"

She lifted her hand to her jacket. He turned back to his work.

"What do you think?" he asked, sarcastically.

"Pardon?" she said, unfurling the letter.

He said nothing.

She lay the letter on the desk beside him, covering a tiny sewing kit. "Did you write this?"

She realized that he had already answered.

Fuck this, she thought. She did not even take the letter with her when she turned to leave.

X

Ming's journey back to the dock, the walk up the pier and out over the sea which she loved and coveted so much, was utterly ruined. She thought of him only, the taxidermist at his bench. All titillation was gone from her. She did not even have the space to crave her lighthouse.

It was a little after one in the afternoon by the time she reached the long, shallow beach's dock at its southernmost point. The crowd had followed her the whole way, even as she meandered furiously onto the beach itself. She fondled the key to her suitcase in her breast pocket, a spike of anger hitting her sleep-deprived chest that the taxidermist had wrecked her anticipation so. She should have just killed him, gone back to Kis with one of the parrots to show him what weird nonsense had been causing trouble, been done with it. But that was neither his nor Caralla's instructions. She would seem incompetent.

Fuck them all. Whatever this was would not get in the way of her enjoying herself. She would take a few days while she figured out what to do.

She stood at the edge of the wooden dock, breathing in the salt. Turned around.

"When did you lose the ship?"

They all tried to answer at the same time, in fact, some of them had been answering while she still spoke. She managed to extract from the temporal confusion that it had been about three days. Right.

"I am going to take one of these ships out to the lighthouse. I will be back two hours after dawn. While I am gone, you will stay on the remaining ships and keep a lookout for further activity. One of you will go to whoever is operating the train and send it back to Lon Apech with a message for the embassy." She produced a pen and a slip of paper out of her jacket pocket, wrote; *Ship gone, evidence of fight. Dealing with it. M.* She drew two parallel lines under the M to indicate that the message was true. Caralla would not bother to look for them, there was no real need for secrecy. She held it out to a man who had already come forward to take it.

Moments later she was on the deck of one of the three remaining crafts, tapping her rings angrily against its controls with a satisfying, echoing chime. This was better. Release.

The vessel was an oddity of Crysthian generosity, a beetle-shaped ten-capacity oval with lively orange armchairs in a dark blue cabin. There was even a bar, and all of it demonically possessed in the same way as the train. These beasts, intangible and supposedly vicious, could be trapped in any material which had been native to the abandoned Earth. They were not tameable, but they could be controlled, tormented artfully into moving any vehicle. It had been revolutionary, their discovery, breaking the political control of the largest energy producers. Crysth calls them demons to keep them to itself, or to justify their enslavement, or to stop further questions.

Ming teased the controls into life, pushing the whirring machine into action, pumping water downwards until the vessel was near floating a foot above the waves. Its speed was capped comedically slowly – a safety control just in case Crysth ever needed to come and shoot this thing out of the water – but it was glorious to pilot, nevertheless. It reminded her of being a child, pulling impatiently at her mother's jacket in infant wrath to be behind the wheel. Here she was, and going home.

The lighthouse had been built just for her, the soon-to-be ambassador. Beautiful, slanted slightly to the right and with a rough, grey sheen.

She stood on the deck before it with her mouth slightly open, soaking in the anticipation of entering, watching the light inside. A rowing boat was docked, no, run ashore against an artificial beach which made a slope up to the lighthouse's entrance. She stared into its paneless windows, fixing her eyes on each of them in turn as their flicker fought the sucking dark of Apechi evening; seeking the first sight of the woman who waited within. Nowhere. Oh well, she knew where she would find her.

She started forwards and whipped her eyes up its iron staircase. Slowly, slowly now, she ascended. Taking care not to look up, not to ruin the first sight, not to hurry and not to linger. She pushed the trapdoor above her head and saw.

Her *tama*, cross legged on the floor.

Ming stayed there, her head the only thing visible against the darkness behind her, and watched the *tama*. She waited for as long as she could, until the woman seemed about to speak and she crawled forwards, silencing her with a long, deep kiss of relief and lust and ran her hands over the alien body whose otherness she longed to perceive.

"Ming," she whispered. "Hello."

"Hello." Ming sat back on the floor opposite her, imagining what it could be that her scanning, photographic memory saw.

The *tama* seemed confused, but content. She had remembered Ming's name this time. Ming was not sure whether or not she liked that, but she was not thinking about herself, only about that mind, that body, so alien and so intimate. She leaned over and sank the tips of her fingers into the woman's thigh and up until she was cupping a breast. She squeezed until the *tama* winced and looked suddenly afraid. Withdrew her hand.

Ming shook as she pulled the key out from her inside pocket. She tore off her suddenly ridiculous jacket and threw it into a corner of the room. The key twisted and the case clicked its consent; popping open to allow a gap for Ming's thumbs. She lifted the lid and sighed, closing her eyes in satisfaction to see it lying there, waiting. She took it gently and placed it on the floor. Then she burrowed through her clothes to find Fukuyama's book.

The *tama* smiled and extended a hand to the book's spine. She tried unsuccessfully to find a keyhole, like the one she had just seen Ming operate, and then looked uncomprehendingly up at her. Ming let out a groan of pleasure as she realized that the woman had never seen a book before. Not even one of her notebooks from last time? No, she supposed not. Ming managed to smile in a semblance of benevolent encouragement and opened the book herself, onto a random page near the center.

"No!" The *tama* yelled and tried to scramble to her feet, but Ming had been expecting this. She wrenched the woman's arm downwards, causing a yelp of pain which she ignored while seizing the other arm in an urgent vice.

"Look at it," she instructed, her voice commanding now.

Restrained, the woman breathed as if sobbing in dry terror as she fixed her eyes obediently on the page.

Looking back up at her was the hollowly emaciated face of a naked *tama*, watching them over his shoulder in eternal stasis. Fukuyama had blurred out his genitals, but that did not matter. His inner thigh, his neck and his waist were covered in discolored spines, which emerged from his skin in beautiful copses. Some were barely lumps, but most jutted out by inches and broke the skin in blackening, brittle spikes which resembled a pine tree preserved in flesh. They jumbled together, twisting, as if competing for light, and in the tight spaces between them Ming could make out trapped pieces which had broken off and become subsumed by the forest. She longed to find him and run her tongue over those bony spines. She longed to feel the broken shards of disease moving in their cages, hear them rattle as she sucked them out. She wanted to crunch them between her teeth, push them into her cheeks and swallow.

"It is beautiful,"

"No! Ming... pain." She could not tell whether she meant pain in her arms or that the disease was painful, but she did not care.

"Beauty."

"No! Ming... pain... bad!"

Ming let go of one of the woman's arms. "Stay. Look. It is good. Good, you understand?"

She used her free hand to flip the pages of the book until the captive cried out again. Ming looked down and oh gods, it was beautiful.

On this page, Fukuyama had plastered a close up of a *tama* mouth, lips pulled back and teeth bared to reveal spines emerging from blackened gums, pushing teeth out by their roots and curving forwards. Another broken piece was trapped between two crooked spikes just above the incisors. Ming moaned with pleasure and her cunt throbbed to be touched as she fixed her eyes on that one, loose spine.

Ming snapped up her head to stare fixedly into those wide set eyes and said, firmly, "Beautiful. Good."

The *tama* seemed to forget what was happening, saw only that this thing, what she thought of as a Ming, was smiling. Ming let go of her other arm.

"I will show you. Understand? It is good. Good. Happy."

Ming stood and picked up the object which she had placed beside her suitcase before returning to sit behind the other woman, stretching her legs on either side of the nervous body. In response to her touch, the *tama* relaxed and leaned backwards against Ming's torso, burrowing into the warmth. She felt a jolt of excitement and brought the sock in front of their bodies for the woman to see.

She held its tip in her left hand and used her right to fold it down to the wrist, turning it inside out and revealing the crisp red stain left by Agan's tortured corpse. The woman gasped again but Ming shushed her with her right hand, caressing her lips and stroking the front of her neck in gentle persuasion. She lifted the tainted rag to her own face and sniffed deeply. She cursed with disappointment and remembered Peter's pathetic yelling. It was his fault. He had stopped her from collecting more. No matter. No matter. There were still faint patches of it which glistened, wet.

"Look at the page." Ming instructed, whispering into the woman's ear and eliciting a strange gasp.

The *tama* did as she was instructed, fixing her eyes onto the images of violent decay.

Ming bit, gently at first but crueler until the alien's moans of pleasure were intermingled with surprised yelps. She moved her right hand down into the woman's slip dress, down again until she could slip her middle finger into her, imagining all the time those black spines twisting, erupting, reeking out of the slave's skin. She bit, hard, and thrust her morbid garment into the *tama*'s gasping mouth.

XI

"She said it looked like a fort not a fucking, I don't know, castle thing."

"A fort *is*, by *definition*, a 'castle thing'. Shouldn't Military know that?"

"Oh yeah, git boy, that's what we do all day long. We watch slideshows of buildings and go 'fort', 'not fort', 'fort'."

"Can you stop, can you please for the love of the pearl emperor just stop?"

"*The Pearl Emperor Loves Not to Love*," said the two men, automatically.

The three of them were in their formal uniforms, having bickered for more than an hour about what the appropriate attire was for an illicit interview with what they supposed was an alien mutineer. Their rings, medals and identifying badges had been left at home. Ar had stayed, too, none wanting to say it but all knowing that the Apechi simply did not like him. Achira was bad enough, always trying to fraternise with the *tama* – but it had been she who Ming had told to see Rama, after all.

Achira grinned. "Sounds funny when you two say it. As if that's what it really means."

"That is what it really means," said Peter, plonking himself down angrily on a little statue of a bull.

"No, it is not," said Achira, her own voice rising in outrage. "How dare you explain my own faction to me?"

"Yeah," Jasef agreed, "it means the opposite."

"No – now you're doing it too. It means that she is dedicated to love itself, but for the sake of something other than love."

"Well that should be what it says then. Fucking ridiculous," Peter.

"Oh sure, and your mottos are all shining examples of perfect rhetoric, are they? One of them is literally just *Faster Than You*."

"That's because we're the only ones with a sense of fucking humour, Achira."

"Don't swear at her!"

"Don't patronise me, Jasef." Achira.

"Yeah, I fucking swear at everyone, get over it."

"For – for fuck's sake!" Achira covered her eyes with her hand. "We're annoyed and lost and… pissed off. Stop."

Peter folded his arms, adjusting himself slightly on the bull. "At least it's not raining or nothing."

"I really think that it's that thing," said Jasef, indicating a squat, brown cube with battlements arranged around the top and a great neon fish flashing in orange on its side.

"Ming said 'rust-red', though,"

Achira clicked her tongue a few times. "Yeah… but might she describe that as rust-red?"

"It's brown." Peter.

Jasef raised his palms. "Isn't rust-red a bit brown?"

"No."

"I suppose you could say that brown is a social construct," Achira.

"What?" Peter.

"I mean, some cultures don't have a word for 'blue' they just see everything as shades of green."

"You're saying that blue is a social construct too, now?" Peter.

"Shall we just go and try the door?" Jasef.

Achira shook her head. "I was really hoping we'd be able to sort of, just, run into him…"

"As if." Peter. "Plus, don't you think she would've mentioned the fish? It's fucking huge."

"Yeah, that thing is not a social construct. Are you sure we haven't been followed, P?"

Peter screwed up his face in an expression which showed how much of a ridiculous question he thought this was. "We haven't got anybody explicitly chasing us around as far as I can tell, but they always know where we are. It doesn't matter."

"I know, I meant more… us coming this way hasn't piqued anybody's interest, then."

"I don't know fuck from Tuesday in this light."

"Right. I'm fed up with this," declared Jasef, endeavouring to stand up straighter.

"What you gonna do?"

"Where are you going?" Achira.

Peter swivelled a one eighty upon the bull statue, an expression of alarmed interest turning with him as Jasef got near enough the building's walls that the orange glare flashing from its side began to change the colour of his uniform.

"What's he doing?" Achira's voice a stage whisper.

"I dunno," he replied, also in a whisper.

"Is he going to knock on the door?"

"No, he'll pussy out." Still whispering.

A series of sharp, hollow bangs rung out from Jasef's knuckles and into the fog.

"Oh shit," Peter, the two of them rushing forward at an awkward half-jog to stand at Jasef's side.

The door had not moved by the time they were standing together again, but there was something happening behind it. Metal grinding metal, crunches and clicks as something heavy moved inside.

The door, to their surprise, sank into the floor. Smooth, effortless, in jarring contrast with the sounds which had preceded its descent. It revealed nothing behind, just darkness.

"You want Rama," came a heavily accented feminine voice from within. "Here."

Crunching footsteps diminuendoed from the open portal.

"Well," Peter said, purely to punctuate their shared surprise.

It took them a while to realize what they were looking at. Achira was the first to stick her head through when they did. The door opened to reveal only a wall, about five feet in front of it, and another directly to its right. A hallway running left along the fortress' outer wall. A rumbling, and the door began to twitch – they jumped over, into the hallway and, horribly, into its quickly growing dark.

"*Shit, shit,*" Peter, pushing the other two in front of him and away from the door's mechanism which they could no longer see. It was pitch black but for light beginning to glow from a torch implant in Peter's left arm.

"Oh my gods," Achira. "P, what do we do?"

"Come on, she went down here," said Jasef.

"Yes, obviously. She didn't disappear did she!" Achira.

"Sh, shut up." Peter.

They all stayed still, listened to the sound of their own breathing. The light of Peter's implant hit the far wall, showed that they were alone.

"She's either very far away, or she's standing still," he whispered.

Light – the buzzing click of an industrial-sized bulb and flickering into whiteness. The top of the hallway was lined with them, long cylindrical things showing the way.

"Sorry! Forgot light," came the voice, and the footsteps resumed.

The three looked at each other, expressions agitated and

fearful. Embarrassed. They had been afraid of the dark. Anybody would have been, but that didn't matter.

Peter started to laugh, and the others joined in out of relief. They moved down the corridor, a corner, another corridor. They sped up.

"This is dangerous, we're going really far in and we – shit." Peter stopped mid-sentence, still, the others by his side.

"Oh, wow," breathed Achira.

The claustrophobic, winding brightness of the corridors had given way to a huge, square atrium. The ceiling was domed, slightly, and dotted with bright white lights which created a sheltered courtyard of dazzling, twilight beauty. They were standing on the furthest side of one of four arched bridges which spanned a shallow, square moat tracing the perimeter of the central square. But what was truly lovely was the square itself; a pale grey expanse populated by boulders of varying sizes, interwoven with snaking parallel lines in the gravel. It even sounded beautiful, big and empty with water draining somewhere over the moat's shadowed edge.

The woman who had let them in was nowhere, but there was one lone figure in the furthest right quadrant of the square. He had his head down and his back to them, shirt sleeves rolled up, moving rhythmically with a long metal rake.

Jasef cleared his throat, loudly. It echoed strangely in the domed room.

Ed Rama turned, nodded. His movement started to retreat backwards towards them, raking away his footprints as he went. The three of them stood awkwardly on the other side of the bridge, not daring to enter the room without invitation.

As they watched, Rama's winding path reached a large boulder upon which he sat himself cross legged, his rake across his lap. "Come to me, please? Don't worry about the patterns."

"Yes, sir," replied Jasef, surprising even himself as he took the first step onto the bridge.

The others followed, gingerly picking their way over the arched structure for fear of skidding along the layer of fine gravel which lay over it. If they were watching Rama, rather than their feet, they would see that he was staring at the pattern in front of them with such an intense concentration that they would have believed him livid at their destruction of it.

Rama is trying against his exhaustion and his affliction to prevent himself from seeing flickers in reality, moments of future. He is failing.

As they neared, they could tell how tired he was. His face, middle-aged and worn with the ruddiness of dried sweat, was marked with deep blue sockets beneath sagging eyes. His posture, too, was exhausted – leaning over the rake in his lap with his head inclined towards one shoulder. He looked like he had been awake for days, which he had.

"Rama." Peter nodded, holding out a hand to shake.

Rama smiled and waved it away. "Forgive me, I was told it was rude to do that while sitting down, but I would rather not stand."

"Oh, yeah, it's no problem."

They stood there looking at him, all of them realising that they did not really know what to do anymore.

He had not stopped smiling, sadly, weakly.

"Where is the tallest one? I do not know his name," he asked, after a while.

They all started talking at once, but Achira won; "Ar, sir, you mean Ar. He had work to do, he stayed home."

"I'm sure." He looked directly into Achira's eyes now, and the smile faded. "It was our next ambassador who told you where to find me, I imagine?"

"Yes, sir."

He nodded. "Go on, then."

"Sir?"

He sighed. "I assume you're here to denounce me, although your ambassador should know that I did not give the order. I... temporarily – and I do mean temporarily – lost control of one of my friends."

There was a silence. Peter broke it. "You're talking about Zara Ustra's death, sir?"

Rama nodded, contrite. "It won't happen again. Although I realize that it can't; the damage cannot be undone. I imagine Xar wants us all dead."

Consolingly Peter said, "Well nothing's changed then."

"Erm," began Achira, "sir, I actually just wanted to speak to you about what happened at the trial, a few days ago."

"What?"

"I'm sorry – sir, I don't mean to offend–"

"We thought it was a good thing," interrupted Peter, "sir, sorry. We thought it was a good thing you were trying to do."

Rama focused again on Peter. Achira used his distraction to look properly at what she had spotted on his exposed arms – a thick crosshatching of scars, long healed but shining against his skin.

He rubbed his hand against his forehead, "I – I see. I'm sorry I, what?" He paused. "I see. But she is still dead, isn't she?"

"The *tama*?" asked Achira, who received a nod.

The three Crysthians looked at each other, sharing a sensation of thrill and shock. The space added to the feeling, more melancholy than lovely now they were in its centre, seeming to drag emptiness from the darkness beyond the moat's low drain. They have never heard sorrow for *tama* before. The *tama* are barely real to Apechi.

"That means," said Rama, thoughtfully, "oh."

"But sir, if I may return to the previous topic, you're sure you have the situation under control?" This was Jasef's voice.

Rama raised his eyes over the Green uniform before settling on Jasef's earnest face. "That color means you're a plotter, doesn't it? A structurer, a mapper. Cities and agriculture and..." He rolled his hand for Jasef to provide more.

"Business, sir." Jasef swelled with pride. "We are the architects of motion."

"But the Red faction are its masters," Rama supplied, distantly. "How is it that you don't fight, all the time?"

"Each faction operates with a different structure, so we don't get in each other's way." Peter.

Rama frowned, so Achira went on, "That's not strictly true, we do clash. It works because we are designed to." He nodded for her to continue, polite curiosity. "So, the Ethicists have a completely flat structure, none of us are in charge – even, theoretically, the emperor. The Reds are structured so that the ambassadors are near the top, but the emperor and his steward are still supreme. The Militaries are the most straightforwardly authoritarian, and the Greens are split into hundreds of different groups with their own managements. They are designed as balances to each other – no one system is supposed to be able to conquer the others."

He was nodding his head gently, his eyes closing. "So contradictory things can work at the same time, if they find a way to fit."

"Yes, sir," answered Jasef, with absolute certainty.

"So, the embassy does not know that you are here?"

"The embassy does not know that we are here, sir." Peter, receiving a kick from Achira which Rama pretended not to notice.

He lifted the rake from his lap and placed it gently at his side. It rolled away anyway, crashing onto the floor with a soft crash. His bare feet touched the grit as he leaned forwards until his elbows were on his knees, his hands clasped in front of him. "Neither Xar nor the embassy have been responding to my letters. Perhaps you can take the latter a message for me?

I know that Gris Caralla is not inclined to my side, but I need her help."

"Crysth cannot take sides in extra-imperial matters, sir." Jasef.

Annoyance flashed briefly through the lines of Rama's face before he said, "Your ambassador pays almost weekly visits to Xar Kis while ignoring me. She has quite firmly taken a side. She likes Apech the way it is."

Peter's heart thumped; they had been right. "And you, sir? How would you like Apech?"

The older man considered this, staring at his thumbs which he began to gently rotate one over the other. "Unburdened."

Achira nodded as if she understood. She thought that she did. "Sir, can you be sure that our ambassador has, in fact, chosen sides?"

"Yes, Achira, I can." He looked at them, all three of them, making a decision. "You have come to me on the eve of war with praise. Am I to understand that you have come prepared to help me?"

"Yes." Peter.

"No." Jasef.

"Well..." Achira.

"I see." He looked back at his thumbs. "You clash, you are designed to."

Peter rallied. "Sir, do you know why our ambassador would seek to support Xar Kis' dominance on this planet?"

"'On this planet'. Can you know how that sounds to a man who has never seen another?"

"You want to leave?" Achira.

"Wouldn't you?" he asked. "Of course I want to leave. I want to see snow, and cities, and to have a garden. A real one, with date trees. I planted some, you know, when we fetched this sand from Ech Kon. They died. Stupid of me."

"I'm sorry to hear–" Achira began.

"But," –he raised his voice to interrupt– "your ambassador

does not want to leave. She remains, in this desolate and murderous place. Do you not wonder why?"

"We do, actually." Jasef. "It is highly unusual for a black hand to stay in one place for so long, unless it is…"

"Nice? Yes. Why do they have black hands, incidentally? Why the fingerprint on the jacket?"

"That's just a symbol. She goes back home and gets the prosthetics, the black hands," Peter wiggled his fingertips as he said this last, "when she replaces Caralla. They open things, authorize machines and all that."

"Make it so you can't back out." Achira. "You don't give up your hands lightly."

"The more the power the less the liberty," mused Rama. "I wonder, what is it that they know that Crysth must mutilate them so?"

"It's not…" Achira began, "It's the power they have that means they're like that, not any knowledge."

"I wonder," said Rama, and then repeated, "I wonder." He paused. "I think it's time for you to tell me what you want from me."

Jasef nodded, indicating more to the others that he would answer than to Rama that he agreed. "We want information. We want to know why it is you believe that our ambassador is making a poor decision."

"I never said it was a poor decision," he replied, "just not the decision that puts her with me, with the *tama*, with 'the people', as I hear it said." When none of the three made a move to respond, Rama continued, "Xar Kis and I are the same, in a way. No, listen, we are. We both want something that is not Apech, something better. Liberty, strength, pride. Beauty, even. The difference between us is that I would struggle to create such a world for us here, the place he sees as a bridge to elsewhere. I have begged, do you understand?

"It should be obvious to you that what Xar Kis and his ilk want is access to Crysth. They want to be you, young man, who can say 'this planet' with the same ease you say 'this room'."

"But–" started Jasef.

"But we are not you, and you we must be to gain access to your ships. I do not know by what strange designs you determine who can and cannot join you, but I know that our... what shall we call it? Our difference is an obstacle."

Peter swallowed, tried his luck. "So the magic is still bothering you all. Or something. Do you know where it is? Can't you get rid of it?"

Rama looked him in the eyes. "I think I do. And we want to try. Is that not enough?"

"I don't know that I'm certain I understand you, sir. But I think that it should be," answered Achira.

"I knew you would, Achira. Your kindnesses and attentions to the *tama* do not go unnoticed. There was a bit of an argument about it, actually. Would you believe Ustra tried to copy you for a while?" He pulled a strange expression, verging on sorrow. "A very short while."

"Why..." Peter did not want to mention Ustra's death – it would break the spell, their feeling of solidarity or hope in this worn-out man. Such a feeling could not live in his head concurrently with the image of Ustra's young body so cruelly ruined and displayed. "Why hasn't Kis come to get you?"

"To 'get' me. Fascinatingly and alarmingly put. For one, and as I have said, it was not me. I would not have been so... performative. He will know that. It was, however, my fault. He will know that, too, so the question still stands. The fact is that we have the same attitude towards civil war that you do towards 'data' or 'the unnatural'. We remember the damage; we bear the scars of it everywhere." Achira looked down at his arms, he smiled. "Not these.

"We have been seen to throw the first stone, now. Although that is a ridiculous conceit; he throws one every day. It's just that his attacks on our collective dignity are considered normal.

"The *'tama'*," and here they could the hear quotation marks he put around the word, "are almost impossible to organize, and so we need above-grounders on our side. We are a... pragmatic people. Whoever attacks first will be seen to be constituting a threat to the whole. Nobody wants war. Whoever attacks first will lose any sympathy from the undecided."

Achira felt like a fool. Of course it was more complicated than it had ever seemed. It was just that they were always so... weird.

"That's why he seems like the better commander, of course. His solution is leaving, going to Crysth; washing his hands of this place and moving on. Our solution is radical change, which is much harder. The last time we had radical change..." He closed his eyes. "You know what happened. War. Destruction. Lon Apech."

"But why would Caralla help Kis?" Peter felt like he was talking to a blue, a general awaiting a storm.

He laughed, it sounded genuine, if a little manic. Tiredness, perhaps. "I don't know! What seems clear to me, however, is that she prefers a life here than to one in Crysth. Perhaps she regrets her position, perhaps she is fleeing some crime. Her life is extremely comfortable here, as dire as 'this planet' may be. Don't you say the other one will replace her? Then what does she do? Perhaps she will have to leave the embassy, perhaps she is afraid to return. Perhaps she believes that if she helps him, she can retire here and keep his big house warm while he is away."

They were all silent. He was out of breath now and began to massage his temples.

"But Xar is no longer the worst of my worries," he said, slowly, as if unsure whether or not to continue. "A much more dangerous enemy has finally shown his hand, we think. In Ech Kon. My allies were attacked, they have had to flee."

"Ech Kon?" Peter, "I just… Never mind."

But Rama was watching him, suspicion rising behind his eyes as he said, "Do go on." in a way which reminded them that they were trapped in his house.

"Ming's in Ech Kon."

Rama reeled from the information. "Alone? Why?"

"Err," Peter, panicking, wanting neither to lie nor tell the truth, "someone sent a letter to the embassy saying that a Crysthian ship has been stolen."

Rama stood, eyes wild. "You need to get her back. That wasn't my people, they haven't sent any letter. It was *them*."

"Who's them?" Peter, panicking more.

"The– the magic, whatever you call it, it's getting stronger, *they* are doing it. Listen, you need to bring her back and get her to tell your ambassador that we need help. That whatever the magic was is… it's coming back."

"Holy shit."

"Peter," snapped Achira. "Sir, what are you saying?"

His hands were shaking as he gesticulated them wildly around. "It's back, we thought it was dying but it's back. They attacked my friends because…" He looked up at them, went still, "because of the lad Fukuyama. I think."

"Excuse me? The Crysthian, the Red scientist who was here before me?" Achira.

"Holy shit."

Rama resumed his frenzied movement. Pacing slightly in that uncontrolled, arrhythmic way which the Crysthians only expect of Apechi commoners. "He helps us, his research, he was showing what the magic does to us, how it makes the *tama*, and–"

He stumbled – Peter lurched forward to catch him and before he had time to see it coming he had been punched squarely in the face. Achira and Jasef screeched, grabbing at Peter who had wound backwards from the upward blow and looked as if he might fall – then as if he might strike back.

"I am sorry," Rama was saying, "I am so sorry, I–" He staggered backward onto the boulder, his left hand covering his face. "I haven't slept, I–"

Achira saw figures begin to assemble on the other side of the bridge furthest from them, dark, moving shadows. She looked terrified at Rama's face. "It's okay, we can see you didn't mean it, it's fine, he's fine."

Peter bled into his hands, cursing.

"It made me think you were going to hit me," he said. "I'm so sorry, Peter. I'm so sorry, please. I need you to bring Ming back, I need you to tell her it all. We need your help. I'm so sorry."

One of the figures crossed the bridge, became defined in the white twilight. It was one of the men they had seen many times at the Vasa, nobody they had spoken to, but a staple character. He looked as exhausted as Rama. He came to the side of his horrified commander, placed his hand on his inner thigh, spoke things in the language Achira and Jasef could barely understand. This is the first time they have heard it in person.

"Can you," –the man turned to address them– "come with me?"

"Of course," hurried Achira, turning to see even more people behind them and to their right. "Please, don't worry about it. We'll get Ming. We'll tell her everything. She'll know what to do."

"Fucking, hell, yeah it's fine," Peter choked, his head tilted upwards, "it's fine."

"Go with them," the man pointed. "I'm sorry."

Rama's expression was still twisted into embarrassed shock, agonized exhaustion. "I am sorry. I am ashamed. It overwhelmed me."

"No," said Jasef, "please, like he says, it's fine, get some rest. We're sorry we disturbed you, really."

Achira nipped at Peter's back, urging him forcefully towards the direction in which the man had pointed.

XII

That morning, Ming had woken confused before remembering where she was, and then remembered to be angry. The *tama*'s weight was heavy enough in her arms that she had thought for a moment that she was holding Peter.

It was before midday, and the light of Apech's morose sun had penetrated the windows to give the room a gentle orange hue. It was a sad little space, its misery enhanced by the attempts of the lone *tama* to make it seem homely. Worn rags, bits of clothing or lengths of fabric stolen from wherever were patched across the floor, patternless and brown. On the walls stood the odd feather or piece of paper, wedged into place in the concrete's cracks. It was strange, Ming had thought as she bit the other woman awake, that *tama* would collect so many things and yet retain absolutely no concept of ownership. They would constantly make off with whatever trinket caught their eye, only to find themselves staring glassily into the sky above the Vasa a week or so later for theft. But none of them would ever make the connection. Stupid, useless things. Ming had thought about this as she pushed the woman's head down between her thighs.

She had dressed, watching herself in a dull mirror propped atop an industrial sink. She was very angry, seethingly angry, and eye contact with herself only made it worse. She could see it there, unconcealable. It did not matter here with no one to see her, but it did not do to get out of practice. She began to whistle, but stopped when the *tama* joined in.

Her schedule was full of a lot of absolutely nothing to do. Her training said to wait, in situations where the path was unclear, always to wait. Now she would follow the letter of the law as a form of aggression, using its instructions against itself to waste time and to spite all those around her. It was an unusual sensation, absorbed rather than general malice against those in charge – but she was not entirely certain which of them it was aimed at. Xar Kis, for letting Ustra get killed? That seemed unfair, although it was certainly annoying. Ed Rama, maybe, just for existing. Gris Caralla. Peter for loving her, and for being fucking stupid. She felt utterly surrounded by incompetence on this, a planet that Gris would soon have to hand over to her. There would be no more of it then, no.

Slight footsteps carried her over to her suitcase. She knelt, rolling up her right sleeve and taking out a metal cage to strap around her forearm, pressing it hard into a series of magnets under her skin. She flexed her fingers, sent visible shivers of electricity coursing over the gauntlet. She could feel the loathing of the demon inside, trying to push the currents back into her. Her lips curled into a smile. Her fingers sought a knife, she had made up her mind.

She was going to get back to her own work.

Hours later she was more enraged than ever. Not one, she had not found a single thing. No, that wasn't strictly true – she had found dead. So many dead, and useless. As if someone had already been here, predicting her path, killing them. She could ask an Apechi, she thought, winding her way between two of the bronze spirals, but she did not like to make it overtly obvious what she was doing. No, fuck it. This place was going to be hers. But she did not have an image to direct them to, and they would pretend they did not understand if she tried to describe it. She wished she had not made the *tama* in the lighthouse eat her favourite image from Fukuyama's book.

But this looked like a promising space; a long, low circle which curled squat against the ground. *Tama* liked rooms like that, snug and short. She entered, and the moment she did she knew that she had chosen correctly. She could smell living bodies, even if she could not see them. The curving, sheltered space created by the shell-like structure was littered with piles of stinking cloth, bunched up around each other and together, casting deep shadows from the scant light sneaking in over the building's topmost curve. She rubbed the blade in her right hand flat against her hip, absently. Stepped inside.

"Hello," a *tama* voice erupted from a smiling face in the middle of a bundle of clothing. Ming kicked it. Shut up. Quiet. Wait.

"Hello." Crouched down to squat next to the bleeding face. "I am looking for ones with the spine sickness."

The bleeding face cringed and mopped its nose with the rags of its nest. Afraid.

"Spine sickness." Commanded.

The bleeding face did not reply and so she wrenched aside the rags and rummaged to find its torso. Unafflicted. Ming stood, disappointed, and continued her way. Rain pelted the roof above.

The sun was fading outside, no lamps. A remnant of daylight streaked in a murky grey stripe on the outer wall of the spiral's curve. She cast her shadow against it as she walked, the line of twilight severing her neck with a collar of weak iridescent light.

She stopped, suddenly. She had caught it for only a second. A fractional stink which punctured her memory and sent it soaring to ecstasy. She tore bedclothes aside, nobody. Blood stains. There are dying here.

The further she walked into the shell, the more shadows she cast against the eastern wall, the more slivers of decay polluted the air. She was desperate now, she knew there had to be some in here. They could not all be dead. Had they been culled to prevent the spread of disease? Who would do that? The Apechi just left them to decompose. She was almost at the other side. Only one *tama* in the entire warehouse. Nonsense, impossible. Footsteps outside. Never mind.

They must be here. Her shadow accelerated against the far wall.

She saw a hand. Her heart leapt and she stood above it and applied pressure with her foot. A groan. She ripped aside the rags that concealed the body and, oh, gods, yes, she saw him. The dying light did nothing to conceal his deformity. His armpits were so dense with the osteophyte forest that they looked like hair. And there was hair among them, glistening with the sweat of death. She knelt to breathe it in. Moaned as it forced her revolted body to spasm. It had spread down his ribs. He lay face up, his eyes closed but flickering and blood sullying the corners of his mouth.

She lifted her hand to his face and pried open his unresisting lips. None in his teeth. Shame. She tore off what remained of his dress and saw bone piercing the insides of his thighs, ripping his skin in an almost symmetrical pattern of pain. Cauterizing the same wounds they were inflicting. Oh. He bled slowly onto the floor in a great, sticky puddle and she knelt into it, put her hands into it. She licked it and sought the wound with her tongue and blood erupted into her mouth on either side of the shards of bone. She bit, sucking infection into her throat. He was too weak to cry out but gasped and gargled blood. She sucked and chewed and the shards broke. She swallowed them with mouthfuls of pulsing red and brought her face up to spit some of it into his eyes.

He did not belong to the disease, he belonged to her.

She would be the one to take him. She used the knife to smash more and more spikes of bone into pieces, to split them and crush them. She took the lighter from her pocket and she held it to the rags, too wet to catch. She punctured his skin where the bruises of internal bleeding had formed ink stains of purple and black. A butterfly, a kite. Sucking, biting, crunching all the while she punched out his front teeth and could help herself no longer in the fit of her excitement, she drove the blade into his neck. Blood everywhere, deafening her, choking her, she vomited bone and blood back onto the corpse and kept stabbing, kept burning. She wanted to crunch it to pieces, that body. Beautiful, beautiful.

Fuck.

She lay on top of him, wanted to merge herself into the death. She imagined that the sound of the rain was the tattoo of so many pieces of bone, pelting the roof in celebration of deformity. She lay there, drinking and gasping in the blood of the diseased until she could not breathe and so she sat upright, straddling the demolished corpse. What's the point? She tried to wipe the gore from her eyes and sought the corpse's rags. Wiped her face. The fire would not catch. She swallowed more of the blood, willing it to infect her, willing bone to leap up out of her skin.

She lay there for longer than she knew, more oblivious than she thought. Footsteps teased themselves around her, ignored, unheard over the sound of the defeated cracking as her teeth ground bone, chewing thoughtlessly on the disease. She would make a pyre of them, and then the fire would catch. She would make a pyre.

She would not. She knows only in a small part of herself, but she has given up. She is just going through the motions now, pleasure and misery.

Later, much later, she will return to her lighthouse shivering and covered with dry blood and heavy with gore. She will be cold, too exhausted to be angry. Dizzy with it. Images rushing before her eyes. Spots and stars. She will find the *tama* worried, waiting. She will find a parrot on top of her suitcase. It will have three heads. It will have a note tied to its leg. She will read it, drop it, rush to the window and stare out into the blackness, gaping in the direction of the taxidermist's crowded lair.

A gift. For the parak who would be cured.

XIII

"Why were you so quiet, anyway?" Achira leaned down from her bed to poke Jasef's side, laughing.

Jasef slapped her hand away. "Honestly, I really needed the bathroom."

Laughter, all three of their voices.

"Ow, for fuck's sake, 'Chira – can you do that softer?" Peter, his newly stitched face leaning back against Achira's pillow and her feet tucked beneath his elbow.

"Sorry, sorry." She changed the grip of her hands working the muscle in his calves, "Although you did say it would be my turn in ten minutes approximately fifteen minutes ago."

"It's not you who got fucking battered in the face. To each according to their need."

"Yeah," agreed Jasef, his eyes closed to better enjoy the gentle euphoria of a narcotic cube which he had been convinced to share.

Peter looked down at him from the bed and poked his nose lazily. "Such a gentleman."

Ar emerged into the doorway with a bottle of dark rum to refill their mugs. He was wearing his suitcase over his arm.

"Ar, are we leaving already?" Achira, propping herself up. "Shit."

The man nodded and looked around the room questioningly.

"Have you got Peter's letter? It's on the table upstairs." Jasef.

"Nah it's in my pocket." Peter reached into his jacket and produced the square of paper, addressed to Ming, which Ar pushed into his suitcase without opening. "Is the parrot in your room? I'll look after it for you, mate."

"Sorry Ar, I thought I had another hour or so. Let me, let me pack." Achira yawned.

"No tiredness! *There is nothing in the world so innocent as sleeplessness.*" Peter squeezed her foot, and she yelped him away.

"Was that supposed to be Kafka?" Jasef raised an arm to slap at Peter's face. "Because it's the other way around. The sleepless man is *guilty.*"

"Well, what if she has nightmares?" Peter took Jasef's hand and stretched his palm. "Oh yes, it says here that you don't have the knowing of literature. Right next to your lifeline, Jasef knows nothing of literature, clear as day."

Jasef giggled and wrestled his hand away. "Shush, you, I've studied pre-departure literature *extensively*. Achira, what?"

Ar perched at the edge of the bed beside Achira, patted Peter's foot with a smile.

"I need to sleep on the train." She laughed a little. "I'm *drunk*."

"I still think I should be coming," Peter complained. "It might be dangerous. And if anyone's rescuing Ming it's me."

"Rescue?" asked Jasef, sitting up.

"Yeah," Peter, "might be dangerous."

"We'll be fine. We'll be back straight away, literally just collect her and come back. What do you think she's doing right now?"

"I don't know, mate." Peter paused to think. "Surfing."

They laughed and Jasef propped his elbows on the bed. "Is there a time change?"

"You know what, I never thought about that. Probably, but I couldn't even guess in which direction."

Ar shrugged, took a swig from Achira's mug.

"The train goes east so... oh fuck me if I know." Peter sent plumes of his vape into the air, an action usually forbidden by the stringent laws of Achira's bedroom.

"I never know what time it is anyway. Always damned midnight." Jasef huffed, letting Achira ruffle his hair. "Miserable place to be. Imagine growing up here."

Ar clicked his fingers, Achira focused on him again. "Oh, yeah. I'm coming."

"Don't leave me alone with this guy," said Peter. "I should go. Plus Rama likes you, doesn't he? You should be there when we go back."

Ar shook his head, signed, *back?*

"Yes, of course! As soon as possible. Tomorrow."

"No!" said Jasef. "We have to wait for Ming at the very least. What if she knows what's going on? That's what he told us to do."

"Jasef's right, P."

"Fucking boring."

"You just want to get punched again. *Look at me I'm Peter fuckity fuck* BAM," laughed Jasef, thrusting his fist into the air with the last word.

"Is that supposed to be me? I do not say fuckity fuck."

"You do a bit," conceded Achira, kicking him again. "Have we got another cube?"

Peter rummaged in his seemingly infinite jacket pocket and produced another square, which he clicked, nicked his own wrist with the blade and then passed to the other two. Achira watched Jasef fail twice before doing it for him. He smiled at her in glassy gratitude and downed his rum in one go.

"Steady on." Peter drained his own tumbler with a wink. "Fuck I can't wait to figure out what's going on. Ming's going to be fucking thrilled when she hears all this."

"Is she? 'Cause it sure sounds like whatshisface, Fukuyama, caused some trouble on his way out." Achira.

Peter made a long humming sound and then said, "Did we

see him go though? Did you see it with your eyes?" He snapped his fingers in front of Jasef's face.

"Hey, hey, come on that makes my eyes go funny." Jasef swiped Peter's hand away again.

"It's the drugs mate. But, guys, what if, what if there's more students here what we haven't got the knowing of?" Peter was wide-eyed with conspiratorial excitement.

"There aren't." Achira. "We all saw each other at some point at the university, there are no more coming here any time soon."

"How can you be certain?"

Jasef rolled his eyes. "You would be, too, if you hadn't been wasting your time in Irregular Combat."

"Illogical Combat! And don't you come crying to me when you get attacked by a legion of specters. Bound to happen at least twice." Peter grinned while making grasping notions at the bottle by Ar's foot.

"Specters?" Achira.

"Yeah, I made that up, but you gotta watch out for dinosaur people."

"Hey, they are a misunderstood race, and you are being speciesist." Jasef slammed his palm on the bed.

"Am not! They'll bite your foot off as soon as they look at you! Fought off an entire battalion of them single handed in my first year, don't you know."

"I did hear they actually have quite a sophisticated religious hierarchy built around amputated human feet," agreed Jasef.

Achira gaped in annoyance, "What, the hell?"

"Oh, who's Madam Fuckity now?" Peter. "You've never heard of the dinosaur people?"

"No!"

"Well," said Jasef, lowering his tone, "legend has it that they were oppressed for thousands of years, by the shark people of Old Grimopolis, before Crysth arrived and liberated them from their tyrants."

"You are having me on."

"Nope. One of them teaches submarine bomb placement at the academy." Jasef.

Ar burst into silent laughter, signed something none of them could understand.

"You are having me on! You bastards." She tutted at herself for having believed them. "Dinosaur people!"

"How is submarine bomb placement less ridiculous than Illogical Combat?" Jasef.

"What else did you learn, Peter? Don't lie I'm too drunk and tired to be confused."

"See! I told you sleep is bad." He took another hefty pull on his vaporizer and blew it in Jasef's greedy direction. "Well, we mostly did pull-ups, learned how to control all the bioware, and shot at things. Not all that interesting."

"What bioware?" Achira, accusingly. It would be rude to live with someone for this long and not tell them that you had body modifications other than the visible.

"Oh just strength and speed stuff, all of us in the faction have it. You don't get the big guns until you get into proper service. Don't worry, I'm not spying on you in the shower."

Jasef chuckled and sank back onto the floor. Ar clicked again, wanting them to focus.

"Yeah, Ar, uhh." Achira, "I'm coming. Now you two promise not to go back to Rama."

"I promise," said Jasef. "But him?" He waved his arm around until he was touching Peter's arm.

Peter frowned and then winced as the expression tugged his stitches. "I don't see why I can't go."

"Yes, you do. If you leave, everybody in Lon Apech will know about it. They don't care about us." Achira, to nods from Ar. She pushed Peter's legs off the bed. "Get out so I can pack."

"Aww," moaned Jasef. "We're not in the way."

"Yeah, don't be a fascist," said Peter, shuffling towards the wall to accommodate Jasef beside him.

"You're not staying in my room when I'm not here," she said.

"Fascist."

"Fascist," agreed Jasef, allowing himself to be enveloped in Peter's arms.

"Fine," she breathed. "We'll come straight back, won't we? Don't really need... you two, promise me you won't go back to Rama. And no fooling around in my bed. Promise."

Jasef nudged Peter. "Do promising."

Peter held his hands up. "I promise."

Ming had reacted to the news that the train was returning to Ech Kon about as well as one would expect. She's going to be downright apoplectic when she realizes who is on it, but at this moment – climbing from the demon-infested ship and onto the dock – she thinks that it is Agnes coming to check the state of play, which is only regular-grade maddening. So she is running out of time, and she is going to see the taxidermist. He has her figured out, and she has waited for too long. He will know, now, that she had not known how to respond to his note. She has taken off her rings in disgust, sick of the reluctance, the care, the control they exert over her. She never plans to put them onto her prosthetics when mad Caralla finally approves her graduation.

And so Ming stood on the dock, impulsively teasing electricity into her fingers beneath the sleeve of her informal uniform. This is not something that she would ever do if she were in Lon Apech. There is nobody around, which is unsurprising; they are afraid of her. It is normal to torment and kill *tama*, but not to do it so doggedly, in such a sustained, messy assault.

Barely any of them had figured out what it was that she was actually trying to do. Xar Kis was an exception, but he had caught her at it. He had seen a devil in her the moment he saw her and had followed her until he uncovered its exact nature.

She had not restored calm to herself by the time she arrived at the taxidermist's windowless terrace. He had left the door open. Electricity raced around her wrist. The demon could tell how angry she was, wanted her to behave irrationally, let it dance.

She walked into the hallway.

"Close the door."

She jumped, a spike of adrenaline rushed through her and he was right there. The bastard.

She turned, eyes still closed, and pushed her weight against the screaming door.

She opened her eyes, but she did not turn around. There was waiting.

"Tell me," he began, "what you think you are trying to do."

And so she did. In the dark with her face to the door she told the man behind her not just that, but everything she knew. She told him what had happened to the first Crysthian scouts after they had set foot on Apech, described recordings of them displaying impossible strength and foresight.

A man had punched straight through a steel wall. I could see a time when it wasn't there, he had said, but he couldn't explain further.

"What happened to them?"

"Mad. Killed," she replied.

He laughed.

"We thought it might be something dangerous."

"We?"

"The embassy."

"And you?"

"*I don't care.*" She used Apechi. To impress him, or to impress upon him that this is the truth.

She felt his fingers press hard into her spine, run over her shoulder blades, her neck.

"You do not know that I am still unafflicted?" she asked, nastily, inclining her head slightly to the left as she did.

He withdrew his hand as if burned and said, softly, "What do you think that you are?"

She turned to face him, now. He was shirtless, to her surprise, and so heavily, beautifully scarred. More so than Kis and Distan, even. She looked at the crosshatching of ruined skin which crept over his torso without embarrassment or reticence, craving them, envying them. Marks of healed disease. It was as if it had churned his entire body, left him once a pillar of infected bone. "Incomplete." she said, and the word was a whisper, drawn out, loving, savoured.

"Yes."

They looked at each other, relaxing.

"Crysth is monstrous in its strength," he said, watching her watch his skin. "The power to break steel is nothing compared to it. Why have you chased such a small thing as our magic here?"

Her eyes meandered up to his before she replied, "It was not my first choice. But nobody is here to stop me. Nobody is watching. This is," she smiled, "backwater. Not powerful enough, not interesting enough. I will be free here, once I replace Gris Caralla."

"Your empire can be so careless?"

"No. There was nothing here by the time the scouts returned. Any remaining unnatural phenomena have been officially classified as residual. Dying, of no concern." She waited for a response that did not come, and so she pressed on. "You are going to tell me this is not true, I hope."

"You hope, yet you do not know what you hope for."

"I have told you, it doesn't matter to me what it is, just that I can have it."

He laughed, a cruel and humourless sound. Ming curled her lips in a smile to join in.

"I will show you," he said. "You will make yourself useful to me. Then I will show you what you are doing wrong."

He turned, she followed.

"You will never catch it in the way that you are trying. Watching you treat it like a biological contaminant is like…" –he took a long breath through his teeth– "watching someone bury a tree. Why do you think someone might bury a tree?"

He began to ascend. Rolling her eyes she responded, "I don't know. To treat the soil?"

He grunted. "A reasonable guess – but that is because you understand the nature of both tree and soil. You would never be able to guess the motive of someone that didn't. Watching you is like watching someone bury a tree who is trying to produce acorns. Do you understand?"

She lied that she did.

"Good. I am not interested," he resumed, when they were both standing on the floor of his workshop, "in you. And you are not interested in me. But we can help each other. That idiot man likes you, listens to you. More, that fingerprint you were wise enough not to wear today means that you'll be his master. He knows nothing of me yet, but we will do much better together." His tone dripped with regret at this last.

"Do you mean Peter?" she asked, confused, picking her way between the birds towards him.

"Who?"

"The… who do you mean?"

"Farön Kis' son, Xar. Stupid name." Xar is not an Apechi word, nor the name he was born with. It is the name of the first Crysthian ship which landed on Apech. The taxidermist disappeared behind his workbench, from which came the sound of another metal door being opened – this one well-oiled and heavy. "I see you with him, entertaining each other with your stupid little games. I know you are… close."

Ming slowed down, raising her guard again on account of the surprise at hearing methodological, meticulous Xar Kis described as 'idiot man'. She stayed silent as she drew up to the taxidermist's workbench, as she saw the open trapdoor and the man knelt beside it.

"Down there," He said.

She looked into the blackness below, made out the first rung of a metal ladder in the high, grey light. She did not move.

"Well?" he asked.

"You knew Kis' father?" she replied.

"You are stalling."

She looked down into the black square again. "You want me to get into the hole?"

"Get into the hole."

"I do not want to get into the hole."

"I have told you that I am not interested in you. Get into the hole." A compelling point poorly made.

Ming is not the type not to get into the hole.

She lowered herself onto the floor, sought a lower rung with her feet. Clumsy, awkward work. She shot him one last look of suspicious annoyance before his face disappeared over the horizon of her vision.

Her descent was slow and cautious, but the floor still shocked her once it came. She did not trust it, wrapped her left arm around the rung and felt around with her foot, tempted to send sparks of sentient electricity to travel the breadth of the floor, but not wanting to reveal that she could.

She heard him begin to descend, stepped back away from the ladder to wait for him with her right hand on the wall beside her.

She heard him land. He had dropped the last few rungs – more than a few, the speed and weight of his fall told her. That should have hurt him, would have hurt him if he was unafflicted. She felt a rush of excitement to see that impossible strength displayed so brazenly. That is a misunderstanding. This is not strength.

She heard his clothing move, and the sound of a match striking, sputtering into life, and then flames were roaring on either side of her, igniting in two parallel lines along what she now saw as the terrace's outer walls, a mirror of the long rectagonal space above. She spun to watch the progress of the fire and saw the light spreading in all directions until a room, five stories tall and five terraced houses wide, was illuminated in strips of clean orange flame, dancing in straight rivulets until they met each other again on the far side. The room was filled with strange shapes, moving things, but her eyes could not adjust to the sudden brightness fast enough to make out what they were. She closed them against the fire.

"This is how it used to be. Before your kind, before the war." She nodded understanding and he asked, "Your eyes are harmed?"

She opened them, slowly, and found him looking down at her with unconcern. "No," she answered, and tried to see behind him into the flickering orange room. He seized her chin, harshly, and lifted it back to face him.

"What has Kis' son promised you?"

"Nothing," she grumbled through her clamped jaw.

"Liar."

She tried to shake her head, but his grip was too tight. He must have felt the movement anyway because he raised his eyebrows. "Perhaps it is that he does not need to. Will they allow him onto that planet of yours, *parak*?"

She pressed her chin into his hand to indicate a nod.

The walls flickered with tame fire. Her gauntlet itched with desire.

"And he will obey its rules, fawn at the service of Crysth. And you will stay here as our ambassador. You will have slaves to molest and steel to punch through, you will receive students who will mock you. What for?"

He released her chin, but his face made it clear that she was to remain looking at him.

She stayed silent.

"It could be better. For both of you. You and Kis' son." His voice was a whisper, now, and she could hear something else in the vibrant, warm darkness beyond him.

He turned to the room, releasing her, and she followed his gaze to the thing in its cavernous center.

It was huge, it was wrong. Silent and pained, mobile, many-faced facelessness. Once she had seen it, the demon in her gauntlet could see it too. It pounded against her in impotent terror. Get out. A writhing mass of organic decomposition which thrummed and faltered as it raised different parts of itself, shifting in place with a dexterous imprecision that defied identification. Defiled identification. She moved forwards; he did not stop her. She moved more. It did not seem able to detect her; its movements did not change as she approached. Still, she paused five or so feet from its towering base while her jaw dropped in horrible fascination.

"You could sever yourself from that wretched empire for good." He was still whispering, as if he did not want to disturb the thing in its endless roving motion. "Xar is just like his father. Deformed by linearity, enamored with structure. All they saw was those ships, Crysthian might. The solidity of a *parak*. What we had was so much more than that."

"What is it made of?" she whispered, already knowing the answer.

"That does not matter. It does not contain its purpose within itself, it is not the sum of its parts."

A human face appeared at the surface of the constantly morphing flank of the beast, seeming to scream in pain for a fraction of a second before reconforming to the orgasmic pleasure which characterized the expressions of the others stitched around it. The thread pulsed and stretched as the corpses shifted in gulping motions, kneading around each other so that every inch of the thing's flesh was ever throbbing marble.

Ming nodded but did not understand. One day, she will regret that. She will hate herself for not asking the right questions, for asking nothing at all. It is her nature to care only for outcome.

"I thought these were all burned in the war." Her voice was steady as she tried to focus on the weaving limbs and stitching of the creature. It was as if it were trying to take the shape of different animals but was unable to hold them, unable to be satisfied with any of its creations.

"They were," he said, angrily. "But they are only satellites, they can be rebuilt. Your kind do not understand gods."

The word sent a bolt of appalled shock through her body. She staggered backwards – away from this thing she had thought some magical talisman, some totem, even though those who built them before the war had been called priests. She gaped and backed away, back towards the ladder with her eyes fixed wide, mad, on the broiling flesh.

She had known. But she also had not. She had known she was a traitor but she had not readied herself for confirmation that her treachery was so, deeply, deliciously fundamental. Now she must overcome the last of it, anything binding her to the ideology of home.

She stuttered nothing.

"Where are your rings?" he asked, calm.

She looked at her hands, looked back to him.

"Where are your rings?"

She stared at her fingers. "The lighthouse."

"Why are your rings in the lighthouse?" He took a step towards her.

"They get on my nerves."

Flame flickered in the wet sheen of his grin. "This is the source. The one remaining altar. The thing you think of as a disease, the infection you are trying and failing to catch. It is not strength," another step, "it is deconstruction. Reconstruction; the way."

She was still shaking her head.

The smile fell from his eyes. He was beginning to think that he might be losing her. He would kill her without remorse, but would grieve his plan. It was a good one.

"Look." He motioned to the walls, to their base. Piles of debris thrown into deep, moving shadows. Quivering with something that was not the light's gentle motion. "Look."

She looked. She looked until she saw what she was seeing. Mackerel tails with three shoebill heads, a human face with wings and a single foot. At creations as small and strange as those above… but changed. They twitched, all of them, gently, so subtly – but then as she stared one of the great fish thrashed in agony and thumped its parrot head into the wall, letting out a gentle squawk of pain. She jumped, her hands flew back to hold onto the ladder behind her, preparing now to flee. "You can make them live?"

"No. Not me, and not life. The god is reaching out to them, but its purpose is not life."

"What is its purpose?"

"Reconstruction." Frustration in his voice. "It is pleased by chaos; it grants power to the desires," –he stepped towards her again– "of the contradictory. It does not understand us well, but it likes us." Ming shook her head. "Oh, it does. We are agents for it, when we stretch out into the world. It infects us all, weak as it is now, and those of us whose contradiction pleases it, survive."

Her eyes widened. "And those who don't?"

"You know that. *Tama*. Mindless, thoughtless. They cannot withstand the deconstruction, cannot parse it, cannot sense which is right. It first comes when we are children, when we are more contradiction than creature. It takes or it gives, and when it comes back for them later – they die." He smiled again. "You see them. Waiting for it to claim them."

"The spikes… they–"

"They are it," he nodded his head towards the melting

obelisk, "it is them. It is not disease, it is *stigmata*. You cannot catch it because it does not see you. Yet."

That was it. He had her. "So, I can catch it?"

"Yes. But not in the way you are trying."

"How?"

"You must serve it, worship it." He held his hand out to her. "And I can show you how."

She looked at his palm, tried to relax her shoulders but did not approach. "Deities are not... they cannot be understood. They cannot be reasoned with. They... we destroy them wherever we find them."

"So loyal." He smirked, lowering his hand. "I have told you. Your empire understands nothing."

Ming's fingers pressed against the cold metal of the ladder behind her, felt it warming in proximity to the flame. "I'm listening."

"You better be. You want freedom, you want strength. You want to ascend from that... simple form. You want to see."

Her expression of quiet shock did not change.

"I want our god's dignity returned to it." He ran a hand over his scarred chest. "And Kis' son wants power, liberty, decadence. He does not need to bow to Crysth, and nor do you. Last time... we were unprepared. When we saw the ships coming there was too much... squabbling. All we saw was power and might – unity. The god of contradiction takes no pleasure in unity... but it will help him go to Crysth."

"What?"

He laughed, so her voice must have been more stunned than she had intended.

"A sprawling web of cities and rules and connections... so many people and ideas and identities. It will rejoice, Ambassador, it will give Xar Kis more power than he could dream of – petty envoy to a useless planet – if he takes it with him."

Her silence answered him.

"You have seen how powerful he is already, you have seen

the strength and perception that you want, mirrored in his body. And now you see how it is possible. So strong, Farön Kis' child, despite believing his god dead. Despite believing his god never lived. I know he, like you, thinks it was just some faded magic, just some lie. That is his father's doing. But can you imagine, *parak*, how great he could be if he burnt bodies at its altar?"

Ming shook her head again. "That's not how gods work – things like that are symbolic, they aren't–"

"You dare tell me how gods work? Symbolic? It consumes the flesh, eats the flesh of the damned. It lives in the spikes, in the flames. You know full well what it did to your scouts. It liked them, fool. You will tell me that is symbolic?" He snarled and moved his hand over his chest again, "I have read your books. The gods are unpredictable, and many times over has the *parak* failed to grasp their desires. Sacrifices, spires, penance, confession, charity..." He turned to gaze lovingly over his shoulder, watching the god melt and foam. "And even the weak ones have turned their celebrants mad. But this one is so very powerful, and I know how it thinks.

"The god of Apech is a reshaper. It loves to see systems and have them perform differently. Contradiction," he grinned to himself, "without reconciliation. You understand that don't you?" She will wish she had asked what he meant. She will hate herself for not asking him what he meant. "And it sees no difference between one system and another, unlike you. Physics, economics, power, language. All the same."

She just stared, trying not to watch it move behind him, ignoring the organic twitching in the shadows. Trying to think.

"How," she began, after too long, "do you know?"

He smiled, lunged. The electrical gauntlet smashed into the air, sparks flying, but he had known it was coming. He had ducked under its path and out of the way of the malevolent, excitable sparks and pulled her – straight into the body of the godthing. Rotting, pulsing she tried to push herself away, but his hand was on her back. She felt a mouth against her cheek, gaping, sucking exploratory – it pulled her flesh into it and she... bit. Instinctively, thoughtlessly. It tasted like death and she could not breathe but it did not matter. Her tongue found stitches and she could feel the demon in her arm begin to panic. She pushed through the thread, worming her way into the gashes between its moving flesh and it enveloped her – it felt like it was laughing. Dead fingers pulled at her eyelids, childlike and greedy with their pulling and grabbing until – she was released. Different.

She fell backwards, really fell, and her mouth was full of blood. Her blood. She tried to cry out, but her voice was unfamiliar, her teeth impossibly sharp. She could not breathe, she clasped at her throat and felt shining, rubbery flesh... the room was suddenly bright... She tried to speak but slit her massive tongue on backward facing teeth and could not breathe... her hands were spines like trees, like disease... beautiful... She gasped and air filled her lungs once again. Normal. Ming. Wilhelmina's body. Decrepit, weak. She nearly screamed with the agony of not having died like that, like whatever it was. She would have rather suffocated right then than to re-become this.

"Do you understand?"

She gasped, sobs of shock, relief and desire rolling unstoppably through her chest.

"Do you understand?" he asked again, kneeling beside her.

She shook her head, not no, just – wait.

"Do you understand?"

She turned to him, tears falling from her eyes one after the other, great irrational droplets collecting in the corners of her mouth, the dimple of her chin. "What was I?"

"You don't know?" She does not, she never will. "You were everything you could have been, all at once."

"Why?" she asked, for the sake of something to say rather than for wanting to know the answer.

"It shows us these things, lets us know what we can do if we abandon our childish attachments to structure. You were the descendants of ancestors that never lived."

She wanted to feel it again, feel her body changed, torn, rearranged, powerful, impossible. She staggered to her feet, eyes set on the godthing's roving side. She lunged – was caught. She fell forwards, cracking her chin against the floor and sending new blood spilling, touching the flesh at its kinetic base as tongues and eyes and fingers appeared to hold her. He pulled her back along the floor and she spun again to shock him – again, he had known. He ducked the spark and kicked her, hard, in the side. She rolled with the force of it, that unnatural strength, but he had known how not to do real damage. He needed her alive, an agent of chaos, a meddler, a device.

"No," he hissed, dodging another spark of electricity which she had not even bothered to aim. "You serve me first, *parak*, or you will stay that way."

He stood beside her, staring down, hateful and triumphant.

"What," she croaked, "do you want me to do?"

XIV

Achira pinched the bridge of her nose, grumbling to herself as something pushed at her arm. She turned her face, stuck out her bottom lip in an expression of self-mockery.

"Are we nearly there?" Her voice was weak with sleep and a dizzy, sickly hangover.

Ar nodded, *slowing.*

"Oh – already? Have you been asleep?"

He nodded again, smiling. Pointed at her, followed the motion with an upright thumb and a raised eyebrow to say, *you okay?*

"I'll be fine." She sat up, slowly, wincing, and looked out of the window. "Gods it's bleak."

Rain pattered grey and morose against the window, blurring the view outside.

"Need anything?"

He shook his head and she shuffled her way out.

Ar closed his eyes. He had been in fitful, strange sleep, with dreams of Apechi faces stalking university halls, the gardens of his home planet, his high school dormitory. They had a strange air to them, these dreams. A sense of panic tinged with solidarity, a notion of envy edged with fear. If they joined the empire, these people of Apech, they would immediately be more so than he and his race. Something in him recoiled; he was sure it was jealousy. He pushed it down. It was a shameful feeling, he thought, for many reasons. He should not want to prevent Apechi from joining the empire, with all the benefits technological and educational which that entailed. Worse; he should not envy them their appearance. He was proud to be him, and this complex feeling of grudging embarrassment did not change that. He would not make himself look more like a Crysth-born human, even if he could do so with a snap of his fingers. He would not give himself speech the way they had assumed his kind would – offering vocal implants and voice readers as if it were benevolence – and he would not stop adding dermal piercings to his skin, the ones which were becoming so infuriatingly fashionable on Crysth. But he did wish it were easier. He opened his eyes as the train pulled to a full halt.

"Did you see anybody out there waiting for us?" Achira asked.

Ar shook his head.

"They'll know the train is coming back, though? Ming will know, I mean."

He nodded.

"Right. Hope she's hanging about then."

Ar headed out first, spotting as he did a blur of deep maroon through the glass. Ming was there. He twisted the door's mechanism with a smile, stepping down into the pattering rain on the platform.

He had never seen such an expression on Ming's face. It was so distorting that for a moment he had not recognized her – and then he saw the bruises, the stitches in her chin. He had never seen her surprised, angry, frightened – but here she was all of them at once.

It only lasted for a moment, and then she was Ming again. Smiling a confused half nod with her head inclined upwards.

"Ar? What a surprise I – Achira?" Ming laughed, stepping

forwards to try to get them both under her umbrella. "What are you doing here?"

"We needed to talk to you," Achira. "There's a lot going on back home – in Lon Apech, I mean."

Ming raised her eyebrows, "Alright – let's get out of the rain, shall we?"

Huddled together under a sprawling black tarp, they wound their way through the bronze spiral architecture of Ech Kon. It did not take long for them to reach their pagoda away from pagoda, truncated and bright in comparison with the one they had left behind. They peeled off jackets damp with sticky, hot rain and carried them up the staircase.

"So," Ming said, sitting down at the kitchen table, "you've both been here before, haven't you?"

Ar nodded, *are you okay? Face?*

"Me? Yeah, I'm fine. It's nothing." Her voice came down from its enthusiastic high pitch to a more recognizable drawl. "Fine."

"I'm going to make coffee."

"Yeah, thanks. One for you Ar? He says yes, 'Chira."

"'Kay."

"So, what's going on?"

Ar produced a folded piece of paper as Achira spoke, "Peter insisted on writing you a note, but I don't think it's necessary."

Ming took the note with a half-smile, flipped it open.

Ming,

"Where's the coffee, Ming?"

"Oh, in that cupboard up there."

There's all sorts kicking off over here.
We went to talk to Rama like you said

"No, it isn't."

"Really? Try the cupboard down there."

and he told us all about him fighting against Kis.
But he says there's worse out in Ech Kon, he says
the magic that makes them weird you know what
I mean is back and getting stronger. He says that
whoever is making it stronger attacked his people

"There's no coffee in here."

and he says something about Fukuyama helping them.
Fuck is all that about? I reckon they must have stolen that
ship these magic people. Rama wants us to ask for the
embassy's help. Says Kis won't respond to his letters and shit.

"Ming."

We need you to come home and figure it out.

"Ming."

Sorry I was weird the other day. Love, P

"Ming!"

"Sorry," Ming blinked rapidly, lifting her chin to Achira, "come again?"

"There is no coffee in this kitchen."

Ming stared at her, uncomprehending.

"Is there tea?"

"Should be." Ming stood up, her expression still vacant, and began to open cupboards.

"Have you not been staying here?"

"Sorry, yes. I mean, not much. There have been strange things happening here, too."

"You haven't eaten or drank the whole time?" Achira's voice was laced with suspicion, not concern.

"Of course I have, I'm just surprised."

Achira began to scan the kitchen more closely. No unwashed cups, no water splashes, no crumbs – no sign of a hurried and preoccupied inhabitant in any of its features. She looked back to Ming. "What happened to your face?"

The other woman touched her chin. "I can't really get into it. I'm okay, honestly."

"You don't look okay. You don't seem okay either."

"No. You do know a Crysthian ship has been stolen? There is a lot to be done."

"Yes, we know. We went and found out about it, didn't the letter say? Rama told us that his friends in Ech Kon had been attacked by someone who is encouraging the, er, you know, the magic to return." Ming did not react. "Well? Are you going to say something?"

The two women watched each other, neither wanting this to become an argument, both knowing it ought to.

"Rama is a fool." Ming touched her chin again, like it hurt. "Rama is a fool." She sighed deeply. "I actually thought Gris had sent Agnes, when the train was on its way. That's why I'm so surprised."

"Do you need him?" Achira. "Have these magic people been violent?"

Ming shook her head. "There are no magic people. Rama's friends went off with that ship to send us on a wild goose chase, leaving him free to attack Kis."

"No, no he said he was trying to get Kis to help him."

"Seriously?" asked Ming, panic rising that Rama knew about the taxidermist, that he had been able to get to Kis before she did. "He's lying, he's using you. I have told you."

Achira raised an eyebrow. "No, he needs our help. We need you to go to Gris."

"Go to her and say what?"

"That…" Achira paused. "That his friends have been attacked in Ech Kon, that they need our help."

"So, Ed Rama wants us to remove our Military cohort from Lon Apech… just as the dispute between he and Kis is coming to a head… to fight magic people?"

Achira looked at Ar, Ming did so too.

I wasn't there, don't look at me.

"Well, yes," conceded Achira, her voice defensive. "He says the magic's back, says it's getting stronger. Look, we were preoccupied with finding out why Rama wants to fight Kis in the first place – Peter was right, he wants a better Apech. We need to help him."

Ming almost laughed. "That sounded like a Green slogan. What does that even mean?"

"I… We didn't quite get there – it all went… a bit wrong."

"What do you mean 'a bit wrong'?"

"This is going to sound terrible, but there's no other way to put it – Rama accidentally punched Peter."

Then Ming really did laugh, a mean and hollow sound which astonished her audience – she realized it and stopped. *Her control is slipping.* "How do you accidentally punch somebody?"

"He…" Achira waved her hand, lowered her voice to a whisper, "he did that flinch thing that they do, sometimes. Look, he said the magic was stronger, it overwhelmed him he said." She looked at Ming for understanding. "You know, reacting to things that didn't or, don't happen. Like they're nervous all the time or… something. You know."

Ming's eyes glazed over strangely. After a while she said, "So he told you the magic is getting stronger and then put on a little show to prove it."

Ar's pencil had been moving, and now he handed the paper to Achira; "It sounds ridiculous but the ridiculousness is why we need you to come back. We need to get on top of this. And it sounds dangerous over here."

Ming was still gazing out of the window. "You should know better."

"What?" There was a long silence, filled with the weight of Ming's absent consideration.

"What insight do you think you have into the organization of Apech that Gris Caralla does not?"

"What are you talking about? She is willingly allowing people to be tortured to death! She is at Kis' house all the time, she is trying to help him get to Crysth for gods' sake!"

"And who told you that?" said Ming, her voice hardening, "Ed Rama? You saw what he did to Zara Ustra, and you walked willingly into his home."

"*You* told me–"

"I said that before he decorated and hanged a woman's corpse in a cylinder!"

Achira gritted her teeth, seething. "It wasn't him."

"Another *pearl* of wisdom from the man himself, I assume."

"If he was dangerous," Achira steadied her voice, shocked and outraged by the insult, "he would have hurt us."

"If he was clever," Ming mirrored her tone, her anger getting the better of her. "He would leave you unharmed and send you to get Crysth out of his way instead."

Achira frowned, disbelieving but with the beginnings of doubt beginning to flow into her mind – it all felt so much sillier when Rama wasn't in front of her, without the bludgeon enthusiasm of Peter Pïat-Elementov at her side.

"Did you see the writing? The writing on the wall of the cylinder, were you there long enough to see it?"

Achira rubbed her eyes. "Yes," she half-lied.

"And what did it suggest to you? *Parak*." Ming looked over at Ar again. "Why do you think that was there? They don't know that we can read it, do you know that?"

"I…"

"It was a threat. Kis has his flaws. Flaws can be worked with, reasoned with over time. That is what we are doing. Rama is anti-Crysth. We thought he was harmless but now he'll even steal ships, kill, do whatever he can to prevent unification." She paused, "He will even put on a show of strangeness to make sure you believe this nonsense about magic, believe this place is unnatural."

"Isn't it?"

"We don't know! You know we don't know. We haven't got anything back from Fukuyama and the labs yet. Kis is cooperating, Rama is not."

"But, Fukuyama… he said Fukuyama was helping him." Achira paused. "No, if he's so anti-Crysth then why did you tell me to go to his house?"

"I did not know how violent, how desperate he had gotten. I did not think I needed to rescind the suggestion once we had seen Ustra – I assumed, and shan't again, that you would be able to work that out for yourself." She's just making all of this up on the spot. She's very good at it.

Achira dropped her gaze, winced as a shock of pain went through her head. She breathed out and went to sit beside Ar, resting her head on her palms.

Ar looked between the two women, shaking his head slowly. *This is why we wanted to come to talk to you.* He followed this up with a series of complicated gestures, devolved into miming until Ming understood that he was asking, *Rama stole the ship?*

"Yes." This is true, the taxidermist forced them to flee onto the waves and has told her as much. She doesn't care. "But what's worrying me is that this means Peter and Jasef are alone in Lon Apech doing gods know what."

"We told them," said Achira, her voice muffled over her hands, "we made them promise not to go back to Rama."

"That's not what I'm worried about."

What? signed Ar. *What's up?*

"Kis won't go to Rama. But he would go to them. He'll know they've been to Rama."

"What?" Achira sat up straight again. "What are you saying?"

"I'm speculating," said Ming, using their horror, her dramatic pauses, to plan her next move. "But if Kis were to get curious and Peter were to say something stupid to him..."

Ar stood up, indicating the trapdoor with rapid pointing movements which very clearly said, *let's go*.

"We don't have to panic. He wouldn't... Oh, I don't know. Kis is very, very upset." She looked back to Achira. "And you have been seen – you know you will have been seen – to have paid a visit to the person who murdered Ustra."

Achira and Ar felt ridiculous, childish. Ming was right. It was so obvious, here in the tepid grey light of Ech Kon, that they had done something utterly foolish.

"I don't know what to say." Achira.

"Nothing. It's done now. I'll tell Gris about what Rama told you but she'll know as well as I do that it isn't true. We don't need to panic."

"Shall we go now?" Achira stood up, her voice low, cowed.

Ming darted her eyes back to the window in a way which made Achira look too, a quick, furtive look as if she was looking at something she should not.

"I need... someone to stay here. Keep an eye."

Me, signed Ar, *I will stay*.

"I think you should both stay," answered Ming. "Or..."

"What?"

"Can you stay? I'll want Ar to help reason with Peter, I think."

"Oh." It was obvious that she did not want to, and Ar was shaking his head in an *it's fine* sort of motion. But Achira was embarrassed, hungover, her suspicion had worn off and she wanted to make up with this woman whom she hated. "Look, of course, I'll stay."

"Thank you so much. You don't need to do anything, this place is so close to the beach and to the village – just keep an eye out for large groups of people, keep an eye on the horizon for that lost ship, anything unusual. Alright?"

"Yes, yes. How long–"

"I will be back no later than the day after tomorrow... I think. I'll go, see Peter and Jasef, see Caralla, then come straight back. Maybe with Agnes, too." She's lying.

"Okay. Okay, I've got it."

"I just need to go and get some stuff, I mean, go and tell some of the Apechi that I'm leaving." She climbed onto the ladder and paused to take what she believed would be her last look at Achira before descending. "Thank you. Ar, meet me by the train in an hour."

XV

Gris Caralla considers herself to be in possession of many bad habits. She is indulging one of them now, sitting at her office window. She really does enjoy smoking.

It is the dead of night, quiet enough that she can hear the tobacco burn.

The window protrudes from the rest of the building, suspended over the metal canopies below. They could be real in this light. Towering ferns arch fanlike between the bubbling heads of coniferous fakes, parasitic mistletoe erupts from webs of metal bark. It's all too still. She exhales. The smoke joins the mist.

She cannot sleep. She would take something for it, but it is clear to her now that time is running out. None to waste. She had once thought that she might survive Apech. No longer. The only thing that really makes her understand the fact of her death is imagining all the cartons of long, thin cigarettes which will go unsmoked in the embassy's attic. She does not examine why this image makes her feel so melancholic, why it pulls her heart into her throat. That would be to let fear – or, worse, sentimentality – get in the way of her task.

A task eight years in the making. Too slow and now too fast. Part of her suspects that the reason it has taken so long is that she knew it would take her with it. The black hand possesses her, the responsibility will consume her. But it cannot take from her the enjoyment of a cigarette.

She watches the embers twirl into the darkness below, lights another.

Hers is a thankless task, because nobody else can know.

Sometimes she allows herself to wonder whether she would have come here had she known what she does now. She had volunteered to go into that room, observe the recordings from this strange planet. Somebody had to, it may as well have been her. She had been the first to suspect that the scouts' madness could be contagious, was transferring in some way however small to those who had been interviewing them. It was then that she had enlisted a deimancer. They had been able to feel it. Something there. Some grim sentience lurking on the edge of reality, changing it, playing with time and disrupting causality. This could not be allowed.

Gris Caralla understands the creatures or sources of power which Crysth terms 'deities' to be flaws, mistakes in the rhythm of the universe. She believes them to be manmade. She knows that they can be weakened and battered into powerlessness through the destruction of their corporeal bodies – altars, satellites, icons, words. Sometimes people. The deaths of the polluted. Crysth is a genocidal empire. Smash or grab.

Gris Caralla had thought that she might survive, for a while. Take the secret to her natural grave and kill it there with her. The deimancer had thought this possible, that the god of Apech was already so weak from the ravages of its own people's war that it may simply expire, that it was nowhere near strong enough to spread. Alas.

What is bothering her is that she still does not know how it moves, or even where it is. She could almost laugh but she just smiles, because she knows that the reason she cannot find it is because she knows that it exists. Now she does laugh. It is looking back at her, she thinks. She thinks that it can read her mind. It cannot, but it does like her – if such a thing can be said to have likes. It doesn't matter. She has found a way to destroy it without having to know where it is, and without infecting anybody else with the knowledge that it is there to be destroyed at all. She is quite proud of this, how few Crysthian deaths it would take. She wonders how many other black hands this has happened to. By 'this', she means dying far away from home with no friends and no family and nobody to know that it was a martyrdom.

No, that was not true. She has Agnes, but she cannot think about him. That she may have to take Agnes with her is the only real regret of her life.

She thinks of Ming, which brings her some more unnamable emotions. Guilt? Suspicion? The girl was getting impatient, angry. She knows that she is not getting the full truth despite being months away from becoming a black hand herself and is finally sick of it.

Images swarm at the edge of reality. Her skin itches.

Gently flashing lights broil technicolor into the fog. One of the moons tries to shine through above.

The visions look like this.

It starts with déjà vu. Caralla knows this and so she is already away from the window, the stem of her last cigarette thrown beyond the ledge. You can stop them if you can focus, pull yourself together. Sit down, breathe.

The grating sound of rough prosthetic fingers turning a faucet.

She is too tired to fight it, can feel it overwhelming her. Swimming around the room. She puts herself on the floor with her back against the desk. She is not afraid. Her knees complain. She stares at the floor.

He does not look real. His skin is wrong, always moving. Sometimes animal, all teeth and hair. Flickering.

This vision of Xar Kis is not trying to conceal his power. He is holding a golden chain from which swings a railway spike, like a priest with incense. He is playing with physics. It is dancing impossibly in the air, a haunted puppet.

He is not alone. The other man is kneeling. Face down. High nose. Long hair. Green uniform.

Kis steps forwards and the spike smashes against Jasef's face. His mouth opens and he falls – moments later Caralla hears his scream of pain. She can hear Kis' anger, too. He talks quietly when he is angry, very quietly. She realizes now and only now that he does this so that he cannot be heard in the visions. She laughs again. It all seems so obvious in retrospect. From here, the furthest edge.

Distan now, too. Ugly creature. Even when everything about him is in constant motion.

Open it, Jasef is saying. Muffled, from far away. I won't open it.

Caralla's eyes bulge. She knows what Distan is holding – an orange folder, a sealed document box which belongs to her.

She will be betrayed. Everything she had suspected is true.

She closes her eyes, turns over so that she can use the desk to pull herself up, eyes still closed. That just makes it worse, really. It's disorientating, the thing does not know where to put the vision, so it seems to be everywhere at once. Nauseating, but she has to stand. Agnes, she is saying, not calling for him but speaking him. Using his name to ground herself, make a plan. No. Not while it's in your head. Not while it's in your head. She keeps saying his name. She thinks that the god won't be able to hear her think if she drowns herself out.

She does not know that it can lie.

"You get out here, check on those two. I'm going straight to the embassy," said Ming, as the train pulled to a halt at their pagoda station.

Ar yawned, *sure? You look tired.*

"I don't have time to wait. Plus, if I looked good then Caralla would think I'd been slacking." She smiled and then winced at the gash on her chin. "Let whoever's on the controls know, will you? I'll see you when I get back."

Ar nodded, stretched, and waved to her before hopping off the train.

The demon in the engine began to stir. Its torment bore her towards the embassy station.

It was late evening by the time she came to the gate. She wound her way up its path, trying to interest herself in the gleaming metal trees as she went. Chainmail willow branches, curls of steel twisted into bunches of wisteria. It would be playful anywhere else, a game, a feat of creativity. Here it was just cold.

She brushed her hand against the call button and the elevator doors slid open. She keeps touching her jacket's inner pocket.

Embassy staff bustle about their business and nod to her with a self-consciously increasing respect; it would not be long, now, until the office she was headed to was her own. The door swung open to the rhythm of her predecessor's hands.

Gris Caralla sat at her windowsill.

She knew immediately that Ming was changed.

There was an unblinking intensity to her now. Always had been force in her, but this was different. She was not present. It was like making eye contact with somebody who was considering an insult, who was on the verge of saying something irretractable. Caralla watched her, curious but hiding it behind her cigarette.

"Did you win?" she asked, after a while.

Ming smiled unpleasantly, stalked further into the office. Touched the wound on her face. "In my battle for Crysth's honor? Should see the other guy, et cetera."

To her surprise, Caralla found herself sending little shocks of electricity through the gauntlet on her left wrist. How a person could radiate so much aggression was incredible to her. She usually liked it, in fact. Saw it for exactly the kind of thing that a black hand should be able to do. But now it seemed unhinged. A wounded animal.

"What happened?" The ambassador's voice was soft, sympathetic. "Are you alright?"

"Of course." Ming avoided her gaze as she came to sit beside her and took a proffered cigarette, not because she liked it but because she always did. "I fell over."

Caralla was absolutely stunned by the outrageousness of the lie. She decided to laugh, "That is not true."

"No, it isn't. But it does not matter. I am embarrassed, and nothing will come of it. Allow me my mystery."

The ambassador shrugged. That seemed to be all, so they sat and smoked for a while.

"You keep touching your arms," observed the younger of the two. "Are you alright?"

Gris Caralla resisted the urge to snatch her prosthetic away from her forearm. "Kind of you to notice. The gauntlet has been pinching of late."

Ming's eyes narrowed at this, also clearly a lie. "It did not occur to me that you would wear your gauntlet around the embassy."

"Does it bother you that I do?"

"No." It did. "Where is Agnes, anyway?"

"He will be back any minute. He and the blues have been out patrolling the streets with Distan. For protection against domestic terror but, you know. Rama has not left his building. He has sent me many more letters, however."

Ming nodded. "Kis?"

"Likewise. Haven't seen hide nor hair of him since the cylinder, which I find extremely worrying."

"I do not think you need to. They're probably both just waiting for the other to decide whether or not it's war."

"Yes," murmured Gris, "it is, I imagine."

"Oh, absolutely. Should not take too long, though. Rama seems to have lost control of his people."

"I agree, but tell me why you think so."

"He would never have killed Ustra. He's..." she moved her hands as she sought the words, "Concerned with his reputation. Which means that someone did it without his permission. He has also lost his base of support in Ech Kon."

"Yes, I know. He says they fled on the ship. He seems convinced someone is coaxing the magic back specifically to spite him."

The student laughed.

"Any of it true?"

"They did take the ship, and they had been fighting. There's no evidence of any unnatural force, though. I think he's trying to distract us while he goes for Kis' throat. But I haven't quite worked it out yet."

Caralla frowned, pushed the fingertips of her hands together until the pressure splayed them flat and her palms touched. "Then why are you back?"

Ming looked at her straight, now. Pleasure in her expression. "You don't know?"

"Clearly," came the response.

"Ar came to Ech Kon to bring me back," she whispered this, reminding Gris of the quiet nastiness possessed by Xar Kis. "They went to see Ed Rama."

Gris watched her, waiting.

"They think," Ming licked her lips, an uncharacteristic expression of delight in the reveal, "that we should be joining Ed Rama's cause – that Crysth should be fighting the good fight for the liberty of Apech."

Gris rolled her eyes. "What have you done about it?"

"Me?" said Ming, affectedly taken aback. "I was not here. It is you who they think is misguided. He told them that you aren't answering his letters, that you are an obstacle to him being the liberator of Lon Apech – and they believed him. I have dissuaded them from the conviction, but..."

"But what?" she snapped.

Ming raised an eyebrow. "It does not look well."

"That they were so impertinent as to visit Rama, or that they believed him?"

"Both." The younger woman emphasised the plosive sound. "They want to believe you either incompetent or malevolent."

"Clearly."

There was a silence.

"I shall speak to them."

Ming nodded. "That would be a valuable gesture."

"Gesture."

The younger woman shrugged. "Conversation, if you prefer."

"You are being insolent."

"I apologise if my manner is improper." Ming shifted in her seat, an effort to show a more contrite pose. "I am tired, I am hurt. A day's journey has been added to my labors."

"That did not sound like the end of that sentence."

"It was not. A day's journey has been added to my labors because the embassy has not been taking care of the research students here."

Caralla nodded. "Thank you for your honesty."

"Thank you for allowing it."

The ambassador laughed, a noise of disbelief rather than humor. "As if it isn't enough that I have to deal with this Rama-Kis squabble on top of everything else."

The word 'squabble' brought Ming's attention fully into the room. Her master's lack of concern over Kis' position was somewhat unexpected. He was their friend, their plans worked with him in place. He had been the head of all their negotiations concerning trade, diplomacy, everything. "You seem very certain that Kis will win."

"Aren't you? You just said that Rama has lost control, his people are fighting each other. Putting him down should not take long."

Ming considered this. She certainly had said that, but she had not been thinking about it. "Yes, but if he has lost control, who has gained it? He is the most reasonable commander of the opposition. Imagine if *she* takes over. It is a shame that this has to happen now, when we are so close to getting some real industrial capability down here."

There it was. Ming saw. Caralla seemed to have forgotten that this is what they were doing, to be surprised by its mention. "Yes," she said absently.

Retire, Ming thought, you geriatric fool.

Caralla was miles away.

"Ambassador?"

"Yes. No." She turned to look at her properly again. "I need you to be honest with me now."

Ming's face went cold, she stared back at the ambassador. "I always am."

Caralla smiled. "Yes."

There was a long silence.

Caralla lifted another cigarette to her lips, it muffled her next words as she spoke. "Where is Fukuyama?"

"Fukuyama?"

"Fukuyama," confirmed Caralla, exhaling.

"Crysth. He's back home."

"No, he isn't."

Completely out of your mind, Ming thought. "He… isn't?"

"No."

Ming was silent for a time, but when her voice returned it was a whisper once more. "Where is he then?"

Caralla waited.

"You thought I knew," Ming continued, after a while, "this is what you were talking about when we were on our way to the cylinder. You thought I knew that Fukuyama was missing and that I wasn't saying anything about it? Why?! Do you even have his research? Everything is hinging on those documents!"

"Watch your tone."

Ming shook her head from side to side in unconcealed, open-mouthed disbelief.

"And don't look at me like that."

"Oh – I'm sorry – how am I supposed to be looking at you?"

The ambassador clenched her black fist and Ming's head flew backwards, cracking her skull against the wall as a jolt of savage electricity whipped across her face. She gasped, staggered to the side away from the window and for an unbelievable moment Gris Caralla thought that she was going to strike back.

"You," she began, standing up to confront her student, "are privier to the inner workings of Xar Kis' mind than I. Do not think that I do not know this."

Ming turned to look at her commander. Outraged. Livid. The force of the impact had made her bite her tongue. She swallowed a shard of tooth, blood.

"I assumed that Kis had taken it upon himself to…" began Caralla, "remove Fukuyama from the equation. I believed that you were sparing me the precise knowledge that he had done so. I thought the damned documents were with you."

"Why?" that whisper, Xar's whisper. "Fukuyama was helping us."

"Was he?" asked the ambassador, back in control. "Have you forgotten all that talk of bringing labs and witches down here? Yes, so you do see. All our meetings and letters and scientific back and forths will have been for nothing if this planet is deemed unnatural, dangerous. Kis will never get his embassy, we will never get our drills."

Ming stared, realizing for the first time that Caralla wasn't ignorant of Apech's curse – she too was trying to hide it.

This was a defining moment in Ming's life. She saw that she was not the only one with the power to deceive. She had lived her life within so many veils that this notion truly had never occurred to her before. She had thought herself the only crooked black hand. She had believed that Gris Caralla had the empire's best interests at heart, nothing else. But here Caralla was, all but admitting to conspiring against the empire in order to bring a hostile, magical, dangerous planet into the imperial fold. For fame? For importance? It did not matter.

"You thought we had… assassinated him, as a favor to you," said Ming, to make sure, to confirm that she was right.

Caralla nodded, her expression hard. "To us."

"We did not. I thought he had left." Ming allowed herself to be handed a tissue, used it to dab blood from her mouth. "I would have told you if we had killed him. Did you think I was trying to spare your feelings? We had a little farewell party. I saw him board the train."

Caralla shook her head. "He never showed up to the port. I… made my assumption and told them that he had opted to stay a while longer to conclude his research. Good gods."

"Yes."

Caralla covered her eyes with her hand. An expression of disappointment rather than regret. "Oh. Gods."

"So where is he?"

"I do not know. More importantly, where is his research. You are absolutely sure that neither Kis, Ustra, nor Distan got… bored of him? You're completely certain?"

Ming shook her head, looking down at the bloodstain cradled in her hand. "Utterly."

XVI

Achira woke. She had no idea what time it was. Her mouth tasted awful, sticky. But the headache was gone, so that was a win. She rolled over, looking around the unfamiliar, bare room. She had not bothered to dress the bed, just wrapped the covers around her before collapsing back to sleep. She remembered the conversation earlier with a renewed, completely sober embarrassment, and wished she had never come. She struggled out of the tangle she had created in the sheets.

Sun outside; not past noon. Train gone.

She breathed deeply, enjoying the clear air before the taste in her mouth became too much of a nuisance. Back upstairs to her suitcase, to the bathroom.

She opened a nearly round, almost mirrored cabinet behind the sink and was met by the white and blue design of a Crysthian toothpaste. Her thumb eclipsed its logo, a satisfying pop as the cap flipped upwards. Nothing came out.

She stopped, stared at it. Squeezed again, nothing. With mounting annoyance, she began to unscrew the lid, peeled off the seal, replaced the cap. Ran the tap. Closed the mirror. Watched herself brush, eyes inspecting themselves for redness, signs of aging. Nagging suspicion returned to her mind.

She looked around the room, walking around with her toothbrush still moving across her teeth. Nothing in there had been used. Ming had looked awful, granted, but she had to have showered. Her clothes had been clean, her hair had been clean.

She stepped back out onto the landing, chewing the bristles thoughtfully as she went, pushing doors open. Several rooms, and none of them with the sheets on the mattresses, none of them disturbed. She made her way back to the one she had slept in to make sure, but she already knew it had been untouched by anyone but her. Days had passed since Ming had left the capital; it was impossible that she had not eaten nor slept nor pissed nor disturbed a single thing. Nobody had been here. Ming had not been staying here.

She spat into the sink.

Well, she thought, rinsing out her mouth and drawing up to look herself in the face again, what has our Wilhelmina been up to.

XVII

What Xar Kis thinks of as his palace is nothing and everything like Lon Apech.

Too many tapestries. They thought that these great cloth things were intended to cover walls entirely, and so cover them they did. They're all clashing, too. Some are draped around the horns and antlers of creatures that will never grace this planet alive. All are gifts. The Greens are excellent at pumping out cultural artifacts whenever the empire is in need.

An elephant's trunk winds around a candlestick. The effect is quite kitsch.

Visitors can barely walk for trinkets. It forces you to move a certain way, like a museum. Like every museum at the same time. It is usually densely populated, nonetheless. Staff or guards or allies or friends can be found lounging around the place, blending in with their surroundings, affecting the poses on the paintings innumerable.

There's a fountain that's quite nice. A marble horse at its top. Young lovers sometimes sit at it, shy and comfortable. A little paradise to them.

But the master is keeping to himself. Only his best lieutenant and some servants have seen him, and he's been murderous even to them. The house is quiet.

He walked out of the private wing, velvet flowing around

his heels. A friend is coming, the people he sends to tail her have just told him. He sent them hurrying back to her, making sure that she is not followed by other spies. He has missed her, he is hurt that she is only just coming to see him now, even though she told him she had no choice but to leave.

There is glass in his windows. A rarity, here. Stained beautifully in reds and blues. Spotlights are affixed to the cement outside some of these, throwing a reminiscence of daylight through the coloured panes. She walked past one on the other side of the wall.

Outside. The back of the house is designed with baroque secrecy in mind, and so her path takes her winding through scores of verandas, turrets, balconies. Anybody who did not know the way would get lost on the vertical stone maze. Half-hidden stairways, walls which had to be climbed over. Total nonsense. A waste of time. Nobody would dare sneak into his house.

She stopped for breath after a minute of her ascent, leaning her elbows against the side of a fifth-floor balcony which should have overlooked the square below were it not for the city's fog. She watched the lights dance and brawl, listened to the birds. You could smell the Vasa from here, she decided. A drop of toxicity in the steam-wet air.

She did not look around when she heard a door open behind her, she knew he knew where she was.

"Good evening," came a servant's voice. "He's waiting for you in the atrium."

The man bowed his head to her as she began down the steps.

She was still fighting her way under a tapestry when she heard him call her name.

"Finally."

"Missed me?" she asked, weaving her way through his treasure towards the sound.

Her step faltered only slightly when she saw him.

He was wearing the gown that Ustra had been killed in. Was he? Had it been black or maroon? This one was maroon. It was sort of wrapped around him. Torn at the seams, more him than fabric, more hole than dress. Strips of it tied onto his shoulders. He was covered in blood, sweat, suchlike. She allowed alarm to show on her face as she took his hands. He knelt before her with his cheek to her hip, and she ran her fingers through his filthy hair.

"Xar."

"I did miss you."

Her expression, unseen above him, was appalled. Had everybody gone completely mad while she was away?

She examined her fingers. It wasn't just blood in his hair but sticky, industrial dirt. She'd missed something good. She noticed then that there was nobody around, that the mansion was empty, quiet.

"Xar? Look at me. You haven't killed everyone, have you?"

He grinned, showing his grey teeth in childish joy. "Of course not."

"Where are they?"

He shrugged. "They were doing Military posturing with Miré. He's back upstairs now."

"You're making me dirty."

"No I'm not, I'm not touching you."

"I can feel you touching me."

He sat back on his heels and looked up at her. "Happy?"

She checked her suit, considered asking him whose was the blood but hesitated for fear that he might have to say that it was Ustra's. She did not have time for him to be like this. Then again, she thought, the corners of her mouth turning upwards in an expression which he reflected as she watched him, it might help. Give him something else to worship, the way he had the girl.

"I have something to show you," she said.

His face lit up into a delighted curiosity which jarred

dreadfully against his aging skin, his ringed eyes. It was like seeing someone inhabited by the wrong spirit, a body of misery possessed by a ghost of sin. "And I have something to show you. Upstairs."

Ming sighed, pleasure rather than impatience. "You first, then."

He stood, fluidly, and turned. She followed, her eyes tracing up and down the ribbon of scarring which ran down his spine. Old welts from healed disease. Unusually neat, oscillating in Rorschach patterns which spoke either of a particular resilience against or a particular compliance with the affliction's touch. It was, she knew, also partly because his father had taken a hammer to the god's osteophytes as they had twisted their way out of his young skin, torturing his son with tears in his own eyes and teeth bared against the screams. Revolution. Now, though, their horrible symmetry was disturbed by newer marks – scratch marks, so new that his flesh was still shining in red complaint.

"What have I missed?"

At the room's furthest edge Kis bent at the waist to lift the lower corner of a tapestry, draping it over their heads and revealing an elevator on the other side. They stood in the little canopy it created, him holding it above them with outstretched fingers while the machine descended.

"We caught someone," he said, "trying to take a message from Ech Kon to Rama."

"Oh," she grinned up at him, touched her jacket pocket absently. "Someone we know?"

"No."

"What have you been doing to him? Still alive? What was the message?"

"Was when I left, but it's a close thing. Be patient." He frowned. "You look awful, you know. What happened to your chin?"

Struggling to push the fabric back out of the elevator before the doors closed behind them, she answered, "I'll tell you later. I need to show you the thing for it to make sense."

He shrugged in an annoyed, do whatever gesture, ripping a strip of fabric which had been tied in place as he did. Ming tutted and swiped it off him, annoyed by it and by him and by how ridiculous he looked.

"I like it," he protested, but allowed her to rearrange him into a slightly less offensive configuration of cloth regardless.

When they step out of the elevator, they will be walking towards what used to be Fukuyama's laboratory. They still think of it as a laboratory, but anyone else would recognize it as an irreparably occupied territory. Don't be misled by the lab coats, the servants just think they're cool.

The lab had become theirs the moment Fukuyama left. Evidence of their attempts to infect Ming with the Apechi curse are left scattered over tables and drawers. Dying *tama* are handcuffed to hospital beds, all of them far enough along in their poisoned half-lives for the virus to have returned to their flesh. There is a smell of plastic and metal in the air, which is for the best.

It had been Distan's idea to try a blood transfusion, which had not worked. Ming had almost died trying to replace pints of her own with the rotten slime they could still coax out of the ossifying bodies. Then they had tried powdering and inhaling the bones, which had just made her sneeze black for days. They had tried cannibalism, and kept trying it for long after it became obvious that it didn't work. They had managed to sneak in a few children, but rarely enough that they wouldn't have to fear pitchforks at the gate.

Miré Distan closed the laboratory door behind him, sealing the captured messenger away. In his other hand was a large orange folder.

"Ahh," Ming said, her eyes widening with the delight of recognition and realization, "I see."

Grinning without knowing what it was she saw, Miré held

open another of the hallway's few doors while she and Kis passed through it. "Welcome back," he said.

This room was spectacularly weird. Nothing like anywhere else. White floors, shimmering walls. Blue pools and birdsong from long-tailed, paradise creatures which inhabited the branches of a petrified cherry-blossom. The tree had been twisted and tamed in life, spiraling unnaturally before it exploded into salmon-hued petals. The sound of running water, a glass dome overhead. Artificial dusklight pushing through. Real plants turning leafily, greedily toward bulbs which were hurriedly turned off by the few servants who made permanent residence on this floor. Slabs of artificial rock decorated the walls. Onyx here, speckled jasper there. Brass circles creating an unbalanced symmetry underfoot. A long, white table which tapered into a point at one end, an elephant skull sitting pathetically at the other. It's a copy, of course; the apartment of a former and spectacularly tasteless Crysthian emperor.

Ming slipped her shoes off at the door and sat, cross-legged, at the table's tapered end. A shaking hand offered her a wine glass, which she took.

The lords of Apech sat on either side of her, watching in silence as her eyes flicked over the contents of the folder.

"This should be easy to edit." She placed a few of the sheets of paper flat on the table. "It looks like it has been designed that way. Anything referring to," she raised her voice to show that she was reading, *"residual unnatural forces* is in its own letter. We can just remove them." She snapped shut the orange folder again, with an air of satisfaction.

Miré Distan said, "I couldn't open that. It wouldn't open for me. It's not even locked."

She flashed him a brief smile before downing her glass and saying, "It is locked. It will only respond to processed fingertips." she wiggled hers in front of him. "Which you don't have."

"Yet," he added.

Kis scowled, not liking to get ahead of himself in anything, and swiveled the excluded papers towards him. "You don't seem surprised that we've found this."

"No, but you go first. Tell me what you've found out. You got him to talk, I assume?" this last said to Miré.

"A one-man orchestra."

She knows but she can't help herself but ask, "Fukuyama is out there in Ech Kon?"

Miré's monosyllabic bark-laugh preceded his response. "Yep."

"Fucking traitor."

Drumming bloody fingers on the table and watching his own reflection in his wine glass Xar said, "How did you know? Did you find him?"

"Fukuyama? No. I guessed; Gris Caralla just told me he was missing."

Both men's eyebrows descended in instant suspicion.

"Our man in there told me that Fukuyama has been with them for months. Why didn't she tell us sooner?" Miré.

"She didn't know. She thought that we'd killed him. He was making too much of a fuss about the residual..." Ming doesn't know what to call it anymore, "magic that's still here. We all knew he was going to cause problems. She thought we'd just done away with him."

Kis drank as he listened, his head bowed, dry lips blackening with the alcoholic dregs.

"And, what, just decided to sit here with that?" Miré jabbed a stubby finger in the direction of the orange folder, spilling wine onto the table. "Why would we do that?"

Ming looked over to Xar before saying, "I have no idea." She paused. "She is behaving very strangely. She did not want me to tell you that I was going to Ech Kon, remember?" Another pause. "And she hit me earlier."

"She what?" said out of a smile in the corner of Xar's mouth.

"She hit me. With her gauntlet, too. You know aggression

is a sign of dementia?" They laughed so she added, "I'm glad you're amused."

"What is she playing at, though?" asked Miré. "And why did that traitor scientist run off with Rama? He was a coward, he was afraid of everything."

"You gave him damn good reason to be, Miré," Kis.

"What, this is my fault now?" he demanded.

"Not what I said. Tell Ming what else we found out."

Miré glowered for a second, pre-emptively defensive whenever he is alone with these two; he knows that their conversation will inevitably leave him behind. "Rama's rebels have been holding Fukuyama in Ech Kon, waiting for Rama to overthrow us and afterward renegotiate the terms of Apech's integration into Crysth."

"Which worries me, because it means he really was planning on making a move. I have no information which leads me to believe that he has anything like enough support, but..." One of Xar's fingers began to circumnavigate his wine glass' rim, his eyes following it. "I could be wrong."

Miré nodded, waited for more, then resumed his own story. "But then a few days ago–"

"Hang on," interrupted Ming, "what do you mean 'was planning'? Have you dealt with him already?"

"No," and that was a growl, "I have not. He has been hiding in his hole, protecting them all. But he has sent me many letters." His finger stopped suddenly in its path and he looked up to the future ambassador before adding, in a tone of scarlet hatred: "He wants to make friends."

At any other time Ming would have laughed, but not now, not with that gown still wrapped around his grieving body. Instead she whispered, "Has he lost his mind?"

"Perhaps. He suddenly seems more afraid of whoever attacked them in Ech Kon than of a future with you and I in charge of Apech." He allowed himself a flat smile. "He also assures me that he was not directly responsible for Zara's death."

"As if we didn't already know." Miré.

"He must be quite desperate if he is willing to admit that he is losing control." Ming was watching Xar's face very carefully, her fingers moving compulsively to her pocket. "Have you responded?"

"I have said that I will consider opening negotiations with him if he surrenders her to me."

"And?"

He shot her a look. "Do you hear her screaming?"

"Apologies. Stupid question." They sat in alcoholic silence for a while, the servants using the opportunity to rush in and refill glasses before Ming spoke again. "That's why he'll never win."

"What?" Miré.

"He is obviously terrified of this new force in Ech Kon, and yet he won't offer a single sacrificial lamb. We may as well wait for his own morality to kill him for us."

Kis smiled. "He believes that this 'new force' in Ech Kon is the source of our... unnatural happenings problem. He even tried that angle on me, said that our integration to Crysth will be much easier if the curse is completely destroyed."

Ming frowned – she doesn't like that. It makes sense and is therefore dangerous. Fukuyama must have been talking quite a lot. But all Ming wants is the magic. The magnitude of her unspoken alarm was such that Miré gloated in it, watching her squirm. He said, "We should destroy it. That's what Farön would have wanted."

Xar's eyes narrowed at the mention of his father's name and he said, "Farön Kis is dead."

Ming quietly returned Distan's gloating back to him so he said, "Caralla would like it too."

"Caralla is behaving ridiculously. She needs to go." Ming.

"You have wanted her gone since before you arrived." Kis.

"Yes, well now I want it more. She isn't trusting us fully, she is wasting time, she is being strange. It's only a matter of time before she makes a much more consequential mistake than this." She took another sip. "I will have to get this folder back to her immediately. They remember when and who touched them."

"Will you tell her the truth about how we found it?" Miré.

"I don't know yet. But I interrupted you – you were saying?"

"Oh, yeah. So, a while ago his little seaside rebel party was attacked by people who he says were using the," –he waved his hands around, looking for a word– "magic. Using it properly."

Kis watching Ming, now. Waiting.

She held the last mouthful of wine in her mouth until it became sour, swallowed, and said: "Properly?"

Kis smiled. He likes it when she's greedy. Their eyes met.

"Yeah," agreed Distan, with evident distaste. "Fucking around with the world."

"Do it," whispered Ming, watching Xar's expression. "Just once."

Distan retreated from the verge of protest as Xar raised his hand into the air. He wavered it over the table, fingers rippling, then smashed down through five inches of stone.

Ming opened her mouth in an obscene gesture of longing. He had not needed to hit hard. A hand-shaped chunk of table, swatted to the floor. All he had needed to do was focus on a time when the table was not there. He does not know why or how this works. It isn't what it seems.

"It's getting stronger," he massaged his hand, which must have been causing him significant pain despite the apparent ease with which it had sliced through the rock. "That is a fact. Rama knows it, too. We all do."

They settled into silent, oozing rage at their enemy.

It wasn't long before the nervous movement of Ming's right hand drew Kis' eyes. He followed it to her pocket, back to her lap. To her pocket.

She noticed him noticing.

"What's wrong?" Distan's voice was frustrated, whining, picking up on the tension between them but not knowing why.

"Ming has something in her pocket," Xar murmured, in what sounded to the servants like his most dangerous tone but to Ming's ear like flirtation.

"I told you that I have something to show you," she replied.

"Then do so."

Ming closed her eyes, felt her fingertips begin to ache as she squeezed them against the cold metal in her pocket. It had been too long since she had eaten. She could feel her body complaining, exhausted. Fueled by wine and lust.

"Show me," he said, to her eyelids.

She opened them. "I don't know how."

To Distan's disgust, the unifier of Apech's son pulled Ming towards him. Deferentially. The servants withdrew further backwards.

Miré did not see Kis' lips move, the shape of the words as he put his hand into Ming's jacket, stole the little object from her grasp. He just heard him begin to laugh.

"Of course," he said.

"Where the hell did you get that? I can feel it." Distan.

Ming and Kis just looked at each other, unspeaking their desire. Not for each other, although their interactions had been tainted with it when Ustra was there to serve as a bridge between them, but for the goal. Power, joy, freedom, control.

"I met a priest," she whispered to him, her tone low enough to go unheard by any but the two aristocrats.

Kis' face stayed quite still.

"What?" Distan's voice broke her concentration, she turned to it.

"The man who attacked Rama's... mob."

"Did you kill him?"

"No. And nor do I believe I could have."

Distan said, "Xar."

"It's getting stronger, Miré," was the reply. "Rama's right about that."

"There are no priests." Distan. "There never were. They were just... fools worshipping poisoned magic. It's going away. Ming can catch it just as it's fading, but it'll be gone for good in a few years." He sounds like he's reassuring himself. This is what they have told themselves is true.

"Xar," Ming said, firmly and with a longing viciousness that was so utterly her. "I've seen it."

Distan's fist came down heavy on the table. "What is this? Why are we listening to this? Xar?"

"What have you seen?" he asked, again watching his finger on its ceaseless path around his glass' edge.

She told them. With the awe and terror of a crusader newly converted she sought language for the memory of its pulsing flesh, stitches taut over endless faces, bodies pulled apart and pushed together and filled with something that was not quite life. The taxidermist, his warning, his invitation. She drank. They responded with learned revulsion.

Crysth hated gods, mistrusted magic, enslaved demons, tamed witches. It hoards and controls. It hates so much that it names them with words it doesn't believe in. Ming has been raised with that language, that revulsion, and so have Kis and Distan.

"I'm supposed to show you," she said, after there had been silence. The talisman from the body of the godthing lay there, black and ragged against the crisp whiteness of the table. Looking like a tail, or a root.

Xar had seen a ghost of himself pulling it out of her pocket. The god had shown him what it wanted him to do; paying all its attention to him, trying to remind him what it felt like when it first turned itself to him as a child. Distan can see it, his sanctified eyes make out an increasing ferocity in the mess which the god sometimes makes of afflicted skin.

Ming risked leaning over to Xar, clumsily, tipsily. A hand on his filthy arm. "Do you believe me?"

He looked at the hand. Touched it. "Unreservedly."

"I don't," grumbled Distan and then added, quickly, when two pairs of bloodshot eyes whipped towards him, "I mean, I believe that Ming believes. I do not believe the needle."

Kis twitched his lip in a warning snarl, which Ming saw.

"I am supposed to show you," she repeated. "I need a real person and a *tama*. From the lab."

Distan's expression was a parody of suspicion, but he stood with a wave for assistance from the servants to retrieve the requested flesh. Kis watched Ming in silence as she drained her cup again. She met his gaze as it was refilled by that still visibly shaking servant – a young woman who obviously knew that she had heard too much, who was quivering with the certain horror of it.

Ming turned her mouth into a smile. Kis had noticed the shaking too and was excited by it – despite whatever he might be feeling about the priest. He stood upright. A weak erection was losing its fight against the weight of Ustra's skirt.

"Stay," he said, his hand flying to the servant's wrist at a speed incongruent with his gentle tone. "Sit beside me."

Her face broke into anguish, like she might sob. She pulled herself together, rightly realising that tears would only make it worse for her, and took a seat to his left.

"She's just going to watch," said Kis, seeing the look on Ming's face

"Do you know what's going to happen?"

"I can see little hints of it in the air, but no," he denied, but he was being playful. "It will, however, be a thing to watch. Won't it?" The question was directed to the servant. "Drink." he said, putting his own, full glass into her hand. She obeyed.

Ming knew what he was doing. His voyeurism was such that he would try to double himself, to create another to watch for him – watching himself watch. He wanted their minds addled, his watchers, so confused that he might take them over entirely. The girl seemed to know this too. She was gulping as much of the wine as she could stomach, as if obedience would save her, as if she were anything more than a prosthetic which would be destroyed after use.

But Ming was drunk. She had not eaten enough. Bleeding and not sleeping, too. Lightheaded, exhausted. She might even be a little concussed. She could not believe herself. If Gris Caralla found out that there was a god here, found out what she was doing... A wave of anxiety passed over her before she quelled it, pushed it away. She fixed her eyes on the girl who would not survive the hour, the look on her face. That was certainty, that was dread. Ming smiled, comforted by it. Crysth would never allow worship, would destroy anything or anyone that tried to insist on it – but all this could be worried about later. She'd be the ambassador anyway, not Gris Caralla. She'd keep it secret. She rubbed her eyes, took another sip of wine. She'd hide it. This kind of thing must happen all the time.

Ming emptied her glass again before she stood to Distan, proffering the needle to him between thumb and forefinger. "You have to do this, Miré."

"Why him?" asked Kis.

"It has to be done by someone whose mind survived the... spikes. And you don't want to."

Distan took the infected needle and thread from her, examining it between his stubby fingers in a way which made the cursed object seem ridiculously small. She needed contradiction. Deconstruction, reconstruction. And she did not know what any of that meant.

"Attach them together, with that. Leave the needle in the flesh of the weakest." Ming.

Distan examined the thread. "How?"

She heard Kis laugh behind her.

"Just... really?" his expression was totally blank. "Push the needle in to one bit of skin, pull it out, then push it into the other, pull it out."

Distan turned to look at the breathing bodies and grinned with realisation. "Anywhere?"

"Probably."

The Crysthian walked back to her seat, focusing on her drink so as not to have to witness the inelegant parts of the operation; Distan figuring out how to get the bodies into position, figuring out how to use the needle. It was off-putting. More, she was drunk enough to be resentfully annoyed that Distan had dragged in her most beautifully afflicted *tama*, she was sure he had done it on purpose.

She ignored the growls and tuts of Distan's fastidious experimental labor as her cup was filled again.

"Miré will you hurry up?" Kis.

"I am trying!"

Ming clicked her fingers for more wineturned to watch Distan's efforts.

He was squatting with a knee touching each of the bodies' outward facing chests, fat thighed and wrinkled in his concentration. She could not make out what he had managed to achieve with the needle, but it seemed to be going about as well as was expected. She leaned forward to see what Kis was doing. Only vaguely awful. She tipped the last of another glass into her mouth.

"Ming, come help me," complained Distan.

She sighed, stood unsteadily, and joined him. He'd used the blood of one to paste the other's hair – shaggy from long imprisonment – forwards onto its face. Surprisingly good idea. She leaned forward to shove her hand under its armpit, rubbing her palm around the spiked cavern, breaking the longer, sweat soaked spines between her groping fingers...

"Can you hold off for a moment and actually help me?" snapped Distan.

She withdrew her wrist. She couldn't stand straight. She rested against his shoulder. "Sorry, let me keep steady on you."

He grumbled consent and bent his wrists outward so she could see the gristle.

"You're not pushing it in deep enough. The skin's snapping."

"I can't get it in any deeper the neck bones are in the way."

"Just use the meat, it doesn't have to be perfect. To the side of the bone."

She watched as his wet fingers tried and failed to push the tiny, bone blunted spike into the body's skin. "I can't fucking do it!"

"How about this part?" she pushed her thumb into the tendon where Distan's neck joined his shoulder.

She saw him nod. The needle disappeared into the dying flesh, and kept going, he pushed it until the eye disappeared. The body was too weak to cry out, probably in too much pain to feel it. Ming watched in bleary fascination.

"Now what?" he asked.

"Pull it back out."

Distan made a rumbling noise in his throat that could have a been a growl, a moan of frustration. And then he said something stupid: "I'll kill you if this goes wrong."

She did not even wince, no fear, no bitterness, but replied in the same calm whisper that he had threatened her in. "And how do you think he'll react to that? You see him now. Imagine if he had lost both of us."

"He doesn't love you."

"He does not need to."

"What, exactly, are the pair of you doing?" came Kis' voice from the other side of the room.

"It!" roared Distan.

Ming lifted her hand above her head and clicked her fingers; footsteps rang out in immediate, desperate response. The servant skidded, sliding across the blood in his panic to obey and sprawling himself at high speed into the wall behind the morbid tableau. Ming stood at the sound of her wine pouring onto the floor. Raised her hands in annoyance and looked to Kis.

"Oh, kill him." He was not talking to her. The girl beside him stood with an expression of screaming pain and wobbled over carefully to the prone servant. She paused for only a moment, his desperate eyes locked with hers, before stamping them out with the high heel of her shoe.

Ming gesticulated at Kis as the screams and gore splattered out beside her. He caught her meaning and looked around for another servant to replace the man being inexpertly but frantically beaten beside her.

"Does nobody care that I am succeeding here?" snapped Distan, uncharacteristically disinterested in the theatre to his right.

And then Ming fell backwards into the wall. Distan leapt up too, smashing his back into the door beside her. The servant abandoned her victim and sprinted, pathetically, back to Kis. The connected dying were changing.

The disease – the affliction, the interest, the divinity – had sparked. Caught somehow, brought to life by it only knew what, latched onto something which spoke to it, fed it. It had started to rumble, crackle, suck the peace out of the room and send the little birds shrieking in terror. It grew. It pushed its spikes outward and upward and they blackened and twisted as they went. Too big, too fast, fighting each other, flickering, buzzing with some deafening, distant thunder as of water underground. They threw shadows from light that did not exist.

The body on the left was swallowed first. It folded like knitted yarn, trembling as it curled into the other's back, wrapped itself around towers of black bone. Once one was consumed the other fell backward, lay staring empty to the ceiling. Ming could hear Kis shouting something from the other side of the throng but could not make it out. The shifting bone had become a tree-root tumor, spilling onto the floor and there taking shape – shrinking and molding into the semblance of a man. Tall but stooped, forged in the bone of the contaminated and the skin of the tormented. There stood the priest. A silhouette of him, a memory of him. It lifted his hands as if to examine the gore dripping from their twisting manifestation.

"[*Speaking Apechi, unintelligible*]?" The voice was cold, dry. It rang with the despondent, distant vibrations of a fading bell. It made Ming's teeth itch.

"I cannot see," it continued, its curiosity adding a twitch of childishness, naivete to that awful voice.

"What is this?" demanded Kis, breathless. Ming still could not see him.

Distan was reaching under his shirt. Ming grabbed his arm and said, "Don't."

He withdrew the blade anyway.

"Is that Kis' boy?" came the hollow, bone-grating growl.

"I am Xar Kis." This was a snarl. Ming still could not see him, but she could tell that he had approached the apparition.

"Kis' child."

Oh, that would annoy him. Distan threw his blade at the back of the shadow – it clattered to the ground. The thing did not seem to notice.

"The fuck did you do that for?" Ming shouted over the pulling vacuum noise that accompanied the creature, the sound of it and Kis yelling each other down.

"You brought it in here!" he yelled back, spittle flying into her face.

"So!" she shrieked, staggering back as he jerked away, left her to stand beside his master; to confront the beast.

Ming sidled the other way along the wall, stepping over the groaning, beaten servant to approach from the other side.

"Don't talk, just listen! You cannot hurt me, and I do not have time. This is not me, you stupid brat. *Can you understand me?"* Kis was shocked into silence at the sound of his native tongue, lifted his chin defiantly to the shadow of a face that could not see him. *"Can you understand me?"*

Ming drew up beside him, watching the flickering shards of bone rile and broil with the movement of the not-priest's mouth.

"Yes," replied Kis. Ming saw that his knuckles were bloody.

"I can make you stronger, listen."

"No."

"Listen…"

Ming stepped backwards, recognizing the intimacy of this, a pledge of faith, a revealing of a secret, a meeting of generational enemies. She sat on the table, watched the priest's shade broil, whisper, flicker around itself. It felt like the air was disappearing from the room, a sapping of some unseen energy. Distan turned to look at her, briefly, his expression unreadable. She could no longer understand what the shadow was saying, had lost the thread, was too tired. The servant was bleeding onto the fucking orange pack. She picked it up, tried to brush it off, made it worse. Slumped onto her chair. Fucking hell. What were they saying? She closed her eyes.

XVIII

Fuck.

Angry, confused. Hungover. Raging anger. What had happened? Where was she?

Darkness, a bed. Another person. A man holding onto her like she was a toy.

"Xar?"

He grumbled into her shoulder.

She pushed him off her, sat upright. Heard him rustle around, low light as a lamp glowed into life.

A huge four-poster bed in a windowless room. Candles on the walls. Statue of a bull. Shit. What the fuck time was it.

"Where the hell are we?" Her mouth was rancid, sour, dry. "I need to get out, what happened, when is it?"

"It's fine, been a few hours."

"Where are we?" Her tone was enraged. Why had he brought her to bed like a fucking child?

"Calm down," he said, bored. He sat up, indicated a jug of water and a bowl of figs on the bedside to her right.

She drank.

"You need the sugar," he said, watching her ignore the fruit.

"Where," she shoved one into her mouth and bit, "are we?"

"My father's bed," he said, matter of fact.

She put the jug to the side and looked at him in an expression of sullen anger which made him laugh.

"I've got some of those headache things over here," he crooned, fumbling on the floor.

"Why are we here? What are you playing at?"

He was still filthy, ruining the patterned sheets with grime and crimson waste. "It felt fitting."

"Where is Distan? What happened with the... thing?"

He placed the capsules into her hand. She swallowed them before taking more fruit.

"Distan needs more time. He's in shock."

So are you, she thought, seeing that Ustra's dress was still wrapped around his lower half. A miracle of self-control prevented her from voicing the thought aloud.

"What happened?" she was snapping at him, looking for her clothes, spotting the data pack in the gloom.

"Can't you leave in the morning?" he asked.

"No," she replied. "I should be back now, Gris will be watching, she'll know I'm not there."

"She won't," he whispered. "Mine are all out there, causing a fuss." He hissed this last word in a dramaturgical sizzle of sound.

Ming relaxed, somewhat, sitting back onto the bed and looking at him with the same annoyed severity. "She'll know you've done that, too. Shit."

He propped himself up on his elbow. "What's she going to do about it?"

"She is the ambassador. She controls communication with Crysth. If she suspects something, wants to bring Military here, then all she has to do is push a button. You know that."

"I've had enough of her."

Ming flexed her fingers at him in sullen exasperation and said, "Finally."

He laughed.

"So? What happened?"

"Let's see. I was insulted, patronized, and generally berated by an otherworldly abomination which manifested in my very own house."

Ming checked his expression before permitting herself to smile and saying, "Sorry. I don't think he's a fan of your father's."

"No. No, not at all."

She lay back down, facing him and mirroring his pose before asking, much more softly, "Tell me what you think."

"I think that the man is a lunatic."

Ming's heart dropped. She felt cold. "The priest?"

He laughed again. "He is not a priest. He is a lunatic. But a powerful lunatic, I can't argue with that." Silence while her heart raced, waiting for him to go on. "He shunted Rama's crowd into the sea for me, apparently. Proof of concept."

"So he–"

"Which is incredibly irritating." He held a finger up to silence her, something he had never done before. "Because if he had consulted me beforehand, I would have told him to kill them all and send me that orange folder. I could well have missed it."

"But you didn't."

He shot her one of his dangerous looks. "You may have been trained in the art of scheming, but I have been doing it for a lot longer. I want my plans airtight. I was born to this."

She returned one of her own and flexed the largest of the implants in her flesh. "So was I."

The hard edge fell from his expression as he reached out to touch it, touch her. She allowed his fingers to roam – but not far before she said, "What is your plan?"

"I am sending you back to him. You are going to tell him that I want them dead, and that I want Rama and Khora even deader."

She nodded obedience. "I already tried getting him to get rid of Achira for me."

"Why?"

"We don't get along. He told me to go fuck myself, but I'm sure he'll cooperate with you."

"He said that he could prove that the thing is what Crysth calls a deity. If that even matters. He says the horrible little manifestation trick would work better the other way, that the god can pull somebody touched by its power straight through its own heart – he just needs a little flesh to show it who."

"I don't understand."

"He wants you to slice me up and take part of me to him so that he can show me how fancy his magic is."

"Are you... going to... be sliced?"

"Absolutely not. There's a chunk of Miré's shoulder in a vial beside the folder."

She laughed, so did he.

"It'll be good for him," he said. "See the sights, kill some stragglers."

"Yes. But then what?"

"Then I'll know exactly how strong this man is, his forces – whatever they are – will be weakened by a clash with Ed Rama, and I'll have the 'god' in my territory to confront."

"So you are open to negotiations?"

"I am open to whatever gets Ed Rama the nastiest, most ignoble death possible. If I can happen to make it seem to everyone that it wasn't my fault that this happened, then all the better. You know I can't openly attack him myself. This way, a hostile force invades Lon Apech, Rama happens to tragically and bravely get in its way, and then I find a peaceful reconciliation in the aftermath." He held her hands to his chest, and she saw that the one he had put through the table was an atlas of brown and purple bruising. "But the embassy is a problem."

"Yes. I have been wondering what I'm going to do about that. Of course, Gris Caralla knows that there is... something unnatural here. But we can't very well parade a thing that thinks it's a god through the streets can we."

"We'll figure that out when we come to it. Or you will."

"Oh?" She imitated his accent. *"I want my plans airtight."*

"Delegation is an important part of leadership," he whispered back.

"Yes. I wish Gris would hurry up and delegate to me. I just can't figure out what to say to her to make her give me the hands."

"I don't want you to go. I'll be bored."

She looked at him, disgusted, and let her eyes roam to his rings. Trinkets from Crysth. Nothings. She remembered Zara, took his uninjured hand in hers, and began to spin the ring he wore around his thumb.

"Do you think you'll find out all manner of state secrets? You'll tell me if you do, won't you?"

"When I get the hands?" She clicked her tongue. "I doubt it. Well, maybe. But nothing interesting. I fear the state secret is that everybody from the deckhands to the emperors is incompetent, unimaginative, and motivated by cowardice."

He looked disappointed. "What about magic? The technomancers? Deities?"

"I think I know all we know about them. More than most about deities, actually. They're dangerous because they're unpredictable." She repeated the official definition, *"A source of unnatural power which possesses desires and intentions independent of the sentient beings which tend it."*

"Can it think, then?"

"We don't know."

"Can it hate?"

She raised her eyebrows. "Xar Kis, are you afraid of it?"

"Of course not, I–" she slapped him hard across the face.

"What," he growled, pushing her over and holding her beneath him, "was that?"

"Proof of concept. It doesn't matter. Deity or not, world or not, all that matters is what happens to you."

"World or not?"

"Yes. You know. Have you ever... all the planets and systems and..." she rolled her eyes, "whatever we encounter on all this relentless exploration. Haven't you thought about it? Don't you think it's strange that there are people everywhere? Human beings. Everywhere. It's pretty uniform. It's suspiciously fucking uniform. You know there was a time when we thought we were alone? Just Earth, just us. Even then they thought that meant something had to be wrong. How could there be an entire universe with nothing in it but us?" She winced as he bit at her shoulder. "Don't leave a mark. Even the first human beings scratching around in caves thought that the world was designed for us. We've known it all along, instinctively. It's in our blood to know what we can't bear to realize." A pause. "If it's designed, then it isn't real."

"Is that what you think?"

"Yes. It isn't real," she whispered, and he could hear the smile in her voice. "I've seen another one before. A deity. Up close." She spoke as if this is seductive somehow. "I was young, but I knew then that it was all wrong. I think it's us that are unnatural, not them. I think anything with that much power is the real world, the real thing. I could feel it. I felt it again in Ech Kon. This world is a plaything, a puppet the moment you can see its strings. We can take control of it. We can be real." She watched his head move down her body and said, "Stop that."

He slumped. "Please."

"Not in your father's bed. It's creepy."

XIX

The man's hands were so rough that Achira could hear them roving over the leather of the controls, bringing the lighthouse closer. The hands of a man who had done real work in his life, the hands of someone who built things. He was wiry, too, with a sullen shyness which made him seem a lot younger than he was. He had not said a word to her but had been the one to peel away from the house when she had asked somebody to tell her where Ming stayed, asked how to get there, confessed that she could not drive the ship.

The ocean was lively beneath them – salt spray jumped at the windows. Water the same colour as the sky. Grey-blue, murky, light bouncing from scattered cloud. Beautiful, really, but Achira was not thinking to look at it.

The lighthouse itself was hideous. Squat and crooked on a lone rock, grey pebbledash with uneven, small windows. Not even a real lighthouse, of course. Why would they ever know what such a thing was for?

A whisper of calloused skin against leather and the demon-haunted metal rumbled still – the last of its momentum sliding them over the water. This man must have made the journey many times; he knew exactly when to kill the power.

"You'll wait for me?"

He nodded.

"Thank you very much." She stepped out onto the vessel's deck.

It was brighter than she had imagined. Her hand leapt up to shield her eyes. The ship made her clumsy, uncertain of herself. She did not know how to disembark from the thing; a platform floating a foot above the water's surface. She would have to jump, get her feet wet. She unhooked the gated railing from its eye and looked over the side. Barnacles, seaweed, moss-looking stuff. She could see to the bottom. A dirty pool of water which was only teased and stirred by the tide. The water was warm, like Lon Apech's rain.

She was self-conscious of the eyes of her temporary pilot behind her.

She pushed against the metal door and swung it straight open – well hinged, light, surprisingly so. She had only seen a lighthouse in cinema, ancient film. She had expected it to be heavy, bolstered against a blustering wind of deadly oceans the like of which Apech had never seen.

"Hello?" She stepped inside, closed the door behind her.

There was a staircase, like the one in their pagoda but shorter. She started to ascend; her eyes fixed – fearfully, somehow – on the trapdoor above. She stopped below it, listening to nothing.

"Hello?"

The metal was cold against her palms as she raised it and immediately she knew somebody was there, sitting on the floor – she dropped it again in shock.

"Hello?!"

There was no response. She knocked. No response.

She pushed again, stronger this time, allowing the door to flip all the way back with a crash and leave the entrance open, give her the safety of her hands. She raised herself up.

A young woman was sitting with her back to her, her arms rising and falling quickly, rhythmically, pulling at something on the floor.

"Hello? Are you alright?" Achira stared, frightened by the woman's silence, her dogged fixation on whatever labor occupied her hands.

The woman stopped, suddenly. "Ming?"

"No," Achira stepped further up the staircase, her entire torso emerging through the floor. "I'm not Ming. Is that okay? I am a friend of Ming's."

"A Ming?" the woman turned, showing Achira a face flowering with bruises, blood. She had something black hanging out of her mouth, sticking to her chin.

"Oh, gods are you alright? What happened?" Achira pulled herself onto the floor and towards the woman, squatting by her side and – seeing it.

A photo album, its pages ripped and scattered in the woman's lap but legible. A man's back rising out of the gloom, dark spines twisting from his skin, bending his body in pain. Another, a hand with its fingers locked around curved shards of black bone.

"What, what, why do you have this? Where did you get this?"

The woman's fingers returned to the book, tore a piece of paper, placed it into her mouth.

"What are you doing? Stop!" Achira grabbed her hands and lowered them, the woman cringed, tried to pull away and so she released her immediately, watched her scramble away. "Are you eating it, why are you eating it? Why do you have this?"

They stared at each other, frightened incomprehension.

The woman was so hurt. Bloody, thin, blue and red with fresh-looking welts across her arms and legs.

"Are you…" Achira tried to relax, a horrible suspicion taking over her mind and dragging cold rage along with it, "are you *tama*?"

The woman did not respond.

"Right then," Achira softened her voice to a gentle murmur,

"I'm going to stand up and I'm going to look around here. I am not going to hurt you, I just want to see what's been going on." She got slowly to her feet, the woman watching her the whole time. "I'm going to walk over here first, and then I'm going to be opening doors and cupboards and..." Achira continued her prattle as she wandered around the space, noting odds and ends stuck to the walls, pieces of fabric hanging loose like decorations on pieces of protruding steel. "Grey is actually quite a fashionable color on Crysth, or at least it was when I left..." she pushed open a door, a bathroom. "Do you mind if I go in here? I'm going to keep talking like this because I know that will make you feel better about where I am and what I'm intending to do, but I'm going to run out of things to say soon. What are these? Ming's clothes. Definitely Ming's clothes." She touched the maroon pile on the floor with her foot; they were filthy. She bent to pick up a shirt, "Is this blood? Is this your blood? Can you come here? There's probably hot water and you're bleeding. Why are you bleeding? Did Ming do this?"

She stepped out of the room and beckoned to the woman, who she saw had returned to her bibliophage endeavor.

"Stop that, will you please? Why are you bleeding?" Achira held out her hands to the woman, who only stuffed paper into her mouth with an increased fervor. "Stop, stop!"

A low, elegant grumble outside.

Achira hopped down the staircase, two at a time, shouting – but the man and the ship were gone. Turned, already gaining speed away from the lone rock.

"Hey! Hey!" she screamed, waving her arms as if the sight of her would remind him of his word.

She stared, breathing hard, horrified by her sudden seclusion. Would the tide rise and drown her? No, of course not. She could row back. No, she could not. Perhaps the woman inside could. The woman inside.

She turned back in, raced up the stairs.

"Are you *tama*?" she shouted, knowing the answer but not

knowing what to say, what was she supposed to say? What was she supposed to do? She tore into the other rooms, spotting Ming's suitcase, snarling with rage and wrenching it open. A start of shock, a flash of colour. Some, what, parrot thing. It was wrong, mangled and changed and sewn and dead. She turned it in her hands, revulsion growing over her face – it twitched. She'd swear it twitched and she dropped it, backing away horrified towards the bed, blood-stained sheets, the smell of sweat.

Not real, this can't be real. Part of her laughed as she thought that – unbelievable. Of course it was real. She was alone on a rock on an alien planet with a mad *tama* and it was all Ming's fault.

That low grumble again, louder. Her heart thumped and she tore to the window, staring over the water towards the growing noise and disbelief – another ship. Heading straight for them. She flew downstairs once more, getting back outside to watch it near, turning her head to watch the other retreat. Had it been escaping this newcomer? She did not know what to do. To stay or flee. To flee where? She looked at the rowing boat. No.

Someone on board was waving. A large overhead wave, a man, swaying his arm through the air in greeting. She did not return the gesture. It seemed friendly. He was shouting something. A single word.

"Ming!"

He was saying Ming; he was absolutely saying Ming.

The ship was beginning to turn, its front-end veering to the right as it navigated around the lighthouse. She could see his face now, and he could see hers. Confused, both of them, nearing each other without moving. She approached the ship, realising as she did that the filthy trousers hanging off of him were the faded maroon of a Crysthian Red.

"You, who are you?" she called, running towards the vessel, splashing into the shallow water.

"Where's Ming?" he called, his voice alarmed and demanding as he unhooked the railing on the deck's side, jumped easily into the shallow pool.

"Ming? You're Crysth? Where did you get that uniform? Who are you?"

"I'm Fukuyama. Who are you?"

"You're Fukuyama? You're Fukuyama! You're gone."

They stared at each other for a time before he said, "No, I'm not."

"You're not Fukuyama?"

"No, I'm not gone."

She looked past him, saw more figures emerging onto the side of the ship.

"Rama said..."

"You spoke to Ed Rama?" he asked, stepping towards her. "What did he say? What news was there?"

"News? I–"

"Are you with us?" he snapped, taking another step towards her.

She raised her hands defensively. He was small, slight, skinny and ill-looking but there was something frantic and unpredictable, kinetic about his movement which made him seem not quite right, not quite safe. "I don't know what's going on, I don't know who you are – you, Fukuyama's book. Your picture book it's in there, there's a *tama* – she's hurt."

"Ming's girl? Shit, shit." He spun around to look back towards the ship, then back to Achira. "That one won't let anyone near her but Ming. It will only make it worse if we help."

"Wait, what? What? You know who she is?"

"Yeah, she's – hell. We thought you were Ming. Why are you here? Who are you?"

"Achira," said Achira. "I'm Achira. I've been here for a while, on Apech I mean, we – I came to see what Ming had been doing–"

"Ming's not here?"

"No."

"No, no, Where is she?"

"Lon Apech."

"Damn, damn it." He looked as if he might burst into tears, his expression falling from wild anxiety into a childish sorrow. "Why doesn't anything just, just work?"

Achira's eyes did not leave him. Wary, hands still up.

He bit his lip, looking back at her. "It's a damn good thing for you that we're here, it's all – it's all gone wrong over there. Hell. Damn it."

"What," said Achira, in a voice she was failing to control, "is going on?"

"Did you say my book was up there?" he asked, "My photographs?"

Achira nodded.

"You found it there?"

She nodded again.

"I knew it. Ming brought it for me, didn't she?" he said, grinning suddenly in a way which pulled his face back into that manic mobility. "I knew it. Look, look. We thought you, you were Ming but you're going to have to come with us – what's this about Rama? Are you, are you with us?"

"Are you with him?"

"Rama? Yeah. Yeah, we're with him. Look, are you with us or not? Do you, er, do you even know what's going on? We're the, er, we're the resistance, I suppose, I suppose that's what we are."

XX

"But where is the rest of him?"

It was past ten already. Ming had slept long and deep, unexpectedly blissful in her refreshed certainty of Xar Kis' trust, their new mission. Caralla's omission.

"In our defen–" began Jasef but stopped when he saw her expression.

Ar's parrot chirruped away in the silence.

"Ming, we really thought we were doing the right thing at the time," Peter, not looking up at her.

"Yes and look where that's getting you!" she hissed, dropping down from her perch on the kitchen counter. "Now I've had to come back from my work, Achira's on her own over there, the entire of Lon Apech thinks we're on team Ed murdering Rama and there is a disembodied hand pinned to our actual house!"

Peter suppressed a laugh, which she caught.

"This is funny, is it?"

"No! Just, I'm so sorry it was the phrasing. You know I laugh when I'm nervous, I can't help it." He looked up at her forlornly, an expression so cringingly humbled that she nearly burst into laughter herself. "I'm sorry, we're really sorry."

"Where is the rest of him?"

Peter and Jasef looked at each other, pained.

"Down one of the vents," said Peter, losing whatever telepathic battle had been waged between them.

"What?!" She strode over the window to look outside. "Which one?!"

They all stood, crowding around the open window, staring into the midmorning twilight. Clouds of industry billowed out of the vents, thick and white and fading into the tropical mist.

"That big one," Peter pointed, "with the little stone wall around it."

Ming bit her lip. She would have loved to see the body fall.

"I don't," she said, bringing her hand to her face automatically to disguise her expression and changing her sentence midway, "why would you do that?"

"Ming," started Peter, risking a touch of her arm, "we were, like, really fucked up. Really, really fucked up."

"Who gets high and starts tearing up dead bodies!"

"It wasn't like that, Ming, truly we did not mean to it was just..." Jasef grimaced as he spoke, "it seemed like the right time to deal with it, and we were arguing about it, and the vent was just there and, you know, having one's state a bit altered felt like as good a time as any to–"

"To rip apart a corpse."

"No!"

"We really didn't mean that bit," interrupted Peter, "he was just super, fucking, gooey."

"Gooey?!"

"Gooey." Peter.

"Gooey," agreed Jasef.

"He just... came apart?" Ming asked, curiosity audible in her rising tone.

"Like a horrible shoe. A horrible Velcro shoe," said Peter.

"He's sort of," Jasef began, "well he was sort of pinned up there by the spike in that palm. We lifted him up but once we got his torso off the other spike gravity took over and he just... you know. Ripped."

Ming looked behind her at Ar, who seemed as though he might be sick. "I think we're going to have to stop talking about this."

Ar nodded, retook his seat at the table.

"I cannot believe," said Ming, walking over from the window to join him, "that I have had to come back for this. That I have had to come back to this."

"Ming, I am so sorry. We thought it would be better for you to return with him gone. We are genuinely contrite, sorry, in full understanding of our foolish–"

"Oh, knock it off Jasef, I am not in the mood." She narrowed her eyes, looking at him with a new, growing interest. "Actually. I need you to do me a favor."

"Of course, of course," he said, pulling up a chair beside her.

"I have a data pack downstairs, an orange." All eyes widened in excitement. "It needs to go to the embassy this morning, and I don't have the time or the patience."

"I – of, of course I'll take it. Are you sure I'm authorized to touch such a, such a–"

"What's in it?" asked Peter, marveling.

Ming's expression dropped as she looked up at him. "Something for Gris Caralla and nobody else."

"Peter how could you be so impertin–"

"Impertinent?" she snapped at Jasef's interruption. "You've all been *impertinent*. She knows you went to Rama, by the way."

"She... she does?"

"Of course she does, she's the ambassador she knows everything that happens here."

"What did she say?" asked Peter, morose, resigned.

"I am sure she will have words with you herself, before long." Ming rubbed her face again. "Jasef, that thing goes to her. Nobody else. Understand? Nobody else touches it."

"Yes, yes, of course."

"I'll write her a letter to go with it, you can take that along too."

"Yes, absolutely."

Ming stood up, casting a furious glance at Peter as she did, and descended back to her room.

She was expecting it when the knock came. "Ming?"

"Yes?" she snapped, folding the little note in half, not bothering to seal it.

The door opened. Peter's worried face appeared in the crack.

"You're going straight back to the coast?" he asked, apparently not daring to step all the way into the room.

"I have to. I'm busy. I didn't have time for this. You've been so stupid."

He stood still, watching her tidy away her table, turn to look at him. "I'm sorry about all this. We really thought that it was the right thing to do."

She watched him, looking him in the face and for the first time seeing some specter of defiance behind the warm light of his eyes. She did not care. It did not matter anymore.

He watched her, his concern over her crimson-slashed chin leading his fingers self-consciously to the welt on his own face. He felt something coming from her, something like secrecy, frustration, some new facet behind the carefully controlled apathy of her rank. Perhaps it had been there all along. Somehow, he did not feel the overwhelming anxiety he usually felt when she was annoyed with him. Perhaps it was something changed in him instead, a sensation of feeling owed or cheated. His fate was tied neither to this planet nor to her, but she had made him feel crushed to imagine himself without her. But here she was, ready to leave again, obviously thinking nothing of it, not even going to show him that she understood him as existing for her any differently than did Jasef or Ar.

"Will you give this to Jasef?" she said, holding the note out to him. "The data pack is in this drawer; nobody touches it but him."

"Yeah, sure," he replied, still and even newly shocked at her coldness, taking the paper between his fingers. He felt hollow, dry. This seemed to him like an end of something that had never happened, wasn't real. Something that he could not be allowed to mourn. The staircase creaked as she descended.

XXI

Soft laughter comes from behind her.

She is on her knees and weeping with the fury of it, smoke stinging her eyes, closing them. Black fumes spiral around her face and penetrate her throat. It will not catch. She pushes the spikes into her skin where he will not see the scars. Her calf, the side of her tongue, under her hair. Cutting herself, trying to get them into her.

Soft laughter comes from behind her. She does not hear it.

She is naked. She has been here before, making sure that there is water to wash herself of her sins. Her clothes are piled neatly by his foot.

She manipulates dead limbs, clambers across this corpse to another, lighter shaking in her hand.

He steps forward, she hears his boots.

Her head spins and she is upright, faster than he expected but not fast enough. He has caught her arm – the flame licks his chin, shudders in the cocoon of her clenched fist. She meets his stare through eyes drenched with blood and sweat and tears.

Well, he says, lowering her wrist, drawing her closer. Her eyes flick to her clothes on the floor, the weapon concealed within. He sees the gesture, knows what it means, tightens his grip on her arm. He could break it without much more effort.

208

There is something in there that could hurt me? he asks.

She relaxes. He relaxes.

Probably not, she says.

What is it?

That's what you want to know?

He laughs again, pushes her back so that she stumbles.

She looks at him, takes him all in.

Don't, she says.

Not if you don't want me to, he replies.

This confuses her. He smiles.

She knows how to regain control. She throws him the lighter, he catches it.

I'm going to rinse myself off, she says.

He says nothing. He watches while water runs from an industrial faucet, into her cupped hands, over her body.

Well? she asks.

He has been made nervous, an alien emotion to him, frustrating. He is clever enough to resist the urge to respond to it with violence. He rolls his thumb over the lighter's wheel, back again, presses against it hard enough to leave a ridged spine along his skin.

I've been watching you, he says, I think I know what you're trying to do.

What are you going to do about it?

He smiles, walking up behind her, staying there. He meant it; he won't touch her again until she indicates that she wants him to. I could help," he says, "if you like.

When Ming returns to Ech Kon she will go straight to the taxidermist's temple. He will be waiting for her. Dusk. All the dead things will be screaming, roaring in their expressions of the god's desire, a cacophony of new, magnificent hope. She'll be reduced to her knees by it, tears falling with rapturous certainty, and he will tell her the things that need to be done.

A world away, hours away, dawn would be breaking in Lon Apech. This meant nothing as far as the aesthetics of the city were concerned, but it meant that the silence was interrupted in Peter's bedroom.

The alarm beeped once, stifled before the note completed. He had been awake, waiting, his eyes unfocused on the folds of linen he hung over his window and his finger poised over the clock's switch. Revolving spotlights and the flashing glow of meaningless advertisements fell over ripples of fabric, eternal motion in the room's constant dark. He moved his hands over his body, thinking.

Jasef had not come home.

Peter showered, trying to make himself feel something. He had never truly wanted to leave Apech before, viewed this venture only as some minor inconvenience to be loosely enjoyed and studied before returning to a position among Avon's captains; or, he had permitted himself to imagine, a certain ambassador's chief of staff. They would not have stayed on Apech for long after the old nutter retired. Three years maybe, just enough to improve the place before moving on to something new and exciting. Secretly in love, forever. He wondered if Agnes loved Gris. Nah.

But now he wanted to leave. Get away from this grim, misted uncertainty of a place. He was heartbroken, and he did not feel like he was allowed to be.

He had become weaker. A layer of fat rippled over his chest. Training would make him feel better. He'd be stronger than ever, look super fucking ripped and cool. Maybe a new tattoo.

Jasef had still not come home.

Peter knew this to be true, but he checked anyway. Checked his room, checked the kitchen, checked his desk. Checked Achira and Ming's rooms. Considered knocking on Ar's door, thought better of it. He'd only tell him not to meddle. He was in the mood to meddle, he was going to meddle the fucking shit out of this.

And he didn't believe Ming. No, he believed her insofar as he believed that Ming trusted Gris Caralla; but he no longer believed that this was all he needed in order to trust Caralla himself. Ming could be too professional, too cold to see beyond the unyielding hierarchical structure of the Reds. Reds were just like that, he thought. Everyone would guess that Military was the most rigid, but they weren't. They had a certain playfulness to them which all the higher up Reds lost. Everything always surprised you like that.

But not this, he thought, not this situation on Apech. This was clear cut. He had spoken to Rama and he had spoken to Kis. Alright, Rama had punched him, but it was still obvious even then that one of them was cruel and the other virtuous. There was no way anyone could be that good of an actor. He was going back to Rama, he knew that. He needed to. Damn the rest of them and damn Gris Caralla. If she found out, if she reported him, he would have more than enough to defend himself. She had done nothing on this damned planet, she hadn't even told him he can't go and talk to fucking Rama. However, he still needed to go to the embassy first. He would risk bumping into Gris by doing so but he could not just ignore the fact that Jasef was missing. Hopefully he had arrived safely and just stayed there – got whatever bollocking was coming to him for talking to Rama and curled up in one of the administrators' apartments to lick his wounds.

He was glad for the walk to the embassy. He felt purposeful, swift and self-assured even in the glowing mist. He felt changed. For the first time, and in a way which was not unconnected with his sudden, desperate urge to return to Crysth, he felt at home in this city. He knew where he was, how to behave, where he was going. The height didn't bother him as he crossed its bridges, didn't even think about it. A plan. Find Jasef, see Rama. How glorious to have something to fucking do, even if he was exhausted enough to feel wired with the energy of it.

He lifted his chin at the guards on either side of the embassy's perimeter gate but made it only a few steps into the garden beyond before he stopped and turned back to face them. His finger oscillated between them at the end of his arm like a loosely jointed compass needle and he said: "What? No, what's up? Don't you shrug me, I can tell something's wrong. Spill it."

They shrugged him regardless. He levelled his left forearm in front of his chest and made light glow from it. It was only a torch, but they didn't know that.

"Ambassador isn't in," the one on the left said, quickly. "Been gone an hour or so."

"Nah that's not it. Why you acting like something weird's happened? No, none of this glancing at each other all secret like, you tell me what's happening."

"She took the entire Military cohort with her." Left, again.

"Oh now we're fucking getting there aren't we. Did she say where they were goin'?"

"No." Right.

"Went that way." Left.

"To central?"

Two sullen nods.

"You know why?"

The nods went horizontal.

"If I get inside and find out there's more you could've told me then I'm gonna come back and glow the shit out of both you." He brandished his torch. "So is that all?"

Higher velocity nods.

A final flourish and a meander through the petrified forest later he was at the elevator.

"Have you people lost your minds?!" he was yelling into the receiver. "I need to get up there right now."

"She said nobody in or out!" replied the machine.

"She obviously didn't mean me, you fucking morons, she meant the fucking Apechi!"

"That is not what she said."

Peter knew what to say to get up there, but it would be really embarrassing if it didn't work. It would even be embarrassing if it did. He went for it. "I am Peter Pïat-Elementov and if you don't send that elevator down here right fucking now I will ruin your lives and so will Wilhelmina fucking Ming."

Silence, which seemed promising. "Come on, motherfuckers." Muttering to himself.

It worked.

Embassy staff followed in the wake of his stride, harrying him through the embassy's hallways and towards Agnes' office, where he used his embedded key to leave them behind. Their anxious prattle told him that Caralla had been weird. Panicked, so they were panicking too. Jasef had never made it to the embassy. They were out looking for him, fearing that he had been kidnapped with an important data pack in hand.

"How did she know to expect him?" he had asked.

"She's the ambassador," had been the response.

"She called back all the blues early this morning. One from central said they'd lost sight of him there," had been another.

Central, that meant Kis. The bastard.

He flipped open a display case beside the window. Beautiful little machine, silver and ornate. Dragon carved on the side. Long single barrel with a tiny cannister attached to it. He shouldered a pack of them. He could go and get something more sensible, but he's wanted to play with this thing since he first saw it.

Gasps from the crowd when he emerged with it in hand.

"What are you going to do?"

"Are we in danger?"

He stepped alone into the elevator and said, "Just wait here."

Central, that meant Kis. But Agnes had gone there, so that was dealt with. He turned the other way, towards Ed Rama.

* * *

Here's how the city feels.

They're like this, cities, all cities – even this false one. Something glimmers around them in the not-quite-enchanted, not-quite-mundane sense of an external temperament; an invisible, palpable and unavoidable consciousness rests on top of them all. Lon Apech is tense. The only ones here who cannot feel this are the outsiders, those whose ignorance perforates the fog in self-indulged vacuums. Peter is not one of these strangers; his motion flows into the mist of the city and he is boldened by it, watched by its people who have gathered in that unspoken way crowds have of milling around themselves, making the individual feel better and the situation feel worse. Clutches of them here and there, with different moods and different causes, but all of them waiting; knowing they need to be together when it happens. Ready to respond, to help, or to hide. The people of Lon Apech know what is happening in their city, the still war between two opposing factions. They have their allegiances and their opinions even if they would not risk their lives for either; but now they can feel the other thing, too.

Most if not all of them are too young to remember the god at its full power. This is wrong, anyway. It has never had full power because those to whom it was beloved had never had a cause other than its pleasure. They do, now. Unity, strength, escape. Their plans will feed it even as it destroys them. It can do that. It is strengthened, even though such a word could never really be applied to something like this.

The people of Lon Apech can feel it growing, as if it is searching over them. It is. Their vision is blurring. It shows them futures and movements and motions. Things that could have happened, infinite pasts flickering into now. They do not know whether they can trust it. Some are growing to love it already, testing the movement of their arms and fists. They experiment with their new power; play-fighting, throwing reality at each other, knowing exactly how to move in such a way as to appear to defy gravity, knowing the future and how to resist it. They should not trust these things, because they do not know what it is. But it is with them, for now, seeming for all the world to enjoy their games as they roll and writhe against the visions it provides them. We see ourselves as separate, individual pieces; that's another problem. All these tiny futures broken – a deadly fall avoided, a punch landed, a kick here – are as nothing to the sequence it sees. An unimaginable map, a structure of giant lines and vectors and rules. It is these which the god bristles against; we only help.

It is a thing inexplicable, flesh coupled with something like knowledge or divinity. It is because of our similarity that it can use us, although use implies intentionality.

There is a place where the city is at its most fraught. Dozens of people sitting on meticulously raked gravel, staring at the pattern in the grit as the god makes it ebb and flow unreal, impossible before their eyes; all the patterns it will be or has ever been at the same time. It is a form of meditation, for them, to watch the sand and concentrate and to fight off the visions. To force it to be still. They are beginning to lose. The god has found its enemies.

They stare at the patterns. Pick up a rake, change it here and there. Sit down to stare.

Peter broke their concentration with the ringing echo of metal knocking against metal, the barrel of his ridiculous gun striking the door.

XXII

Ming leaned against the wall in her lighthouse kitchen, alone. The *tama*'s body cooled. She had killed her in anger and was slightly annoyed with herself because of it.

She lifted her face up to the window before walking over to it, looking out. They will have seen a ship drop her off. Will know she is here alone. Why are they waiting?

She went to pour herself a brandy to help with the act.

Tart and disgustingly unpleasant. Could brandy spoil or did she just not like it? She could not remember.

She sent an experimental bolt of electricity into the stove with her arm, which fizzled out after lighting up with a soft spark. Good. The gauntlet had been acting strangely ever since she had tried to fight the taxidermist. Usually, the demon would send gentle shocks of angry electricity whenever it could tell that she was excited; now it had stopped almost entirely. As if it were tired or injured. She did not know if that was even possible.

She steeled herself for another sip of brandy. It tasted all the better for her being prepared for it to be worse. Come on already.

To the other window, facing back towards the shore. She leaned out of it, forearms resting against the sill and the mug still in her hands. She could make out figures on the beach, no more than usual, no less. How long was the taxidermist expecting this to take?

It would be hours until they arrived, the ship's prow bifurcating the horizon into two equal parts as she watched. Finally.

She broke into a run halfway down the staircase, splashing out into the water and waving madly towards the pearl uniform on the deck.

There were too many of them in the ship. It was uncomfortable, cramped, and rancid with anxious sweat. Ming was being treated like the sole survivor of a shipwreck; expected to be shaken and overwhelmed by the appearance of this last clutch of Rama's power in Ech Kon. It was miserable. A dozen people with broken health and fading hope, looking at this one remnant of order as if they had saved her, or as if she could save them.

She could tell, too, that some were not pleased to have her. Including, perhaps even especially, Achira. They were all grim and Ming was sick of speaking to them.

"Caralla knows," insisted Fukuyama, jittering and jabbering in a mode of anxiety unusual even for him. "She knows and she's protecting it."

"Why would she do that?" asked Ming, and she did not have to feign her curiosity.

"You know she's helping Kis and Distan get into Crysth. It would... endanger the cause, wouldn't it? Wouldn't it? I – you know, you were there the whole time – I'd been saying since day, day one that we needed deimancers. She won't let them down here. She knows it's not just some residual energy. She knows."

Ming nodded in thought. That was not a bad point.

"I, I, I still have some of the proof with me, here. That's why I came, why I ran. Went to Rama." He looked up at her with wild eyes. "And I'm proof, now. I thought, I thought she'd.,. I don't know. I thought she'd kill me."

"What do you mean? What do you mean that you are proof?"

"It's a god Ming. They'll all tell you."

One of the Apechi took a deep breath, "We don't know what a god is. We don't know what you mean by the word. But we thought it was gone. Dying, dead magic, something like that. It's been getting stronger, this past month. They came for us with it."

"But that would help," Achira. "That would help Kis and Distan to enter the system. If there's a deity here then Crysth will help them fight it, get rid of it."

"No, no, no." Fukuyama stood up, shook his hands in expulsion of nervous energy. "You don't understand, it would, it would mean Kis is cursed – all of them here. It would mean that they have already been possessed by the, the god, by its, its, its touch. They would never be allowed near Crysth."

"Fukuyama," said Ming, her voice low and calm, "what do you mean that you are proof?"

He looked at her, his face finally still.

A quiet fell over the others, too, even though they had not been talking. Anticipation, pity.

The man lifted his ragged shirt, above his waist and up to his chest. Thin black spines burst his skin in patches of meandering darkness, spotted with dry blood and the gleam of infection.

Ming stared at Fukuyama's beautiful, tormented side. Stared as a saint watching the rapture take sinners.

"It, it, it'll kill me. I think."

Ming did not believe that it would, but she did not tell him this.

"What is this, now?" Achira demanded, outright anger in her voice. "What have you been telling me, what is all of this?"

"The god is…" Fukuyama's voice broke. He looked to the Apechi who had spoken and sat himself back down.

"The god infects. We do not think we can get free of it once it has someone."

"That disease?" Achira. "That's this god? We can catch it?"

"How," asked Ming, voice totally flat, "Did you catch it."

Fukuyama shook his head, face in his hands.

"We don't know," answered the other man. "If it gets you as a child, you live. The *tama*, they are... some people it just takes their mind, does not break out of them until they are adult, when it kills. We never know why or who." He rolled up a filthy white sleeve, turning his forearm this way and that to show scarring on dry and suntanned skin. Still, this is nothing Ming does not know. "And in that case, they will die. Most likely. Sometimes not," he lied, with a glance at Fukuyama.

"And the visions. The sight. I can see them too, now."

"We..." Achira's face was a mask of horror, "we have to be able to cure it. Back on Crysth, there'll be something we can do."

"What do you see?" Ming, "What have you seen?"

Fukuyama looked up, his eyes red. "Nothing that, that makes any sense. Miré Distan's face, all the time. Movements like blurs. The world shakes. Sometimes I see things happening on Crysth, normal things, like, like old teachers opening classroom doors. It's like dreaming. People walking down corridors that I can't remember existing, I don't know, it's like dreaming but I think that, sometimes I feel like I'm making it happen... Déjà vu..."

"That is what worries me," said an older man. "If it can see Crysth... can it get there? If we lose Crysth we lose all hope of destroying it."

"What?" Achira backed away from Fukuyama and into the side of the ship. "We're talking about a disease that can infect people on Crysth, from here?! Caralla needs to know! We need to get out of here!"

"She knows! Have you heard nothing? She, she will not allow that information off, off of this planet because then Kis will not be permitted into the, the, the capital! And I'm sure you can't catch it by proximity. Stop recoiling, it makes me feel like I am plagued."

Shit, thought Ming, Caralla knows there's a god here.

"I don't think she does know," Ming said. "She would have told me. I have been there, with her and Kis, this has never been spoken of. Not once."

"Would she tell you?" Achira, skeptical.

"Of course. She thinks it's some sort of magic. You've misunderstood her I–"

"She knows," Fukuyama, "because I told her. I explicitly told her, and she told me never to mention it again. That I was wrong."

Fucking shit, Ming thought, she really does know.

"She probably really did think you were wrong! We need to tell her,"

"We agree," said the first woman again, "most of us anyway."

"We can't get past him!" Fukuyama, waving a hand toward the coast. "We're trapped out here!"

"This so-called priest? So you're just going to wait here and die?" Ming. "What the fuck is your plan? Why have you brought us here? We need to be back in the embassy. If there's even a chance that Fukuyama's infection is endangering Crysth they need to know. They need to know months ago."

"We cannot get past the priest. Look how many of us there are!" The Apechi man again.

"Will they attack with me and Achira there?" asked Ming. "If I do not return, then Agnes will come looking for me. He will bring Military."

"That is exactly why we could still just wait. They won't leave you out here." Another of the crowd.

"We leave the ship around the other side of the bay. We can walk to the train from the other side, they won't see us." Ming.

"We don't know what they– they– we don't know what they can see." Fukuyama.

"You're saying we're probably going to get attacked by some actual deity the moment we hit land?!" demanded Achira. "A thing that can infect and cannot be cured?"

"Almost definitely." agreed the woman who had spoken first.

"No." Achira. "We have to wait. If Ming doesn't go back then Agnes and Peter will come looking."

"Not for days," said Ming. "The train is here. And how much time do we have? You have water – what about food, how much? The longer we wait the weaker you get, and the more likely they are to just come out and find us. There weren't any priests or monsters hanging around when I left, so I say we go. Before someone calls the train back and we're stuck." She stood, looking around at them all in anger. "You're telling me Crysth is in danger."

"No," retorted another, one of the few outwardly annoyed by Ming's inclusion among their ranks. "How do we know we don't get to Lon Apech and this… ambassador won't turn on us? She's with Kis as often as Caralla!"

There were a few agreements. Ming turned to the objector. "That is my job. Kis is in charge here – not Rama. If I had the choice, I would choose the latter."

"But," began Achira, incensed, "all those things you said to Peter, Jasef and I–"

"I was trying to protect you! Going about it like… so obvious. I can't let you endanger yourself – and I had no intention of engaging in an all-out war!"

"See," Fukuyama turned to look at Achira. "I told you."

"That's what you've been doing this whole time? Arguing about me? You are the world's most fucking incompetent resistance, do you know that?

"Now the priest and whoever is with him will know I'm with you," Ming said, knowing that they did, having been instructed by the taxidermist to be here. To lure them into the trap. "Are you armed?"

"We, we have hammers and wrenches and, and, that kind of thing," buzzed Fukuyama.

"And does anyone here know how to move the train? If everybody still on the shore is on their side, then we will have to do that ourselves."

Nods.

"We need to land at the closest point to the train. Give them the least amount of time possible to start coming at us." Another man who had been silent until then.

"If they come at us at all." Ming looked back at Achira, trying to soften her expression. "Why don't we have a word on the deck, give them some time to decide what we're going to do?"

Ming leant on the ship's rail, staring away from the shore into miles of empty ocean. Achira stood beside her. A strange moment of peace.

"Why didn't you say anything?" asked Achira, after a while.

Ming did not turn to look at her. "About what? What would you have had me say?"

"All this. That you believe us, that you agree."

"I do not. This is not me disobeying Caralla. This is us being kidnapped by agitators and finding a way to return to the embassy."

"You'll abandon them, once we get back to Lon Apech?"

"If I have to. I will not disobey Caralla."

"You are such a fucking Red."

Ming smiled in a self-satisfied sort of way which would have horrified Achira had she seen it.

"Ming,"

"Yes,"

"Why was there a *tama* in that lighthouse? Why was there blood everywhere?"

"They wander around more freely over here. It's a nuisance."

"She was really hurt."

"They can't think, Achira. They hurt themselves."

"It was all over your clothes."

"I was hurt too, remember." She jabbed a thumb at her chin.

"You lied about where you had been."

"No, I didn't."

"Why didn't you mention the lighthouse, then?"

"It's nice to have a space to myself."

Silence.

"I don't know what to say," said Achira, relenting for the time being. "Everything was normal yesterday. Now I'm in an alien battle and I'm going to be attacked by an actual god."

"Just stay next to me," Ming said, voice lowered. "That's what I wanted to say to you."

"What?"

Ming withdrew her sleeve slightly with her left thumb, showing Achira the shining metal on her wrist beneath.

"Is that…?"

"Yes. But if there is a fight I would rather we not get involved at all, so do not say anything. If they know I have a weapon like this, they'll want me at the head of it."

Achira swallowed.

"And stay next to me."

"I can't believe this is happening."

"It might not be."

The birds screamed overhead, a vibrant, high noise so unlike the strums which the godthing could produce from their dead vocal chords.

"Why did you come out here? To the lighthouse, I mean."

"I knew you hadn't slept in the pagoda. I wanted to know why."

"You don't trust me."

"Would you?"

"Yes," said Ming, and realized that she would. She had trusted Caralla completely, and not been trusted in turn. It was the same with the priest. She did not care. She only needed Kis, and the god itself.

They heard the door open behind them, Fukuyama's jittery voice sputtering through it, "We, we think we need to go now. I... I know it's a lot but, but we need to do it."

"Yes," agreed Ming, "If we go south from here, we can–"

"We do not need," interrupted one of the Apechi inside, "your instructions. We know where we'll land."

Ming and Achira spent the entire return journey on the deck, at once captives and imposters; stolen, necessary, and unwelcome. Ming could barely contain her laughter.

They had landed to the south of Ech Kon. A shallow rising cliff grown over with thick, green jungle. They would have to pick their way through it for hours before finally reaching the tracks and following them on to the train itself.

Those with edged blades went first, cutting a slow valley through the mess of vines and stopping, here and there, to pick at the small, uncultivated and unripened fruits which decorated its sprawl. It was more obvious on land that the two newcomers were considered captives, flight risks. They were watched, hemmed in and ushered through the bushes with wary eyes constantly following. Fukuyama tried to distract them from it, make them feel comfortable with his constant ramble about the trees, the birds, the fruit and the fungus concealed beneath the thatch of forest floor. Achira seemed eager to keep up the pretense of normality, too, for the sake of comforting Fukuyama in turn or for the sake of comforting herself Ming did not know. She asked questions as he spoke, asking him to compare the undergrowth to species he had seen elsewhere.

Ming watched. She watched Fukuyama's strange gait and imagined where the spines were twisting under his ruined clothes. She watched the more confident of the Apechi, making sure she knew what kinds of weapons they were carrying, what she would have to look out for. Machetes, spanners, hammers.

Those at the front of the pathetic caravan were arguing in fast, hissed Apechi. She could not make it out and started joining in with Fukuyama's babble to show that she was not trying to.

"Do, do, do you see how the moss only grows on the side facing the ocean? I don't know why that is but look you can see that we're getting further away…"

Their progress stopped, abrupt, with a ducking movement which flowed along the line of people in an urgent ripple. There was a murmuring from the front, sent down the line. It had just been a pig, spooking the fuck out of the people leading the way. But the spell of temporary comradery, or the tension which forced Fukuyama to want to achieve it, was broken. They were hushed as they raised themselves back up, resumed their painfully slow climb through the trees.

Something changed in Ming's mood. She wondered if that pig might have had poison stitches in its side, one too many limbs, an avian spine curling from its distended stomach… she did not know how powerful the god was, how far it could make its cursed things move. She could no longer look away from the branches and the shadows, inventing extra wings among the iridescent blue flutter of the butterflies which fled their winding, hacking path, her ears sucking life out of birdsong – straining to hear the wailing flatness of a dead scream.

Two miles north along straight silver rails, he is waiting. The station is busy with the awed throng of the faithful, dozens of committed soldiers who cower and grovel in the presence of their god's roiling flesh. It is pumping itself into different figures, pushing this way and that in a churning shapelessness. It is not curious, because curiosity suggests knowledge, but curious it looks. Curious is the best way it can be understood. It is wrong, not real. It should not be here, and it breaks the world around it, ruining time and space and flesh with its touch.

He is impatient, coaxing it forwards and sideways and onwards in ways known only by him. He has to quiet his mind

to do this, resist its influence and push his own back into it –
dream its future, change it. Remember all the time that he is
dreaming. The body is not the god itself, just a way for him
to reach it. He is weakened; the concentration blurs his mind
to the world and in these moments, he becomes as old as he
should be. He is protected by believers who flank him on his
slow, painful progress.

But he is so impatient. He has waited in the quiet and the
dark for most of his life and now he cannot bear it any longer.
He can feel the strength of faith feeding into it. Not faith, but
faith will do. Faith is all it seems to them, so faith is all that
matters.

The flesh is doing something. Bound by infection to
something far away, busy at the task of deconstruction.

This is an ambush; in case that was not clear.

The rebels' greatest hope is that the taxidermist will expect
them from the beach, has arranged his monster in such a
way as to catch them as they emerge from the waves, that
the confusion will give them enough time to get away before
it comes to confront them. But there is a traitor among their
ranks, leading now in a way which seemed to them as though
her Crysthian body was protecting them.

This is what the taxidermist has told her to do.

They will climb onto the platform, unbelieving and eager,
tasting success and not daring to hope, eyes fixed on the train
and racing to open its doors. But at that point he will no longer
be able to suppress the godflesh hum, the organic throb that
its presence pushes into the air. They will feel it and they will
know the trap is sprung. That is when his guards will attack,
and when the roaming corpse monolith will push into view.

Ming will break character first; calling to the taxidermist's
guards in desperation for them not to kill Fukuyama. She
will realize they may not know his name, scream at them
not to hurt the Crysthian man. Achira will cling to Ming's
side, not yet having realized that these cries are evidence of

cooperation. Ming will betray the plan, rushing to protect Fukuyama from the onslaught of Ech Kon's faithful. Trying to find the taxidermist, unable to concentrate or locate him over the static, toneless shriek which is the god's reality-shuddering presence. The guards know not to hurt her, they will stay out of her way.

It will be a brutal, slow fight. The believers are armed with spears and blades, but none of them are so skilled as to make their justice swift. The taxidermist will be relying on this; he has under-armed and undermanned his own side for the sake of the other task he and the godflesh must perform. Something much more important to him than the destruction of enemies. The work of deconstruction. That labor will be accelerated by the unreal movements of flesh in combat, its devoted using its wild energy to slice impossible motion into their opponents' skin.

It will be obvious when the climax is coming – the air will thrum with electric tension. Audible, time-shattering stillness. High pitched, moaning, the godmelt at its center. The taxidermist will roar over the noiseless orchestra of the deity's strength and in response the closest guard will hurl his own spear directly into the wall of roving flesh. For his lapse in concentration the guard will be destroyed beneath his opponent's hammer, but he will die knowing that he has served his god well. The spear will break flesh, tearing apart the roaming side which will begin to swirl and concentrate and pulse around the point of perforation.

It will eat the weapon's metal. Dozens of flowing mouths swelling around the collision and taking chunks of the steel as if it were their own rotten meat. Its stitching will loosen, swell, hands and feet emerging more and more frequently from the bodies to grasp at the spear's handle, pulling it in, consuming with childlike greed and each of its faces will grimace in a second of unified disappointment as the thing is spent, the last of their meal devoured.

But the rift in the body will not have healed; it will bleed and ooze in a chaos of accelerated, frenzied decay. Chunks will fall from the greening flesh, stinking and fading in a plague of slow death as the flow of those bodies grows faster, showing a pattern in focused morbidity around the wound and the air will scream with the power of it and a single face, a man's face, grinning with idiot complacency in the reanimated flesh, will be centered in the vortex.

It will grow, concentrated, its neck extending and shoulders emerging where there had been feet and genitals and hair and legs and teeth. Rotting spheres of disposable flesh will drip from the wound. The man will reach out, holding his newborn hands in front of him and beginning to regurgitate silver flowing metal. It will run in rivulets between his fingers, molding itself as he caresses it back into the spear it had been but by then he will be biting at his own lips, pushing his teeth out of his mouth with his own jaw and becoming new again, consuming his own face and creating one fresh, biting bone becoming muscle, constant chewing motion, spinning himself. And in this he will become familiar.

Miré Distan will stand before them, woven from godflesh, a thing untrue. Still, absolutely, irrevocably Miré Distan; left without any choice but to believe in the god's power.

XXIII

"Alright what the fuck is going on? Untie him!" Peter swung the gun around, accusing the entire courtyard with its tip before turning to Rama with, "I thought you were the good one."

Jasef was cross-legged on the floor, his hands behind his back but uninjured, the orange data pack open on the gravel. There was a vaguely apologetic look about him.

"He is armed. You should not have let him in here," Rama responded.

"Who you talking to?" Peter.

"Me."

Peter yelped at the sound of the woman's voice suddenly behind him, hadn't even time to turn before his gun was gone. He stared at his hands. She had put hers through his chest. She had put her hands straight through his chest and snatched the weapon from him. He could only repeat himself: "What the fuck!"

The crowd were all arguing now, shouting at each other – some in a language Peter could not understand.

"Khora, please!" Rama, and his tone was unmistakably a plea. "We can't use it, you know we can't use it."

Peter stared at her, the woman who had shown him that his body could be nothing, who was holding Agnes' gun at arm's length like it might explode. She was an ugly figure, her face mottled with red burns stretching beneath a short mohawk. Patterned scars decorating muscular arms. Recognition dawned. "Are you the fucking executioner?"

She ignored him. "I just gave us one less problem. Listen you blue clothes-"

"Nah I'm not talking to you, you evil murdering freak. Magic and shit's happening now?!"

"No, no that was a mistake." Rama held his hands out again in a soothing motion. "We are... look, please let me explain."

"Oh *please, please, please*. I am so sick of listening to you beg," hissed the woman with the gun.

"In their defense, Peter, this may not be as bad as it looks," offered Jasef, to everyone's surprise.

"The fuck? You're kidnapped mate."

"Yes but... Well yes, but I think I can see what's going on."

Rama was still watching the executioner, openly fearful. The entire crowd seemed coiled, tense and angry and ready to spring in entirely different directions. Rama was not in control.

"What you mean?" she barked. "No. Don't have time for this. Blue clothes, Ming gave him this pack – she took papers from it. Why? Where are they?"

"I said I'm not talking to you. Jasef, the fuck is going on?"

"I'm not sure – but can you just, can you just tell me what is missing, what did you want, what are you looking for?"

"Screw it." her voice again. "Tell him."

"Why are you giving orders now?" someone in the crowd, to agreement.

"Someone has to."

Rama held his hands up to the uproar that this caused and said, "It's okay, it's okay. We need to keep calm."

"We were to be sent evidence of Fukuyama's theories. To present to your ambassador." She circled the barrel of the gun at Peter as she said the pronoun. "This pack has Fukuyama's name but only nonsense about rocks. Pages missing."

"What theories?" Jasef. "Please, I think I can help, I think I'm finally figuring this out."

Rama took over. "He believes that our affliction – which is suddenly getting worse, as Khora just demonstrated – is caused by a deity. He wished to request Crysth's help."

"Oh fuck. Wait what?" Peter.

"Why has Ming taken his evidence? What has she done with it?" the executioner, beginning to point the gun in a more purposeful way. "He has given her this pack at Ech Kon, no doubt to fetch to us, and she has done this."

"We don't know that's what happened." Rama.

"Fukuyama is still here?" Jasef. "What?"

"Get over it. What are you 'figuring out'?" She turned the gun to him instead.

"Hang the fuck on, why are we all just standing here talking to this murdering cunt?"

"Khora, no! Peter, we don't have time. It's a long story. Khora is... a prisoner to that task." Rama.

"Fuck does that mean?"

"It means," she began, "that Xar Kis hates my face, and has a nasty sense of humor about it."

"What? Nah. You're trying to tell me he forces you to torture people to death and you just do it? What kind of coward are you?"

"Better me than anybody else."

He scoffed. "No way have you actually convinced yourself to believe that. You scum."

She had barely flinched towards Peter before Rama was in front of her, wrestling the gun away from her as the others roared. He stood over her, gun cradled in his arm, repeating: "We don't have time for this. We don't have time. It is coming."

"Sweet fuck what is 'it' now?" Peter.

"Excuse me!" called Jasef, plaintive. "Look, it all makes sense. All this is saying is that your planet is extremely valuable.

If there's a deity down here, then all of this is secondary. Don't you get it?"

All of them staring at him now.

"Caralla, she… this is it, this is what's going on. She wants the wealth and not the hassle. That's it. That's all there is to it. She's hiding the… magic or whatever it is on purpose. That's why Ming took it."

"I fucking knew it," spat the executioner.

"No," Peter shouted above the new, furious commotion. "Ming wouldn't do that. No way. That's not right." He paused to think, said aloud, "Caralla?"

"It all makes sense." Jasef.

"Shut up mate, you're still kidnapped. Gris Caralla? She's off her head but she's not…. she's not… boring."

"It's all here, Peter."

"No it isn't, it's exactly not here, that's the entire point."

"Because someone removed it. And it was Ming who gave him that pack." Rama.

"And you who kidnapped him!"

"Get over it." The executioner, again.

"We had no choice," soothed Rama. "That data pack… what we thought was in it is our only chance. The magic or deity, whatever it is, it is getting stronger, fast. We can feel it. As if it is getting closer or bigger. We don't know. We needed to see, to make sure everything was right. And it turns out we were right to be suspicious."

"And now what?" Khora. "We have no request for assistance to take to embassy and even Crysthian boy believes that she would not listen if we did! I told you! Fukuyama told you! This is your fault! Letters and pleas, letters and pleas. Your fault!"

"Can someone at least untie Jasef? Why have you even got him tied up, he's helping you isn't he?"

Rama waved a hand to indicate that someone ought to do so. Peter found himself amazed that the gesture was obeyed.

"We can help," said Jasef. "We can all go to the embassy

now; everyone will hear us – it will be undeniable. There will be a tribune."

"What is a tribune?" the executioner seemed incensed by the unfamiliar word.

"A kind of trial," answered Jasef.

There was another din in which Khora demanded, "You think we need more of your Crysth trials?"

"We do not need trials, we need help." Rama. "Every year we've been losing fewer children to… it. But now, I don't know. We don't know. It's back. People are stoking it."

"They need to die." Khora. And the crowd agreed.

"There's nobody there." Peter. "At the embassy I mean. They all think Kis has Jasef, they've gone to get him. I can get into Agnes' office and send an emergency signal to Military. We're well within our right."

Rama interrupted with, "Why would they think he has Jasef? That doesn't make sense."

"I don't know! But we need to hurry up before they get back, don't we? I don't like any of this. We need more people down here. We need someone in the embassy who isn't Caralla."

"Yes!" The executioner. "Blue is right. Come on. We need to act!"

Peter found himself siding with the murdering cunt.

"Erm." Jasef. "I don't feel like there is a 'we' here. Peter and I will go to the embassy and contact the relevant authorities."

"My eye you will. We will accompany you. We will make sure."

"You're not coming into the embassy." Peter. "No way."

She began to argue but Jasef interrupted. "No, really. Do you want to look like you've invaded? Because you will."

"Kis will attack us out there," Added Rama. "If we leave then he will come."

"Then I will go below and make sure we are ready to fight back."

"You have an army?" Peter.

"No." Rama.

"Yes, we kind of do! I have had enough of your doubt, Ed." More agreement. Almost everyone is on her side.

"This is not doubt, this is reason."

"Look at the position we are in! You have put us here. I will get us out."

"We need to leave. They could be on their way back right now." Peter.

Growling restlessness, revolutionaries who have been too patient too long. Who have lost faith in their leader. He cannot control them and so if he wants to remain even superficially in charge then he must stop trying.

"Fine. Fine. We will escort them to the embassy and there wait for help but no more!" Everyone knows there will be more.

"I want my gun back. And I don't trust her. I don't want her anywhere near the embassy." Peter narrowed his eyes at her and said something that had been bothering him, "Was it you killed Ustra?"

"I'd do it again."

"She was a kid."

"No she was not. That Crysth-lover knew what she was. She was twenty-two years old and lived better in those years than she would allow the rest of us in a lifetime. Best for her to die then, to spare for her the shock of living in our world. And we're keeping that data pack."

Peter took the gun from Rama's hands. "Nah."

"Again, I really don't think you want to do anything that makes it look like you are the ones being hostile in this situation." Jasef.

"I fucking," – the executioner pointed at him, bared her teeth – "hate the way you talk."

Peter felt himself warming to her again.

XXIV

"Is a butterfly the same when it emerges from its pod?"

Ming watched with unfocused eyes as Miré Distan's renascent body picked over the corpses of Rama's vestige.

"Well?" urged the taxidermist, irascible and exhausted, lying with his back propped against the station's stone shelter.

"I don't know," she answered finally, "is it? What are you even talking about?"

"The creature dissolves in the pod. Do you know that? The caterpillar builds itself a home in which to die. It becomes nothing. No form, no shape, no brain, no nerves. It is the creature of deconstruction – not a worm growing wings, but a matter gone, rebuilt from the mess of its termination."

Ming turned her attention back to the body of Fukuyama, which she had dragged out of the rain for her inspection. She had wanted him alive. She needed to know how he became infected. "Would it work with Fukuyama? Would he have been rebuilt, too?"

"You misunderstand."

She shrugged, holding up a dead arm to see pricks of blackness pushing up beneath the skin around his joints. "You still haven't answered."

"Hm?" The priest rumbled.

Ming sighed. "Is that the same Miré Distan I spoke to yesterday."

"Is a butterfly the same that emerges from its pods? It is the same question."

"I know what the question is, I want the answer."

"Then you do not know what the question is. He is coming."

Ming turned just as this Distan reached her side, still pulling a wet but relatively clean shirt from one of the fallen believers over his head with one hand. He sat and held his other palm out for Ming's inspection.

"Do you need these?" he asked.

"Nah," she replied, moving the tip of her finger through Achira's badges and rings. "Just don't let anybody know you have them, other than Xar of course. I don't yet know what I'm going to say happened here."

Distan placed the trinkets into the pocket of his trousers, which he had taken from another of the godthing's guard; a living one, who had practically leapt out of them when Distan asked. Watching a man be born from the body of a god will perform wonders as far as compliance is concerned.

"You look weird in trousers," said Ming.

Distan settled beside them with his face turned in curious awe to the tendrils of godflesh which were stretching around the platform to consume the meat of the fallen, pull them into itself, make them into its carnal patchwork. It appeared content, but of course such a word could never be applied to such a thing. Revolving in ceaseless action. Slow and strangely peaceful in its grotesque corpulence. It seemed to like freedom.

Ming watched him. "How do you feel, Distan? What did you see?"

"I feel strong," he said, looking up at the priest with a sheepish twitch of the eyelids. "I feel like I can tell... what the world is made of. It's fading. But I knew it when I was in there."

Ming moved her fingers impatiently for him to continue.

"I just... I can't explain it anymore. I could see and understand everything. Everything made sense. It hurt, letting it take me on the other side. But everything was just in front of me. I understood."

"What happened on the other side?" she asked.

"I... I think it, absorbed me, I–"

"We need to return to the subject of your ambassador." The taxidermist's voice was dagger sharp.

"Oh, she's totally gone off it." Distan. "What about her?"

"What do you mean?" asked Ming, scanning his gargoyle face for marks of resurrection as she spoke to him. "Gone off it?"

He sighed, as if this was all inconsequential and dull. It must have been – what are politics to a man dragged through nothing? "She's got determined that we've taken the Green boy off her. She came with guns to the palace, asking us where he was. We said we don't know about it. She doesn't believe us though."

"What? What?" Ming's face was a grimace of disbelief. "Green boy? Do you mean Jasef? He had, he had our data pack on him. Gris Caralla turned up at the house, armed?" She looked sideways at the priest, who was watching her. "That makes no sense whatsoever. What's Xar doing?"

"He's just holding onto them for now. We reckoned it'd be a good idea to keep them out of the way while he," – he nodded deferentially to the priest – "got rid of Rama."

Without opening his eyes, the taxidermist said, "Good. She was easier than I thought. We can dispose of her, too."

"We're killing Caralla?" suggested Distan, excitedly.

"Back up and tell me what's happened in the capital. This is vital, this is insane."

"Jasef disappeared in central with something important on him, she thinks we took him."

"Did you?" asked Ming.

"Nah, I said we don't know about it. But she's taken all the blue uniforms and shown up, wouldn't come inside so they're just sort of, standing off."

"Then now is an excellent time to act," said the priest, seeming to wake up. "They are all in one place. We trap them, strike."

"Yeah!" said Distan. "Why?"

"We think that," Ming paused, touched her face in concentration, "there is a chance that Caralla is aware that there is a god presence on Apech."

"But Crysth hate–"

"We know" Ming. "Which is why it's worrying. We do not know why she has not investigated or, called any deimancers in, anything."

"Deimancer," scoffed the taxidermist. "Pathetic."

"Yes, yes," returned Ming, impatiently. "But we cannot just erase her from the picture. We need to know exactly what she has known and who she has communicated it to."

"Won't you find out all that when you become the ambassador?" asked Distan. "Also, why would she tell? She's helping."

"That is... Yes. No. I no longer know whether or not she's helping." She raised her voice, seeing that the taxidermist was about to interrupt. "However, Crysth will not simply turn the place over to me if they arrive to find murdered embassy staff. I still need to go back and have my prosthetics done. They will put somebody else here in the interim. Probably not a black hand, probably not even a Red."

"How long will that take though? A month? We'll blame Rama, say they attacked the embassy, you were elsewhere, we fought for Crysth's revenge, we won. All's well. Two birds one rock." Distan.

"No! This isn't... I have no idea how much the implants record. What her diaries say, who she has communicated with. I know none of it. There will be so much scrutiny. You don't understand, this is Crysth, not–"

"Not backward, provincial Apech?" suggested the taxidermist.

"Yes!" Ming. "That's the end of it."

"It is the end of it," he said, beginning to pull himself to his feet. "I've made up my mind."

"What, what do you mean?"

"I will not have another agent in this plan, disturbing the movement of it. If we do not know her motives, she must be removed."

Ming and Distan stood with him. "We cannot," she entreated them, "the fleet will–"

The priest raised his hand, quickly, threateningly, and as he did the godthing pulsed audibly behind her – an electric, angry throbbing which swelled its flesh into the air. "That is your problem. You will deal with the fleet, ambassador."

"You cannot make the entire Crysthian empire my problem."

"Shall. Prove your use."

"We can't... They might not even still be at the palace by the time we get back. We cannot attack the embassy." Her brows knotted suddenly, her fingers moving to an implant in her neck. "They're calling me."

"What?"

She cocked her head to the side as if listening, feeling for instructions under her flesh. "Someone at the embassy is sending me a message to come back. It's an emergency line and it isn't being used properly. No signature. Something must be happening."

"We can move very quickly," said the priest.

"Through the... through it again?" Distan asked, a quiver of excitement in his tone.

The old man shook his head. "No, not yet."

"How?" asked Ming, her own curiosity and lust getting the upper hand over her rigid dread about this new turn of events.

He smiled, tilting his grey-maned head to one side. "Divinity can touch anything sentient. Anything."

"What do you..." she stopped, then followed his gaze to the gleaming metal of the haunted train. "That's not possible. That cannot be possible. No." This last word was a gasp, a whisper, a desire for it to be true.

"Oh, yes," he smiled. "Yes."

XXV

"Prove it's you," came the voice from the receiver.

"How?!" Peter. "What do you want a fucking safety word? Open the damned doors, it's me again you twats."

"They're being very sensible," reasoned Jasef. "Don't get angry."

"You said not to open for anyone!"

"I didn't mean me!" he yelled. "Come on, I haven't got time for this."

The elevator began to descend.

"What was the point of that, even? Overzealous little shits,"

"They're doing the right thing," Jasef argued, stepping between the opening doors. "I hope we are."

"We are."

The elevator rose.

"Please don't mind Peter," said Jasef, stepping into the hallway.

"What's going on?" said one of the group.

Peter nodded to those assembled. "I could not locate the ambassador."

"What? What are we going to do?"

"They're all missing?"

"Wait, hang on, they were looking for you," said another, looking to Jasef.

"Yeah, but I found him. And I didn't find them."

"Where were you?" asked the first.

"I feel uncomfortable discussing that at this time," answered Jasef. "We are about to send out an emergency signal."

There were gasps at this, looks of excitement and concern.

"Are, are you sure?" stammered one.

"Positive," answered Peter, brimming with the pride of authority. "Come on. Agnes' office."

They followed him and Jasef down the hall, watching with tantalized adoration as he swiped the back of his wrist over the door to unlock it.

"You all stay out here," he said, "except Jas. You don't need to hang around, just go to the rooms upstairs. All we can do is wait. Actually, someone bring the elevator back up. Jasef and I will take charge of the receiver from now on. Don't crowd us."

Jasef was already at Agnes' desk, taking the papers carefully from his jacket and arranging them in front of him.

"What you doin'?" asked Peter, closing the door and leaning the gun against the wall beside it.

"Having another look through these... Military is going to want to see this immediately."

"Yeah," agreed Peter, moving around the table and setting to work on a safe beneath it. "You know what, I feel like we're in one of those stories."

"What stories?"

"Like..." the safe door swung open and Peter paused with his hand resting on it, "you know, the famous stories."

"I have no idea what you're talking about."

"You are so humorless. I mean like just political fables that everyone's heard. You know, examples of stuff going funky and getting fixed in weird ways."

"Going funky?"

"Yeah! Like, come on, when we went to land on what we thought was a planet and it was a mess of demon bastards, and the colonel went berserk."

"Peter what are you talking about?" Jasef's tone was beginning to rise into the particular annoyed frenzy which only Peter could provoke.

"Do you seriously not know that one? The transport demons – we thought they were a planet. As we were just figuring out how to secure them in metals and all that shit the colonel in charge of part of the operation went batshit nuts, saying it was slavery and that they needed to be released."

"I have never heard that and that is because it is obviously an exaggeration caused by poor interpretation of some fanatical energy company lobbyists."

"What," Peter pulled his head back out of the safe in outrage, "are you on about? It's not an exaggeration – it happened, there was a war. People died!"

"You just said it was a story."

"Everything's a story when you tell it! Doesn't mean it's made up."

"Except that was definitely made up."

"You don't know anything about it! Shut the fuck up and read your papers. Do you want to distract me while I signal the nearest fucking ship? If I fuck up, we're fucked." His voice was magnified around the interior of the safe.

"What do you mean we're fucked?"

"I was exaggerating, it'd be fine."

"Ah ha!"

Peter pulled himself back out of the desk. "What do you mean 'ah ha'?"

"Exaggeration, making things up!"

"I am not making things up! For fuck's sake I wish they'd hit you a bit or something you are completely insufferable."

"What, like they hit you?"

"Ah! Ah! Now who's making shit up! Rama hit me, not they, and it was an accident because of that, you know, god thing."

"Alleged god thing. They seem uncertain."

"Whatever."

"No – absolutely none of this 'whatever'. We are going to be interviewed – separately – in a case pertaining to us directly accusing a black hand of malpractice. We need to tell the absolute and most precise truth at every turn."

"Fuck yeah I know; I'm obviously going to talk to them differently than I'm talking to you. Don't fucking be so patronizing all the time."

"Will you signal that damned ship? We are being relied on."

"If you'd shut up then yeah," Peter replied, maneuvering himself back underneath the desk.

Jasef sighed, sat himself back in Agnes' chair to watch.

"Got it," said Peter, pulling himself upright.

"Was that it?"

"What did you expect?"

"I don't know, it to take a while. What did you actually have to do?"

"Type in a sequence."

"Show me."

"No. It's Military stuff."

"Oh, come on."

"No."

"You don't want me to see because it's just a button isn't it."

"No!"

"Then show me."

Peter paused, hands resting on his thighs. "Alright it's just a button."

"Ha!"

"Shut up. I called Ming too. We need to go watch the elevator."

They passed back into the corridor, following it around to the embassy's suspended lobby. The staff were gone, leaving them alone in the comfortably furnished space. Peter flopped himself down, closely followed by Jasef who positioned himself opposite. Before long, Peter had leaned his head back and surrounded himself with the weak plumes of soothing smoke.

"Do you think we're going to get in trouble?"

"Nah. We're doing the right thing. We're going by the book. The ambassador isn't here, you got a bit kidnapped... we should be calling Military to us."

"No, I mean, negotiating, planning, scheming with Rama."

"We are not scheming."

"There was definitely a degree of scheming."

"Everyone will understand."

"We have betrayed a black hand."

"Technically," said Peter, sitting back up, "we have not. Don't lose your nerve."

"How have we not? We've plotted to sneak into the embassy while she was out and do something we know she wouldn't want us to do."

"Shh," Peter hissed. "Also, no we haven't. You're thinking about it wrong. We have requested off-planet assistance when we were unable to find our ambassador."

"We did not look."

"That is unnecessary information and you need to stop saying it."

"What, lie?"

"No, just do not mention it. Leave that part to me. I was the one-man search and rescue operation. I believed that the ambassador would be with Rama, I did not find her there but found you instead, as you were the reason she was out, I decided to return with you rather than further seeking her. Easy."

"That does sound fine."

"It does."

"What about the matter of me being kidnapped?"

"Alright." Peter lay his head back again and was quiet a while, thinking. "That's a bit of an issue and Rama's probably going to have to pay for it. But, under the circumstances, I think it'll be fine?"

"Was that a question?"

"A suggestion."

Jasef shrugged, although Peter did not see the gesture. "I don't know."

Peter closed his eyes. He did not know for how long. Anxious, liminal dreams. A disease at their centre. Gris Caralla, a churchyard with graves illuminated from below. A great, dark space lit by a rectangle of fire, Ming's voice.

"Peter."

Was it a sound or a dream? He relaxed, soothing himself beyond the first rung of nonsense before sleep.

"Peter!"

His eyes shot open, sitting up. "What, what?"

Jasef was standing in front of him.

Peter's shin throbbed from the kick which had woken him. "What?"

"Look!"

Peter turned his head, looked back towards the entrance.

The elevator was gone.

"Oh, *shit.*" He stood, wiping the sleep from his eyes and staring at the vacant shaft.

"Oh fuck. Oh no."

"It's either Caralla, Agnes, or Ming," said Peter. "It's fine, it's fine."

"It's so not fine. This wasn't supposed to happen."

"Chill, calm down, don't behave like you've done something wrong."

The elevator rose, breaching the horizon of the floor and settling smooth and soundless into position. It slid open and the sound of panic erupted into the room.

"Quick, get it back down–"

"You help them into medical, I–"

"Fuck–"

"Help me with this, get out get it back down–"

"What the fuck are you doing here?!"

This last was directed to Jasef by a blue-jacketed man with a bleeding wound on his left shoulder.

"What, me, I–"

"Ambassador, Agnes, sir. How can we help?" Peter interrupted, striding forwards to get in Agnes' line of sight.

"What?" Agnes reeled, bewildered. "What are you doing here?! Jasef? Oh, gods."

Caralla was just staring, utterly stunned. The elevator disappeared back into the depths behind her. Injured Military helped each other past and into the embassy's winding halls.

"I came to deliver a data pack–"

"Where have you *been*?" Caralla, beginning to walk over to him. "This is impossible."

"I – I've been here."

"Get into my office, both of you, come, I–" she swiped her black hand through her hair, blinking frantically in an expression of overwhelmed horror which neither of them had ever seen on her before. "Come."

Agnes caught up to them just as Caralla's office door was opening.

"What happened, ambassador?" asked Peter, watching her near collapse into her chair, "Where were you, who attacked?"

"We were looking for Jasef," Agnes. "You went missing in central, that's where we were."

"Yes, I–"

"Why the hell did Ed Rama know what was in that data pack, Jasef?" interrupted Caralla, her voice firm again.

"Ambassador, we have the contents," he answered. "They are in Agnes' office. Rama's outside, yeah?"

"What? What? You opened a data pack without my permission? Rama. Rama had you." she murmured, still looking down. "I saw you in Kis' palace. I saw you."

"Gris?" said Agnes, something warning, or unsettled in his tone.

She looked up at him, unseeing.

"You were attacked?" suggested Peter, in the ensuing quiet.

"Twice, I believe," replied Agnes when it became clear that the ambassador was not ready to speak. "First by Xar Kis' servants, and then by Ed Rama. Maybe. It is only the clashing of the two which saved us."

"I don't understand." Peter.

"We were waiting to catch sight of Jasef in central. We believed that he had been... delayed by Xar Kis. That data pack is of interest to him. He probably considers it belonging to him. We had spoken... I do not know why he suddenly decided to attack. The train... I don't know. We fled, there have been casualties."

"We need to see how many," added Caralla, darkly.

"I would guess at three, at this stage," said Agnes, sitting down and indicating for the other two to do the same. "We fled this far, and then Rama was at the damned gate shouting at us about the data pack. They started fighting each other while we carried on running back here."

Caralla flinched, apparently at nothing. A memory, perhaps.

"Tell us what happened with Ed Rama." Agnes prompted, leaning back into his chair.

"Sir," responded Jasef. "He wants to speak to you, about an urgent matter concerning some... magical entity."

Caralla's red, lined eyes focused on Jasef's face. "Tell me every detail."

"They believe that..." began Peter, carefully and deliberately, "there is some sort of..." he looked to Jasef for help.

"Unnatural presence, maybe a deity. On the planet. They are convinced that there are people in Ech Kon trying to support the strength of this... entity. Rama wants to secure Crysthian assistance in the destruction of this entity."

Agnes seemed to be on the verge of speech, watching the ambassador. "Gris," he said, softly. "This could work."

"No." she snapped, shocking them all by slamming her artificial palms against the desk, "You know why. No."

"Gris," he repeated, "we are losing. And that train just came back from Ech Kon. That's no coincidence. We can get out there and help them, call a Military backup–"

"No,"

"There's one coming," said Jasef.

"What?!" Caralla.

"You've sent an emergency signal?" Agnes turned to Peter. "When?"

"Erm, about… Jasef?"

"About two hours ago."

Caralla stood. "You fools, you absolute fools you–"

"Gris this could be a good thing!"

"No! They cannot be here, they cannot know what's happening, Rama needs to be destroyed, they–"

"Rama wants our help!" Peter. "He is asking for our help and you are ignoring him for the sake of Xar fucking Kis!"

"Are you out of your mind?!" she snapped, "What the hell do you think is going on here? Agnes, stop that signal. Stop it now."

"Gris, I can't. They will come anyway after two hours. That's too long for it to have reasonably been a mistake – they'll think we've been overrun."

"They cannot be here. They cannot be here. It can lie, Agnes. I'm right, it's a deity. It's sentient!"

"You do know!" burst Peter. "You know there's something here and you're protecting it!"

"What?" Agnes stood up, closely followed by Jasef who joined him out of a sense of alarmed embarrassment. "What are you talking about?"

"We saw what was in that data pack," said Peter, lowering his voice to address the blue, "We know how much this planet is worth, why she's helping Kis get onto Crysth."

Caralla flinched again, so much it made them all look at her. She went still, and then burst into laughter before she replied. "You stupid, ridiculous man – what are you saying to me? What are you accusing me of? Out with it."

"You are, you are conspiring to allow a race that have been... altered by some big fucking god thing into the empire. For personal gain!" yelled Peter, gaining in confidence as the sentence progressed.

"Peter that is absolutely absurd–" began Agnes.

"No!" Jasef. "Why don't you want Military here? Why won't you help Rama?"

"Yeah!" Peter.

"Rama is far beyond my help – they all are," she yelled back. "I am too."

"No," Agnes.

"You know it has me."

"We can do something."

Caralla shook her head. "It has me."

"What's happening now?" Peter.

The ambassador's shirt folded beneath her thumb as she pulled it aside. She showed them her flesh, gleaming with spots of new blood. Black spines twisted along her collarbone.

"Fuck," said Peter. "What is it?"

Caralla slumped back into her chair.

"Why," she murmured. "All of you. If only you had just done as you were told."

"They don't know, Gris. We've never told them–"

"And we never will! Crysth cannot know!"

"They are coming. And so is Kis, and so is Rama. A side in this has been chosen for us," urged Agnes, approaching his master's desk. "Kis just attacked us. You know the deity will attack us. We need to face them now while Rama is already out there fighting – we can help. Together, we might be able to–"

"No we won't!" she sobbed, more fury than sorrow. "You saw them, you saw how fast they are, what it lets them do. It can lie, Agnes. It showed me... I was so sure. It seemed so real... Jasef was in there."

"So, it knows we are its enemy and we must start fighting. If we leave Rama out there to die, they will keep coming. What's to stop them collapsing the embassy?"

Jasef let out a little whimper, followed by, "Pardon me – I don't, I don't understand – why would we ever prevent Military from helping us here? Why can't we let everybody know what's going on? When has Crysth ever refused to destroy a god?"

"This one is... is..." began Caralla, her weeping eyes unfocused again, "it is exceptional." She is right. "It needs to be destroyed here, by the ignorant."

"What do you mean?" Peter.

"She means that it will be harder to destroy if those who are trying to do so are aware of it." Agnes. "It can see plans; it can see intention. Something like that. A destruction of it needs to be incidental to another cause." He was talking with his hands, drawing boxes in the air as if he could contain these impossible clauses within them. "It is a thing made of... wanton obliteration. You have to come at it without thinking about it. Not to have a concrete goal that concerns it. It shatters linearity."

"What the hell does that mean?" Peter.

"But, the data pack, those documents – Kis will be allowed into Crysth – why did you... why..." Jasef started and stopped, trailing off.

"Crysth needs to believe that this planet is not only valuable but plagued by an incurable disease. Not a deity, just an infection. It will be... cleansed. For its own good," she said, softly, like a prayer.

"You..." Jasef faltered.

"You're talking about genocide," said Peter. "You are talking about conspiring to trick Crysthian agents into committing genocide!"

"Not genocide," answered Agnes. "Deicide. It is inside them, they cannot be allowed out. It will live as long as they do. That cannot be allowed to happen. You know we cannot suffer a god to live."

"You were... you've been lying to Kis." Jasef.

"Of course I have!" she answered, anger seething behind her teeth. "The work of years, and you have undone it in moments."

"We need a plan B, Gris. It's right here."

"There is no plan B. There can be no plan B."

"We can arm ourselves and help Rama." Agnes insisted, "they caught us off guard last time and in cramped and unfamiliar space, when we were at rest."

"We won't win."

"With Rama and Military on our side we might. We've failed, you're right. Military are going to find out that there's a god or a magic here–"

"It's a god," she growled.

"I know, I know. I didn't mean... look. They are going to find out. We can't sit here and wait for Kis and... it... to come to us. We have a chance with Rama."

Peter and Jasef just stood there, silent intruders at the end of the world.

"It's using me," she said, looking down at her hands. "It's lying to me, making me move. Making me believe things that are not true."

"We can–"

"No!" her shoulders heaved now with a sob she could not suppress. "It's got me. It's really got me. Agnes I... I think it's had me for years."

"We can fight it, we can fix it – we might even be able to cure it."

"You know that we cannot."

"I know that our best chance now is to fight it outright, and hope that we can. Worry about it later."

Silence but for her breathing, the three men staring at the black fingers knotted beneath a shock of white hair.

She stood, slowly, looking at them all with a face blotched with exhaustion and misery – but set. "It can see into my mind. There's hope for you, in this. But it is using me."

"Gris," he said, and it was a whisper, a plea. Just her name. "Please."

Tears began to fall again, without expression, just looking into Agnes' eyes.

"Please don't."

She did.

The body which had been Gris Caralla collapsed into the ambassador's chair. Agnes tried to catch it before it slumped to the floor. He might have been calling her name, it did not matter; she had been dead the moment that she had the impulse. Painless, instant, a shock of haunted electricity from her wrist and the end, wherever that was. Right now, it was the carpet beneath the desk.

Jasef had jumped forward too, arms outstretched, as if both men had thought that by catching her they could prevent what had already happened. Now he stood beside the desk, staring down at the body in Agnes' arms, mouth open, strangely unaffected. Agnes' grief filled the room.

Beyond the embassy, through the winding unlife of the metal garden and into unplanned, unseen, chaotic bloodshed, Rama was sending for aid.

Silence in the ambassador's office.

"We need to get out there, sir." Peter's voice, a rupture in the static quiet.

No response.

"There weren't many of Rama's people out there. Kis will fight through them soon."

Jasef nodded. "Only a few dozen," he added, flatly.

Silence.

"Come and help me with her."

"Sir... there's nothing we can do," answered Jasef.

"What? Come and help me."

Peter glanced at Jasef, his face contorted with pity. "Agnes, we can't help."

"Why the hell not?" he demanded, raising his head over the desk, his eyes wet with furious, shocked tears.

"The electricity sir, it was instant," Jasef stammered back at him.

"She's gone, sir," added Peter.

"I know! What are you talking about you damned fools?"

"Respectfully... what are you talking about?" Peter's tone had lapsed from sympathy to bewilderment.

"We need to, oh you idiots, we need to use her hands to get out of here. We can't open the door without her prosthetics."

"Oh fuck yeah shit," Peter. "Sorry, we thought, er..."

"Just... help me."

They started forwards, stopped suddenly, fixed each other with attentive, questioning stares.

"What was that?" Peter whispered.

"What?" Agnes.

"Sh," Jasef.

Agnes glanced between them both and then unfocused his eyes to listen with them. A constant, irregular popping, with the tones of something very loud but far away.

"Oh no," breathed Agnes. "Come on, quick, quickly."

"What's going on?" Jasef responded, kneeling beside Caralla in obedience.

"Gunfire. You left sentries down there?" Peter.

"Only a few of them. Hurry." Agnes.

An urgent knocking from the other side of the door, followed swiftly by more when it went unanswered.

"Fuck, fuck. How are they this close already?" muttered Peter, trying to manipulate his hands beneath the former ambassador's back in the least disrespectful way possible. "Jasef, have you got her legs?"

"Err."

"Under the, just the back of her knees," advised Agnes, kneeling now behind her with his hands beneath her shoulders. "Be careful, for gods' sake Peter."

"I, I think I've got her here." Jasef.

"Hang on I don't, fuck. Alright, stand up." Peter.

The three of them staggered to their feet with the slack weight of Gris Caralla between them.

"I wish they'd stop hammering on the damned door." Agnes. "Jasef, this way, you go first."

"Err."

"*Around* the table not fucking over it–"

"Peter, stop swearing. You are holding the ambassador to Crysth."

They shuffled across the room, embarrassed and reverent and to the tune of intermittent banging on the office door.

"Peter," started Agnes, leaning his shoulder against the wall beside the door's hinges to steady himself, "get her hand and put your foot in the door."

"Right."

"Err…"

"What, Jasef?" Agnes nodded his head to the side as he spoke, "get round over here, as far away from the opening as you can."

"I–"

"I don't want them to know that she's dead."

"Oh."

"Ready?"

"Go."

Peter pasted her palm clumsily against the door, applied pressure to her fingers. The prosthetics felt like stone.

Voices came rushing through the crack in the doorway, angry and alarmed and desperate for instruction in the face of attack.

"Oi, no chill out. Calm down – the situation is under

control. No! Look, listen, an emergency Military cohort is already on the way. No, the ambassador is in her safe room. Yes."

"Peter," hissed Agnes urgently, "tell them to gather everyone in the lobby."

"No you cannot – look, hey I'm *trying* to tell you, shut up! Right, get everybody, *everybody* into the lobby. Arm yourselves who can. Alright?"

More voices raised in protest, demanding Agnes, the ambassador, silenced as Peter clamped the door shut.

"Hell," Agnes muttered. "Right, let's just put her here. Actually – Peter go and get her chair, bring it over here."

"Sir do we have time for–"

"Do it."

"Right."

"Sir," began Jasef, as Peter dragged her heavy oak chair across to them, "if we leave her on this side, we aren't going to be able to get back in."

"I know."

"Is that not... a problem?"

Peter placed the chair beside the door and began to help them position her in it. "I don't think we need anything in here, do we?"

"No."

"But... do we not need to communicate with Military?" asked Jasef.

"We can't," grunted Agnes, trying without success to respectfully balance Caralla's head on her shoulders. "We'd need Ming for that. The lines are all Red. Have you buzzed her already?"

Agnes gave up his miserable labour, stopped to look at the ambassador's corpse, rag doll in her chair.

"Right," he said, "let's go."

Agnes held his prize weapon as he spoke. His trophy, his favorite toy, and he would be damned if he could not use it this one last time. The embassy's administrators and Military blues stood before him in awed terror. Crysth was under attack. Military were coming, but they could not sit and wait.

"At this point, we are attempting to make contact with Ed Rama…"

Weapons were being distributed among the blues and those of administrative grey who dared take them. In the corner, Peter had checked Jasef's pistol and showed him how to use its aim assist. His own light machinegun rested against the wall.

"Focus our efforts on Xar Kis and Miré Distan. Their supporters will be well armed…"

The elevator could only take a few at a time, funneling them down into the space below the embassy – conveying Agnes' speech to those below, training their weapons into the evanescent lights of the embassy's garden.

"Expect unanticipated motion. They are being assisted by a form of magic…"

Peter had been surprised by Jasef, taking the pistol without complaint or argument. Don't leave me, he had said, and it had been Peter's voice.

"We have been the victims of an unprovoked attack and we must unite with Rama…"

"What do you think the others are doing?" Jasef had asked as the last trickle of people got into the elevator.

"I don't know," Peter had said, "but I'm glad they're not here."

There were bodies down there already. Punctured with bullet wounds and bleeding into the concrete floor. Rama's supporters, Peter could tell, and Agnes standing among them.

They had pulled their triggers instinctively, the guards that had remained outside, but there was one Apechi still alive – on her knees with her hands in the air, a spear on the ground to her left. She was speaking up to Agnes with wide-eyed desperation.

Her face lit up in recognition and relief at Peter's face; "Peter, you tell him."

"What's going on?" Peter asked, nodding to her in assurance of his support.

"She says that Distan and Rama are up front, they were trying to distract as many of Kis' people away from them as possible to give Rama a chance. Lost them in the garden, then our guards opened fire." Agnes.

"They're in the trees?"

"Yes," she said. "Scattered. We must go back to Ed."

"I recognize her, sir. From when we were with Rama before. She's on his side."

"That's right," agreed Jasef, "definitely."

Agnes nodded, extended a hand to pull her up, raised his voice to command his troops once more.

"Peter," she whispered, "Ed is not stronger than Distan, he will die, he will lose."

"We're going." answered Peter, watching as some of the Crysthians were appointed to stay behind and guard the embassy, some were sent out into the trees around it, some remaining on the path. "Come on."

The four of them set the pace, Agnes, Jasef, Peter, and the survivor with her spear.

XXVI

Ar sat, the orange disk of a dried peach caught between his thumb and forefinger, the parrot's gluttony busy around it. He had not enjoyed his day.

Everybody had been gone when he came up to brew some tea. He had not been able to find the kettle. There was just a note that said "Achira" on the side. He had smiled at that; glad they were playing pagoda detective again. But he missed his tea.

He felt a little abandoned. He also felt that this was a silly notion, that everybody was busy about their business and that Jasef and Peter at the very least would be back any moment, bickering and offering him some horrible bitter ale.

He wanted to be back with Muhr. There was always music with Muhr. Long, melancholic strings which flowed around visual conversation. Recently, he had started thinking with a voice in his head. He did not like that. It sounded like Ming.

Miles away, the train flew. Haunted and demented, manic with the god's possession. Apech whipped past Ming's eyes at the rail's true, uncapped speed; the demon within it aided in a metallic revolution that overthrew Crysth's restraints. She watched her gauntlet, fascinated by its own little zaps of uncontrolled action, bitter with jealousy that she yet remained unaffected. How would it feel, the transient sentience trapped upon her arm, when they were devotees to the same cause?

The taxidermist wanted more variety to fuel the god's strength. Ming had argued, briefly, against it. She had lost.

Ar's head snapped up from the parrot when he heard her voice, shrill, almost pleading. The sound of her footsteps mounting the spiral staircase. He stepped out of his room, his face contorted with the worry and loneliness that had been plaguing him all day.

Ming looked terrible. Her clothes were dirty.

"Ar... fuck it. Jump. Go to the window and jump. Go fast and easy. They're coming. Jump!" she commanded, a flash of trembling desperation hovering around the line of her lips.

He shook his head, expression contorted in alarm.

"I will do it if you won't," she hissed, pulling back to her sleeve to reveal the weapon which he had always suspected she wore.

He held up his hands in fear or supplication. Nothing happened. She seemed to be trying, but the thing was broken or unresponsive. Flashes of electricity falling from it like sparks by a flame.

His eyes widened as he heard one, two, three, unfamiliar voices below. Beginning to climb the stairs.

A soldier rolled, laughed as the whip of a metal chain crashed into the concrete beside her. *Grab it.* She sees herself grabbing it and pulling its owner's body sprawling into the copper tree in front of him, so she does, and he did. She laughed again, leapt up with impossible energy and wrapped the chain around the fallen man's neck. There's another coming behind her, she ducks at just the right time and loops the chain around him. He was trapped, his every move anticipated, she hideously strong as her flat muscles strained against the constraints of intention.

Through glistening, cold branches with multicolored light reflecting in polluted dew, another. This one was losing – unable to keep up with the god's constant fracturing of reality she dips and dives but has become desperate, started to concentrate. It felt like the deity had turned against her. It had, in its own way. Rama's allies came at her, realizing as they did that she could not see them. Wild blind eyes staring at shadows that were not there.

They have become scattered. In the initial, confused skirmish, some had chased the embassy staff into the grounds and become lost in the forest, avoiding gunfire and rallying in pursuit of Rama's stupid, useless, murdering rebels who got in their way. They could hear them shouting to each other as they fought, Kis' servants calling out in fury; they do not know why they are being attacked. They do not know why these cowards have come out of hiding to fight them now, while there is suddenly so much to do. They have not had time to think, they have been scattered and left their master behind and there will be trouble. All of them are trying to converge back towards the path.

The memory of Farön Kis' face smashed into Lon Apech's artificial ground. His son's boots moved through the ruins of him as he addressed his army.

"My father was a great man." A railway spike swung on the end of a length of gold as he walked. It moved in flashing, impossible ways. The god adores him. It loves in flashing, impossible ways. "But the work of his greatness is done. We are united. We are together, thriving in the city he built for us."

Miré Distan lurched behind him, afraid but in awe. He had never imagined, nor dreamt nor glimpsed in vague waking visions, that he would take a hammer to Farön's monument. If the Kis beneath their feet is truly gone, he thought, then the Kis by his shoulder has finally taken his place.

"How many mindless were there before we turned our backs on this power? Can you recall? More than half of us are lost every year, now. You have all lost people. For what? They're gone for nothing if we do not use this." Tendrils of godflesh flickered from the floor, exploratory and tame around the feet of the willing. "This is strength. It is on our side. This is power the likes of which even Crysth's emperors fear, and which will come with us as we explore this world. We have come this far, and we will go further."

Ming stood on Farön Kis' right foot, the taxidermist on his left. All that remains of the statue. Someone had found Ming some black paint. It was drying on her hands.

"Gris Caralla is in our way. Ed Rama is in. Our. Way."

The godthing roared with its quiet thunder, tasting possibility.

Ming's eyes roved over the crowd as Kis spoke. They were breathless, excited, full of terror. They wanted to believe what they were told, they wanted to allow the feel of it into their bodies – stop resisting, give in. They wanted to let it take them and infect them with its scattering, rhythm-breaking logic. Some of them were hitting their weapons against the ground as Xar spoke, murmuring to themselves in louder and louder agreement. Turning to each other and knowing that they were caught in the wave.

The taxidermist whispered constantly.

It suited Xar. Ming watched him, rather than the crowd. Thinking about what she is going to do. Caralla must have sounded an alarm to the nearest Military cohort. There would be a mutiny at the embassy if she had not. This meant that they would have to take her alive, to know what she has communicated to them, to figure out how Ming must shape her lie.

She stepped down from the pedestal and over to Miré, who dropped the head of his great hammer into the sprawling godflesh without fear of doing it harm, turning his attention to her. Waiting for instructions.

"Kill Rama, all of them," she whispered to him, "but take Caralla alive. Scatter the embassy staff, do not kill them unless it is necessary. I will be able to convince them of our version of events." She looked down at her hands. "Once I have worked out the kinks in the story. Go now."

XXVII

Peter could hear the sounds of death coming soft and strange through the forest. Cushioned by the fog, peppered with guttural screams and the tolling bell of weapons striking hollow metal. All weapons trained into the trees.

Those stalking behind them are trained for this. Mundanely. Like it's a fire drill. All of them theoretically ready to obey, shoot, and die. For Crysth, but mostly because that's just a part of getting to be here. The endless rotation of Military duty or embassy work, the freedom of going. This might happen, be prepared. Panic consumed by automated responses, reacting just as they would to an accident in space. They never thought that this would really happen to them, or whatever, but they knew that it might. Cowardice is not even considered; it is not an option. This is unthinking.

That will change when the faithful start to attack.

It started with a chaos of bullets, shuddering noise into the trees because something had moved wrong in the shadows and then someone had panicked and then everyone had joined in. The survivor bolted and Jasef with her. Peter screamed after him, but he was gone. You coward. You fuck.

Thrust into the trees for shelter. Everyone ran. There were people coming after them so they scattered, abandoning their friends and the safety of the pack to hide or just to run. Peter and Agnes chose the former, sticking together and corralling each other through the metal. Guns sang behind them.

"You alright?" asked Agnes, hushed, the two of them stooped between the roots of a great bronze cedar which lurched dramatically to one side.

Peter looked like he was in pain, wincing against some invisible wound, but he nodded. The surge of adrenaline had activated the freak technologies which hugged the bones of higher-level Military factioneers.

"Relax." Agnes.

"Yours not working?"

"I'm just more used to it." He wiped at his brow for no real reason. He was shockingly calm, partly because of the help from his body, partly because the worst had already happened. "That went wrong a lot sooner than I was expecting it to."

"Yeah. What now?"

"Same as before. Find Rama, help him."

"Shit."

"Yep. Let's go."

A lone woman with a huge, glistening sickle backed into the gloom. The blade touched the metal of the trunk behind her with a light, airy ringing which set her teeth on edge. She watched the two of Kis' men who had cornered her glance to each other in satisfied, anticipatory telepathy. Good, she thought. If they try to fuck with me then I'll have more of a chance to get lucky.

One of them made a move forward and so she looked down, concentrating on the ground. She can see his choices. She lowered herself and focused on them, channeling years of intense, manic focus on the sand in Rama's garden. No good.

The other zipped left, gone with invisible speed. The god

knows when she won't be looking, knows the right balance and weight and resistance so that its faithful move like dreams.

The first was more wary. Afraid of that sickle and afraid of his god but on fire with Kis' voice and desire for the body in front of him. Divinely sanctioned destruction, holy obliteration, sacred rape.

She did not know where the other one was and so he must have been behind her. She could not hear him, and she could not look so she thought fuck it and went forward into the other. The one behind her had known she would. He grabbed her as she lurched and she spun, trying to swipe the sickle into his arm but he was gone and the other one was doing the same and she was just waving the sickle around without really knowing where they were. Agony, the flat of the first's blade broke her fingers against the silver handle, the other pushed her forwards as she dropped it and she was down. Tried to roll away but the other brought his boot down on her forearm, crushing it into the concrete with all his weight. The skin on her side split open against a steel fern. She stared up at him, to his face gnarled with possibility and pasts and futures, shifting in constant metamorphosis through which she made out his pleasure – and then it exploded.

His headless body did not seem to know that it was dead. Still upright with the boot on her arm. She looked to the other as the corpse crumpled backwards. That one was staring into the fog, scanning his head side to side in frantic confusion even as bullets whipped into his chest. Some of them went through him, hitting the metal behind him with raucous defeat as the shifting machinations of his flesh decided simply not to be in the way. But there were too many, emptied into him, and he was dead.

"Are you alright?" A high voice, undulating slightly in waves of concern.

She cradled her ruined right arm and looked up through her pain. "You." Relief.

"Can I help you, can you get up?" Jasef.

She said a few nonsense words to him as she struggled upright. "Shit, shit. Get me my weapon, pass it, it's over there."

"I don't think that you can–"

"No choice, come on."

A young embassy administrator rallied with the stragglers around him, regrouping each other and cowering together in the low mist which ran around the trees. He watched the person beside him breathe, watched green then red then yellow lights rove across his face, reflected from somewhere. He found that watching other people calm was calming him.

"We need to keep going," said one of them, a Military deciding to take control. "We know what we're supposed to be doing."

"Do we?" gasped another, to her right.

"Yes," she hissed. "We find and support Ed Rama. We find and kill Xar Kis. We find and kill Miré Distan."

"Where? Where are we supposed to go?" Another, to murmuring agreements.

"The path." Another. "We can reorientate ourselves with the path."

"We were attacked on the path."

One shook his head. "We only need to know where it is, not be on it. We can stay in the trees."

"Right," nodded the Military woman, "this way, this way."

On their hands and knees, many clutching guns they did not truly know how to use, they huddled through the forest.

Ed Rama saw Miré Distan, a lone figure between the embassy's gates.

* * *

The paint had not yet dried on Ming's hands. It was sticking to the wooden spokes she had gripped in each palm. The wood was rough, unfinished, it would be painful if she cared. Xar's bare torso pinned her against the Vasa's wheel, thrusting into her in urgent, growling monomania that she had not even tried to deny him.

She watched the taxidermist over his shoulder. The old man knew, kept glancing at her in something like contempt, something like satisfaction. He was doing work with the godflesh. Unpicking its stitches, talking into the wounds. The god consumed the corpses impaled on the Vasa's three masts, climbing up them with spiral greed.

Ming closed her eyes and pressed her lips to Xar's ear.

"We'll win," she told him, gasping as his teeth tore at her skin. "It's ours."

"Sh." Agnes was still, suddenly, listening.

Peter froze beside him. He waited. He spoke, "I can't hear anything."

Agnes held up a finger, eye-rolling concentration. "There are some of ours to our right, a lot of them."

"Nice control," said Peter, unable to prevent himself from marveling at the other man's use of tech. He could have learned more from him. Should have learned more from him if he hadn't been busy feeling holier-than-thou and fucking. "Oh, shit." he added, remembering how the embassy staff had reacted to sudden confrontation before.

"Yep."

"Can't we let them know that it's us?"

"What, you want to start singing the anthem? They're coming this way."

* * *

The taxidermist crooned and soothed, speaking constantly as he strummed the godflesh apart with his little blade. One by one, the stitches sprang apart, a labor of devotion.

He was saying names. He wanted this moment of emergence to be explosive. He wanted his dark, miserable, secretive life to bring about an orgy of power and magic.

He glanced up to Farön Kis' son, to the *parak* taking him. Good.

He was saying the names of the willing dead. Those of whom the satellite was first made, who gave their lives to preserve the defeated god. People who have been waiting in hell.

He hopes they're angry.

"Alessi. Idris. Gayatri. Fucking... is that Mark?"

The embassy staff froze, looking around to seek confirmation that the others had, in fact, heard their names.

"Peter?" whispered the woman in blue.

Another nodded. "Think so."

"What if it's a trap?" hissed another.

"Apechi don't know our names."

"What if they're using him, holding him hostage like?"

"Shit you're right."

"Don't be ridiculous." The woman in blue.

"No, I think it's a legitimate concern."

They looked at each other a bit more.

One aimed his pistol in the direction of the voice, cleared his throat to announce his intention to his comrades in case any of them felt like stopping him. "Peter?"

"Yes," replied the alleged Peter, "and Agnes. We're over here."

Gunfire raged in the near distance, metal complaints, thinning screams here and there.

"Where's here?"

"Over there."

"No, it's over there." Her again, waving the barrel of her gun in a different direction.

"Oi," the disembodied voice again, "oi. We're coming to where you are. Don't freak out."

"Shit."

They saw movement in the murk, Peter's face emerging as from water, color roving over him. "I've got Agnes behind me," he said, "you all alright?"

"Thank fuck." There were several of these sentiments.

"Language." Agnes.

"We're all going to die." Whoever.

There was a snort in the dark as someone laughed. "Sorry."

"FUCK!" And a thud.

There was a shocked quiet after the stifled screams subsided. It would have been silence but for the gasping, retching sound coming from the body between them. A body which had fallen from the trees. An Apechi in what seemed to be a wetsuit. Then a single, appallingly brutal pop from Peter's gun. An execution.

The corpse between them bled. The fall had been too fast for them to even see.

They looked up.

"Are there more of them?"

There were.

"Run!" Agnes' order was too late, the corpse's comrades were already descending – dropping out of the uncertain gloom of the canopies with a grace the unlucky one had lacked.

"He's here!" one of them screamed, his body still held in the moaning branches of an iron oak and his voice tearing to defeat the sudden roar of bullets coming from beneath. "Agnes, here!"

Agnes and Peter had backed off already, taking themselves apart from the crowd. Three of the figures in the maroon-dark clothes favored by those close to Kis had focused on them, springing between branches wet with mist, slipping here and there and righting themselves as they came after the two Military men.

"Come on!" yelled Agnes, "Bring them—"

They ran, upright and sprinting, smacking into trees but going faster than the figures in the canopies who also had to descend, navigate the wild bullets of the embassy staff beneath them, negotiate with space and the not-real-space the god was forcing them to imagine. They did not trust it to help them anymore. They had just seen one of their own fall.

"Bring them, bring them to the path—"

Semen trickled down the inside of Ming's thigh as she walked over to where the taxidermist knelt.

"Oh," she said to him. "That is cruel."

"Don't you want it?" Xar, his voice low and sensible again behind her. She could hear the offer in the question, to destroy the aberration before them if she said no.

"The bird is a little much, but it can stay."

The taxidermist grinned his insatiable joy up at them. "Wait until you see it move."

"Please, please get away from here." Rama's voice cracked but his lips barely moved, speaking to the man at his side. "I am begging you to run. Away. Please."

Distan picked up his hammer, lofting it into the air with his two gnarled hands. "I am going to kill you, and then I am going to kill him."

"This is not your fight," answered the man. "He is not just your enemy. This fight is ours, all ours. Always has been. And we knew this was coming."

"I love you," Rama told him.

"You can't, right now." The man stepped away, angling his

machete in front of him and watching Distan with focused rage. "Come on then, you sick fuck!"

Distan started to run.

Rama shot to his left at the last moment, guessing correctly that Distan would swing for him rather than his lover and letting the weight of the giant hammer send Miré wheeling backwards – but he didn't. The hammer stopped like it had hit something, Distan moving it as easily as if it were made of polystyrene, and then it was coming through the air again.

The machete lunged, missed as Distan's flesh chose not to inhabit the space it occupied. Rama's hand went to his back and pulled out his weapon – a stiletto with a blade half the length of his spine.

Distan laughed. Rama went to swing for him, but he was being lied to – the real Distan had spun around and was slamming the hammer, overhead, wheeling, crashing through the air as the other man danced around it.

"No!" Rama jumped, landing on Distan's back and trying to stab the knife into his chest but the handle of the hammer had come up already to hold it off.

He could not see the other man, but he could hear him, his breath a tortured moan.

Distan fell back, ramming Rama into the ground behind him and knocking the breath out of him as he did. He broke his grip and rolled off, stood, raised the hammer.

Fire.

The metal shrubbery erupted into screaming flames by the side of the path. Their faces burned with the heat of it, their eyes burned with the light of it. And through its blasting, crackling boom there was cheering.

"Fuck yeah! Yeah! How do you like that you shits!" Peter's yell came triumphant as the fire subsided, followed by the ridiculous slap of a high-five and Agnes' near-sadistic smile.

Agnes nodded, laughing, treasuring the weight of the dragon shotgun in his hands – and then he saw the fighting aristocrats.

"Oh, shit," he said.

"Oh, shit!" Peter raised his gun, aiming at Miré Distan, while Rama rolled away and up in the confusion.

Distan did not know what to do. He backed up, looking between Rama and Agnes as he did, swinging the hammer in a movement which looked like an aid to thought.

"Get further away." Peter's voice was loud, clear, not directed to anyone in particular.

Rama realized what he meant and turned at the last moment to shield the man on the ground.

The rumbling gale of fire. Pain searing across his back.

"Are you alright?" he managed.

"Yes! Go, get off me, look, go!" the other man spat, hammering on Rama's chest to turn him around.

Distan was on fire, but this did not seem to be much of an inconvenience. He was a tower of flame, wrestling with a screaming Agnes while Peter looked on, horrified, his gun aimed towards them in frantic inactivity.

Agnes and Distan were rolling on the ground, the flames subsiding, seeming to run out of air – but Distan had the gun. He did not even pull the trigger, just smashed it into Agnes' skull until it wasn't Agnes anymore.

Rama barreled into him, trying to knock him down with one arm and thrust the blade into his side with the other.

Peter saw that Agnes was dead, still could not shoot with Rama in the way, screamed at him to move, get up, get off him. He knew what he should do – just squeeze the trigger anyway and take both of them – but he did not have the courage.

Distan was winning. But Rama had hit him – once in the side with that blade.

Peter thrust his gun into the hands of one of the embassy staff who had finally caught up, leaving it with her as he dived into the fight, tearing at Distan's arms to free Rama. It was like pulling at a vice.

* * *

The woman with the sickle staggered forward, her body catching up with itself and beginning to realize how hurt it really was. Every footstep sent shocks of electric vitriol up into her nerves, no matter how closely she cradled her damaged arm, trying to stop it from moving. Sometimes the mad ache was so much that she jolted it on purpose, just for the relief of a different pain.

"Your side is bleeding quite a lot," said Jasef. "I really think you should stay still."

"No time."

He continued to follow, wincing as he watched her tortured steps. Part of him was glad for it, a distraction from peering into the impenetrable gloom accompanied by an overarching sensation that war would never do anything so ungentlemanly as attacking someone already this wounded.

"There's fire coming."

"Pardon?"

"Ahead," she gasped, turning to shield her eyes in a movement which he was too slow to copy.

Flame ballooned behind her, throwing the trees into silhouette, obliterating the multicolored glow of the fog's refracted light as it blossomed in the distance. Jasef fancied that he felt its heat.

"How did you–" he asked, when it had died down, but he could hear movement behind them. Lots. The gunfire seemed to stop, the shouts and wails momentarily mute. "It's Agnes' gun. Everyone is going to go towards it."

"We need to hurry up," she panted, already on her way, "they'll catch up, they'll go through us."

Jasef gritted his teeth, ignored her cries of pain and grabbed her around the waist, half lifting her half supporting her to get through the metal forest as fast as they possibly could, both of them believing that if they got to the fire then they were safe, that whatever was happening there was the way forward, the way out.

They burst onto the path, falling with the relief of it. She screamed and rolled herself onto the ground, moaning in shocking pain that left rivulets of glistening fluid on the rough concrete beneath them. Jasef's face was twisted into a mortis of concern, but he looked beyond her to the fray between the two columns of the embassy's entrance.

It was a mess of people. So many of them, writhing in close-armed combat with embassy staff stalking the edges, shouting and occasionally daring to fire with their aim-assisted pistols – often missing even then.

Jasef stared. He knew Peter would be in the middle. He just knew.

"I need your weapon. Please."

She ignored him, so he took it.

"Sorry," he added.

With the sickle in his right hand and the pistol in his left, he walked towards the mass of bodies. If Peter Piat-Elementov was alive – which he indubitably was, on account of being Peter Piat-Elementov – then he was in the middle of that fight. And Jasef would be damned if he wasn't in there with him.

Rama was dead. His body was at the center of the fray, crushed beneath the mass of people trying to either kill or aid Miré Distan.

Peter had lost track of both in the fight, was concentrating on keeping Kis' loyal away from Rama's, who were still swarmed around a central point which must have been Miré.

He had a spear, now, much better suited to this mess than the heavy, barely controllable gun he had brought out with him. Stupid.

He was trying to concentrate, control the flow of technological fury around his body like he had seen Agnes do – and was succeeding. He lunged into the crowd, a fake-out to make the others dive into his exposed flank. He opened one of their chests but was cut by another, using both ends of the spear – someone started shooting at them. Fuck. He shouted out for the shooter to stop but the bullets were actually hitting his assailants, distracting if not killing them as the god rearranged them in its constant, shifting interest.

Peter took the opportunity of their distraction to start singling them out, thinking about them rather than himself, putting them down around him.

"Peter!" Jasef's voice broke over the noise of death and nearly made Peter allow a hit – a chain, this one was fighting with a fucking chain, he'd never had a go at anything like that before – but he glanced it around the spear and hopped back, trying against his better judgement to see where the git Green was coming from.

"Are you – are you shooting that thing at me?! Fucking hell!"

"I am saving you!" He was.

Peter twisted the end of his spear into another chest, turned back towards the main fray. "Give me that."

"What? No."

"Fuck's sake man give it!"

Jasef handed Peter the pistol, which he spun around his wrist before firing, precisely and perfectly, knowing exactly how to adjust the barrel so that the aim assist caught on with each new target. He kept going until there were no bullets left, reached back to Jasef for his spear.

He could finally see Distan again, backed out of the gates and standing with a group of his own. His face was mottled, scarred, teeth missing, blossoming with blood. His left hand held a wound at his ribs, but he was upright.

"He won't fucking die. He won't fucking die, Jasef."

"Where's Rama?"

Peter shook his head.

They stood. The embassy and the rebels within the gates, Distan and Apech's loyal without.

"Why aren't we shooting?" whispered Jasef.

"Stop," snapped one of Rama's. "Shh, don't you hear?"

They looked, beyond the wall of soldiers, into the fog, the shapes of the neon lights on great hollow buildings.

People were coming.

XXVIII

The executioner came running, hurtling toward Distan like a missile. His sergeants got in her way, meeting her with their blades but more were coming after her – swarming the devotees from behind, crashing down into the crowd with wave after wave of people armed with tools, screwdrivers, wrenches, anything.

Distan turned his head back to the embassy, focusing his eyes momentarily on Peter.

"Are those... *Tama*?" Jasef, stunned.

"Yes," a rebel voice, "they are. Come on!"

They ran.

So did Distan. In the wrong direction, sideways, towards the embassy's walls – away.

Peter let out a roar of victory, of fury, and chased after him.

"Peter!" yelled Jasef. "No!"

Distan looked back, knew he was being followed, was mobbed briefly by a collection of *tama* armed with tools and dressed in rags but they were nothing to him. Nothing but allowing Peter to catch up.

Peter thrust the spear forward, Distan caught it, and now they were gripping either end of the thing – staring at each other. Peter pulled, bringing Distan briefly toward him with the shaft and then Jasef was by his side with the sickle.

"Yeah?" Distan, looking between them both with an expression of demonic contempt. "Yeah? Come on."

He had let go of his wound, now, was holding out his empty, bloody hands and waiting for an attack. This close, two armed men did not seem like enough.

"Why chase me? Just to stand there?"

Peter lunged forward again but it was just a dive, trying to space himself out from Jasef, communicate somehow to the Green that they should be on either side of the enemy, not directly in front of him.

"Pathetic." Distan began to stalk sideways, arms still out, watching them both as they split apart. Jasef got the hint.

Distan turned his attention to Jasef, seemed to dismiss him outright, focused back on Peter.

He was moving like a spider in a web. Picking on invisible threads, gravity taking him in directions he should not be able to move so lightly, sometimes appearing to be caught in the wind only to end up back where he was, still in that arachnid, hunter's stance.

"Xar's got Ming." He drew out the sound of her name. "They're up on the Vasa." Something must have changed in Peter's face because Distan's became all the more vicious. "She fucks him, you know."

"Ignore him," warned Jasef. "He's lying."

"No I am not. Go see for yourself."

"You just don't want to fight, you coward."

"Got me there," Distan agreed, his tone artificially light. "I don't want to fight. Because if we fight, then one of us dies, and I want to be able to see your face when you realize that she's on our side."

Now it was Peter's turn to laugh. "You dumb fuck," he said. "You fucking fell for that shit? Caralla was going to have you all killed, none of it was real – none of it was even about you. They just wanted to take down that fucking, god thing."

Distan's face had changed, his mouth gone still.

"Yeah, how do you like that!"

"Peter," cautioned Jasef.

"Was?" asked Distan, lowly and levelly.

Neither Peter nor Jasef responded.

"You said, was going to. Didn't you. Is Caralla dead?"

"No." Both.

Distan leered. "Liars. She's dead."

Peter attacked.

Distan was strong but he was wounded, critically. He was dead already, unable to twist his torso and struggling to see despite the god's erratic assistance. Unarmed.

The final blow had been from the sickle. A hacking wound to the side of the neck, from behind, while Peter had him impaled on the cracking spear.

Jasef cried when he was finally down.

It had been hard work for Peter to remove the spear from his still-heaving chest. Twisting it out with the sole of his boot on Distan's sternum as he stared back up at him, an indiscernible something in the shape of his expression, on the tip of his tongue.

"What?" Peter had asked. "What?"

But Distan had not been able to reply.

They stood over the body for a while before Peter decided that was enough. Of gloating, or mourning, or guilt.

"Give me the sickle, Jas."

"What for?"

"Everybody is going to need to know he's dead. Good for morale."

Jasef looked from the sickle, to Peter, to Distan. "No. Absolutely not. That is… barbaric."

Peter closed his eyes. "Come on, don't do this."

"We are not cutting off a dead man's head! A trophy?! Barbaric!"

"Jasef, you tried to cut his head off while he was alive! What the fuck kind of logic is this?"

"That was fair, he was fighting back, then."

No, he wasn't, thought Peter. But what he said was, "Jas just give up now, I'm going to win this one because we do need to show everyone that he's dead. He killed Rama. This will make them feel better, rally them up a bit."

"He did?"

"Yeah."

They were quiet again for a moment.

"No." Peter began again, correcting himself, "I don't know who killed Rama. It could have been anyone. But they both went down and only this motherfucker got back up, so it should be him. That's how it ought."

Jasef nodded, held out the sickle.

"Thanks."

It was not an object designed for hacking through bone. Jasef had to go away.

Severed heads are also a lot heavier and harder to carry than Peter had thought. He realized this had been a terrible idea a minute after beginning but he couldn't admit that. There was too much blood everywhere, he could not get a proper hold of him so had opted for a two-handed, bile-raising carry with the horrible artefact outstretched in front.

"We need to finish them." All the executioner had said, grimmer than ever beneath the massacre of scarring that was her face.

The *tama* hummed as they went. Tuneless, undulating music without rhyme or rhythm or rule. Embassy staff walked between them, mixing with the dead rebel's army with an effortless, wordless comradery. The fear of death and the certainty, beneath it, of victory. Of rightness, and good.

"Vasa!" yelled a *tama* voice, its owner swinging her weapon with the thrill of speech, adding the sound to the flowing buzz of song.

"City!" answered another, choosing whatever Crysthian word had entered his projector mind purely for the joy of saying it.

Peter laughed. He was limping slightly and fighting waves of disgust at his own putrid, iron smell, but he laughed.

"Train!" An embassy blue, feeding the orchestral engine with the noise.

A rebel turned to look at the Military who had spoken, before smiling and shouting, "Home!"

Metal. Moon.

Without pentameter or score. Light. Fruit. Neither chorus nor verse. Fog. Embassy. Words as eternal punctuation, no grammar.

Sword. Ship.

There were more joining them as they went. People who had not been in the fight. Apechi commoners, armed with whatever they could be, mixing tentatively with the *tama* until they went from hundreds to almost a thousand bodies flowing through narrow, haphazard streets. Saying nothing but coming shoulder to shoulder with the enslaved. Standing once again beside people they had grown up with but whom they had been forced to forget. Fearful, searching glances at Rama's rebels. Seeking the forgiveness which they lacked the courage to request.

"Spear!" yelled the executioner.

Nobody but the *tama* could make the hum. It was too scattered, any semblance of a pattern breaking itself before it could be recognized.

It all felt different now. The electric thrum of whatever horrible celestial thing waited for them came thundering like an invitation, a summons, no longer a deep foreboding rumble but a galloping call to arms. The air was charged, and the power was for them.

"Crysth?" Jasef's voice was a suggestion, asking the swelling army's permission to add it.

"Lon Apech!"

One of the *tama* had Distan's head. She was holding it in her shirt, drenched in blood and sweat and toxic dew from the city's reeling fog. Those guarding Kis needed to know, the executioner had said. There are hundreds of them. We need to give them a chance to surrender.

They were emerging into central, now. Still with that same, ever-changing song. Hammer. Tension. Wave.

Lon Apech began to clear. Its cramped, vertical unpredictability giving way into open-spaced gigantism. The mist thinned, giving the flickering neon lights attached to the city's architecture more dominance over its cavernous space.

They were slowing at the front. Peter picked up his pace, swinging the machinegun he had re-acquired onto his shoulder and lurching at an off-center gallop.

"You see them?" The executioner.

He did. Or he saw something. The Vasa with figures on top. Shoving itself into the fog with the tips of its three spiked masts so high as to be obscured. People standing around it, waiting.

Coming towards them through the fog.

Slowly.

"They're not people." Peter, almost to himself.

The executioner was shouting, calling to the legion inching towards them. She had her fingers in Distan's mouth, her thumb pushed carelessly into his butchered neck. Swinging him around by the jaw as she spoke.

"Jasef," said Peter, "get back."

"Why? No. Absolutely not."

Near-screaming now in some Apechi triumph which was making those behind her cheer and yell – the crowd's noise still heightened by the *tama* with their mad, random explosions of sound. Khora raised the head to the advancing figures, spun, threw it – impossibly far, as if it were something designed to be thrown, as if something were pulling it through the air toward the Vasa. It is. It wants its flesh back.

The onslaught lumbered on, unmoved.

"Jasef. I don't think they're people. I mean, I don't think that's people."

* * *

"I need you." Her voice was softer than he had ever heard it before, her arm cradled around his chest.

"It's Khora, Ming. Can't you recognize her voice? It's her."

"Xar," she put her other arm around his waist, pretending she had the strength to hold him. "It won't bring Ustra back."

"No, but it will make me really. Fucking. Happy."

"They have guns."

"They will miss."

The taxidermist was standing by their side, watching over the edge with his fingers curled over the ship. "It was this woman that killed young Ustra?" he asked, genuinely interested. "What spinelessness."

Xar snarled his agreement.

"But the *parak* is right," continued the old man, "we need you. This is…" He hesitated, perhaps in annoyance but with no change in tone, "your city." He was very aware of the horde of people around the Vasa's hull, clinging to it, clinging to Kis.

Ming had not felt Kis relax; she tried to communicate this to the taxidermist with a look, was ignored.

"The god will make them miss." Kis.

"She will die at their hands. There is no escape. She is dead." The promise was a lullaby hushed into the back of his neck. "She's dead."

"Then why can't I do it?"

The sound of the distant woman's shouting, rolling and swelling with her army's support, subsided for a moment. And then something was coming towards them in the mist.

A small, spinning object. Round and apparently accelerating towards the ship.

"Down!" the taxidermist had ducked a moment before Kis and Ming, who were both staring at the advancing shape with a breed of well-mannered curiosity.

They all dropped, the three of them on their hands and knees behind the Vasa's side – tendrils of the god's interest growing over their fingers in ticklish excitement. There was a wet thud as the thing hit the floor.

"It wanted him back," commented the taxidermist, in his tone of passive interest.

"What?" asked Ming, then saw for herself. "Oh, oh shit."

Kis had already scrambled after it, trying to pull his friend's head out of the pulsing layer of flesh which coated much of the Vasa's deck. The god argued with him – sending its low static hum of noise into spikes of annoyance, or playfulness, as he tugged.

"Give, give him!" Kis tried to command.

"Let it have him, Xar." Almost compassionate there from the taxidermist. Ming was impressed.

Kis obeyed, releasing the sides of Distan's face and allowing the crawling skin to send its mouths and stitches and wounds to consume it with their throbbing appetite.

He watched, they all did, but Kis watched without blinking, as if he owed it to Miré to make sure the beast did not waste a drop of him, to stare until every tooth and hair had been crunched in its holy deconstruction.

"Deconstruction." The taxidermist.

Ming will regret not having asked him what that really meant for a very long time.

Kis turned to the two of them. Something far more fearsome than anger in his expression. A vacant, soft acceptance. Horrifying calm. He raised an eyebrow at Ming.

She crawled towards him, placing her hand on his forearm and looking up into the storm on his face.

"Go on then," she said, "but don't you dare die."

"I don't think that's people."

The others were beginning to realize it too, now. There was

something wrong with the way they were coming. Something wrong with their scale and size, something wrong with their shape.

"No. It isn't." The executioner spoke in Crysthian to the men by her side.

Arhythmic humming cushioned them as they stood, but the words were gone.

The things neared, lurching through the mist. Roving, moving beneath the shifting lights as if they, too, were transient, unpalpable things. Thirty, forty of them maybe. No more. But they were larger than the human shape they seemed to be mimicking in a melting, broiling fantasy of being.

"Oh fuck. Oh fuck me, is this a god? Is this your fucking god?" Peter levelled the gun to his hip, changing his stance and taking a few more steps forward.

"Something of it." She turned and raised her voice in frantic Apechi to those assembled now behind them.

"Peter what's going on, what the hell now?" Another embassy Military, surrounded by her comrades.

"They're the magic Agnes warned us about. We'll be alright. Keep going! Don't be fucking scared of it!" He began to fire.

The rest of the Crysthians followed. Calling to each other over the din of song they arranged themselves at the head of the united army, sending their bullets into the square. The people still standing by the Vasa ran, getting to its other side and out of the way of the onslaught. Peter's gun was getting hot, but he could control the pain, concentrating the useful little whatevers in his body to his skin. The action also distracted him from the very real fact that the bullets were doing nothing. That the beasts were still advancing.

Round after round. He stopped. *Jasef* was all he said.

"I know. I know. Take your spear."

"No, give me the sickle. You want the spear. They're big. Don't get close to them, stay out of reach."

Jasef obeyed, turned to look at the executioner who was watching in knowing dread as the last of the gunfire died down.

"Cylinder!" he yelled, suddenly, turning heads towards him. "Bolt, screw, gear!"

The executioner nodded, raised her own voice. "Sand!"

Rock. Square. Water.

"Gris!" yelled Peter, brandishing the sickle in front of him and turning to the embassy staff, screaming his order. "Get around them! Shoot at the people on the fucking ship! Around!"

Birds. Sun.

"Peter!" Peter spun to Jasef's voice, followed his gaze–

"No."

It was Ar. Not Ar. It was Ar's body. A bluish hue, a mass covered in throbbing stitches, moulded together with unfamiliar flesh, all of it writhing like a mass of falling clay. The little pink bird stood out against his dead chest, wings pinned into a permanent sprawl, its beak opening and closing in a flat imitation of song.

But the face. That was worse. It was Ar, but with an expression which could never be imagined to cross his own. It was smiling. A sort of innocent, orgasmic pleasure overwrought by a psychosis in the eyes. A narrowed, studied focus. Rage.

"You bastards!" Jasef ran.

Some of the *tama* followed him. They needed no instruction. They knew what this was, somewhere deeper than marrow.

Peter went after it, too, this towering not-Ar. It needed to go.

The others had made contact too, the humming raised into a scream as they threw themselves into the god's reeking flesh. To live, to kill, or to die and become a part of it.

It killed by biting. The process was slow but inexorable, latching whatever of its orifices could be pulsed to its surface onto the victim's skin and chewing in sickening, insistent pleasure. One of the *tama* had already lost her leg up to the thigh as its mouth expanded around it but was still attacking, going for it at the seams, trying to rip it apart. Her comrades pulled at her, screaming and hitting at it, being absorbed themselves. Jasef was dancing, heeding Peter's advice and needling at it with the end of the spear from as far as he possibly could.

Peter was faster, despite the injury. He could zip in and out of its wheeling arms and pluck at it with the blade of the sickle, teasing and snapping the threads holding it together. They kept at it, kept playing with it. Whatever motivated it kept pushing it back up, inflating and brawling in the cage of its flesh, but they were winning. As they tore it apart its joints became weaker, destabilizing, falling not without life but without strength. Not enough of it together to keep going. It sank into the ground, into rivulets of unsupported, glutinous flesh until Peter could hack at Ar's face – desperate to destroy him, to save him from inhabitation by whatever evil thing had taken him. The bird still screamed.

Another came. This one was even larger than the un-Ar, a great five-armed thing which contained the bodies of animals – tusks and hooves suggesting pigs, horses. The *tama* mobbed it, an onslaught of them, some without weapons, chewing it as it swallowed them, trying to rip bristle from bone with their dying jaws.

Jasef looked around the square, at the seething pockets of battle, people desperately trying to tackle the relentless pending of the liquescent godthings and Kis' real, living allies joining the fray. Kis. His gaze sought the Vasa's deck, up to the ship's prow – a Maroon uniform. Ming.

"Ming!"

Peter had not looked around at the name. He was trying to grab Jasef's attention too. "Come on!" he was saying. "Over there!"

Jasef followed his finger to the executioner, standing not ten feet in front of Xar Kis. He clutched a silver railway spike in one hand and a hoop of golden chain in the other. She ran at him, Peter lurched forward–

"No! Peter, listen, listen!"

Peter turned. "What, what?! He's right there!"

"Ming is on the Vasa! Ming is on the ship!"

The light in Peter's eyes changed, he looked up. "Where?"

"I just, I just saw her. I swear. She's up there."

Peter shook his head. "We can't, we've got to get Kis, we've got to–"

"No, listen! She can get us back into the embassy. She can talk to Military."

"Fuck." The larger man turned again, looking at the whirling mass of aggression which had become of Kis and the new rebel leader. He was winning. Peter could tell just by how much they were both moving; Kis seemed to be making barely an effort, glancing every strike of her spear with a careless flick of the wrist. "Hey!" he yelled, addressing the nearest group of *tama* and embassy staff which were mobbing one of the godbeasts, this one made of scales, reeking of infection and brine, fins and giant, unblinking black eyes. "Hey!" the embassy staff turned to the familiar voice. "Look!" he yelled. "Get Kis! Get Kis!"

Finally, they saw. Half of them split, running after the instruction, running to save the executioner in her final moments.

"Come on." Back to Jasef, now, grabbing the man by the shoulder and heaving him along to the Vasa.

"Are they... alive?" asked Ming, watching by the taxidermist's side.

"No."

"Are they dead?"

"No."

She thought about it. "Do they act like they did before?"

"Before the god took them?" this seemed to puzzle him. "I suppose so."

The last of them slinked over the side of the ship, not yet humanoid but just a mass of creeping flesh. Smacking into the concrete below, piling upon itself. Hair and shell, the eternally gaping mouths of predatory sea-things, birds, hands. They broiled together, pouring over the edge and pushing themselves upright, begging themselves into the shape of legs and a torso and as many arms as it could manage at once. Onward.

"Have you seen Kis fight before?" asked the taxidermist.

"Yes. But only for fun." She waited, and when the man did not say anything more, she continued, "He'll kill her."

"You were not sure."

"I am sure. I just don't want him out of my sight, or injured."

"Wise. I assume you have worked out what you are going to say to the Military interveners?"

"No," she said, beginning to walk towards the prow of the ship. He followed her. "I need to know who is left first, how much the embassy staff know. What Caralla has already said. We may need to execute the survivors."

"Should you not have a rough idea?" he answered.

"Not yet. If I think too much about it now then I might get attached to an aspect of the process that no longer works with new information. It's harder to rearticulate an old lie than to form a new one."

"You better be right."

They could still see Kis, a figure without features but Kis nonetheless, standing in front of Ustra's murderer.

They attacked each other. She was a whirling circle with her spear, he was slow and controlled.

"See," she said to the taxidermist, "he's… fine."

But suddenly Kis was surrounded, alone. Enemies were heaving around him, seeming to have noticed all at once that he had come down from the safety of the Vasa. Waves and waves of them just throwing themselves at him, embassy staff trying to get a shot, the executioner dancing backward for breath as they worked to exhaust him.

* * *

Jasef reached the Vasa's ladder first, zipping out of the way as Peter punctured what remained of the loiterers by the ship. Peter was getting stronger as he moved, adrenaline carrying the empire's guarded innovations around his body. He spat blood and sweat, throwing down the sickle in exchange for a long, fine dagger dropped by one of the faithful.

Jasef turned back to the ladder, the spear slipping in his hand as he tried to climb.

"You've got it," he heard Peter say beneath him. "I'm behind you."

He couldn't see. Up on the deck, not a thing. His hair was in his eyes and he didn't have a hand free. He pushed the spear onto the ship and wiped his face –

"Jasef?"

The taxidermist wheeled around before Ming spoke, saw the man emerging over the edge of the vessel. He dived towards the ladder, grabbed the intruder by the front of the shirt and heaved him bodily onto the deck, throwing him forward into the layer of godflesh still pulsing around the masts.

Jasef rolled, onto his side and upright. Turned back to face his assailant with his hands outstretched as if to defend himself but the old priest broke straight through him, punching in a single, precise jab aimed straight at his throat. It collapsed, flattened by the force of the blow and Jasef crumpled again, clutching at his deflated neck and choking on his own body, gasping with sickening, inhumanly guttural pain while he died.

"No!" Peter was up, on the deck and on the taxidermist's back before the man could even turn around, wrestling with him and stabbing mercilessly, repeatedly at his chest with the defeated soldier's blade.

Ming staggered backwards, mouth open. She looked briefly over to where the *tama* were still swarming over Kis and realized that she was alone. She tried her gauntlet – nothing. Just weak little zaps of electricity as the demon revelled in the heaven which faith had afforded it.

She leapt forward, pulling at Peter's arm and screaming for him to stop.

"What the fuck are you doing!" Peter howled, managed against pain and hope to get the old man down onto the crawling, shifting deck, kicking at the back of his knees with his arm still wrapped around his neck.

"Stop! He's controlling it, he's controlling it! Stop!"

But it was too late. In its endless, fickle or incomprehensible desire one of the thing's many mouths had latched on to a bleeding hole ripped fresh in the taxidermist's waist. It sucked and chewed, audible above the buzzing soundlessness of its presence; a wet, fertile smell of soil and meat and body and ooze.

Peter pushed Ming away and dived over to Jasef, pulling the suffocated, juniper-clad body away from the inquisitive vines of patchwork flesh.

More and more mouths were converging on the taxidermist, now. Ming had him by the shoulders. She screamed and pulled but all she could do was watch it latch onto his face, masticating jaw and tongue and teeth until the taxidermist's screaming was nothing but a lubricated bubbling in the throat. She backed away, watching in cold, unbelieving dread as the body was consumed.

She kept going, backing up, looking to Peter who was cradling Jasef's abandoned body. Expressionless, tearful, bereft.

"He fought, Ming, he was fighting the whole time. If it wasn't for him none of us would know what the fuck is going on. He didn't even know how to use the gun I gave him. He was fighting the whole fucking time."

"He was brave," she said, aiming for conciliatory while focusing her eyes on the forgotten dagger.

"I called him a coward."

"It doesn't matter." She began to edge towards him, trying not to look at the weapon and give her intentions away. "He knew he wasn't."

He looked up at her, stopping her in her tracks. "What happened to your hands?"

"What?"

"Your hands," he said, his tone going strange, "they're... black."

Ming went to dive forward and so did he, but at that moment something crashed into the deck between them – shocking them both back away from the sound.

The executioner rolled into the godflesh, the railway spike still thrust into her neck and out of her gaping mouth, but she wasn't dead.

"Oh, shit!" Peter scrambled onto his feet.

Kis' hands had already emerged onto the deck, pulling the rest of him back aboard his ship.

"Oh, shit," repeated Peter, looking from him to Ming to the dagger.

Kis showed his grey teeth in a leering smile. "Hello, comrade. How are you?"

"You shut the fuck up. You don't fucking talk to me."

Kis laughed in response, turned to Ming. "Where is the old man?"

"It ate him."

Kis paused. Looked at Peter as if for confirmation. Then, slowly, "It ate him?"

The executioner gargled.

"Xar. It ate him."

Peter looked wildly between them both, said Ming's name. She ignored him. The executioner died on the floor.

"It. Ate. Him?" repeated Kis.

"How many times do you want me to tell you?" Ming said, her voice rising as she straightened her body, "It ate him. It chewed him up. He is gone."

"Then who is controlling it?" Xar.

"Fuck is going on?" Peter.

"I don't know." Ming answered the first question but her

answer worked for either. She looked over the deck, towards the ambling flesh monoliths which stalked the square, sucking and writhing at the united army. "Gods," she shot Kis a rueful smile, "I think it might be them."

They started to laugh.

"Ming?" Peter again. "What's going on?"

But the pair were just laughing. Xar brought his grin over to her but she held up her hand to keep him away. "Wait."

"Ming?" Peter.

She looked over at him. "I'm sorry, I'm just so," she paused again to laugh, "it's just so funny, isn't it?"

He stared.

"Peter," she began, suddenly serious, "where are Caralla and Agnes?"

He stared back. Eyes whipped to Kis and back to her, down to her hands. "Embassy."

Ming smiled. "Are they dead, Peter? I need to know. Crysth needs to know what happened here."

"Military are coming. I'll tell them."

"I don't think you will." The words rolled from Xar's tongue as if they were kind.

"They're dead," decided Ming, lowering her hand and finally allowing Kis to do what he had wanted, to pull her into him, for her to lap at the executioner's blood at his throat.

"No." Peter breathed, "No fucking way. Ming. Ming!"

She looked over at Peter, looked back to Kis. As if she was bored, wondering why Peter was even still there.

"Him?! Not him. You're choosing him?!"

Her expression changed, fell into a disturbed confusion which had her tilt her head to the side as she said, "You think that's what this is?"

The soldier couldn't bear it any longer.

Peter lunged, springing himself forward at that phenomenal speed and even then he was caught by Kis' left hand. He tried to punch with his other arm but was caught again. Ming turned, disinterested, began to ascend the steps to the wheel as they grappled. She had a massive fucking explanation to come up with and needed space to think. Her mouth tasted like metal.

She heard his boots on the steps behind her at the same moment in which she spotted a distant, blue light in the sky. It punctured the fog to the left of Apech's weak moon, advancing slowly towards them through the unimaginable volume of space.

He stood behind her, breathing heavily and reeking of everything.

"They're coming?" asked Kis, looking up at the same, faraway light.

"Yes," she answered him, running her painted fingers along the Vasa's wheel. "And we are waiting."

1

"In the mind of the rebel, laws do not have eyes."
– Swazembian Proverb, Sangha, circa 5051

The dance of water had ended. The swirls of purple, the swishes of yellow and green, spilled over Swazembi's upper Sangha province and dissolved into vapors. Lileala wasn't physically there, witnessing the spectacle, but she could feel it, nonetheless. Her intuition always peaked during the summer rains, and she had a way of sensing their patterns, the way they swarmed, swelled and spiraled.

When the rains finished, she knew. She saw the signs. Above her in The Outer Ring, the planet's tourist center, the jacaranda trees unfolded, and scraps of violet petals trickled through the air shafts into the underground city of Boundary Circle. The petals were strewn along the private outdoor track where Lileala was stretching and running. The sparse petals were a distraction, disturbing her focus as she ran past. She hadn't seen the Surface since she was an elder-child of twenty-six, but she could recall it clear as water; the flowers thrusting into the warm winds, the tree branches whipped into a long frenzy.

She slowed her pace to a trot and thought hard about stealing a glimpse. If only she could come up with a way to sneak out. She glanced over her shoulder, then searched both ends of the track. There was no trace of her trainer. Good.

Slipping a finger through the small, glowing halo above

her wrist, she whispered, "Otto? Otto, are you there? Otto?"

The halo shimmied in rapid circles, but it didn't produce an image, not even a foggy one.

She hurried past the five-kilometer marker.

"Otto," she whispered again. "I'm on track level Y, but I'm sneaking off. Be there in a few minutes."

Lileala darted toward the end of the track, ignoring the colors that suddenly began flickering beneath her feet. The colors chased her, brushing against her shoes the way water folds around the heels of a swimmer. The faster she moved, the faster they came. They raced up her shoelaces, then billowed and foamed just above her ankles.

"That's it, I give up," she said, sighing. She wanted to laugh, and maybe she would have, if the situation hadn't been so annoying.

"Okay!" she yelled out again. "Baba Malik, I know you can hear me! The Drifts. Call off the drifting colors, will you? Please?"

The colors withered. Then Malik turned the corner wearing the expression he always did when he accused her of being lazy. "Lileala Walata Sundiata! I take one short break and you're giving up already? You've been training for a mere thirty minutes."

"Is it your dial?" Lileala asked, scanning his wrist. "Is that how you knew?"

"No, Miss Rare Indigo." He pointed to a clear cord that was clamped to his collar and draped over his left shoulder. Colors were fluttering from a rear opening of the device and onto the floor of the track. "I had this made just for sly ones like you. If the heart rate slows or you get too far out of my range, it syncs with the Sea of Vapors. Then –" he made a sucking noise, "– swish! It suctions drifts right out of the Surface."

Disgust disguised itself as a smile on Lileala's face, but she knew it lacked the sweetness of her real smile. It felt rigid, and the dimples that normally pinched her cheeks were absent.

"Clever. But I don't like that thing; it's tacky." She wiped her hands on the sides of her leggings and ran them through the coils of her hair. They spilled around her temples in scattered clusters. "How does it work, anyway? What is it? I mean, what's it called?"

Malik gave her another disapproving glance. "Doesn't matter. If you'd stop slipping off, I wouldn't need it. Honestly, I didn't have these problems with your predecessor."

"That's not what I heard."

"What?"

"Nothing."

"I heard you," Malik scoffed. "And just so you know, Ahonotay may have been silent, but she was not uncooperative."

"But Ataba Malik, I'm tired of exercising. And I need to see someone."

"Is that so?" he asked. "Rushing off to see Otto again?"

"Is it okay?"

"Sure, if you want to contend with this!" Malik waved his fingers around his device and laughed as skinny streaks of red drizzled down his back and formed webs around Lileala's feet.

"Ataba!" she yelled. "Stop doing that!"

"Just having a little fun with you." He sighed, "Go on then, but be back in Point Two Hours; and if you're not, you're going to run even harder."

"Okay, okay." Lileala glanced at her dial. The halo in the center of the dial device was spiraling and taking on the outline of a face. "Otto, finally. I'm leaving, but I'm stopping by The Ring first. Be there shortly."

"What?" Otto whispered. "Lileala, it's midday. You can't –"

With a shake of her wrist, he vanished. Lileala concentrated and blocked out his attempts to reappear. She wanted to stroll through The Outer Ring on her way to see him. If she didn't avoid him, he'd try to talk her out of it. Diving into her satchel, she pulled out a string of amber beads and a yard of patterned cloth that she wrapped around her lower body. Her fitted leg liners weren't suitable for public appearance, but the woven textile would hide them.

After tying a knot at her waist, she tossed the beads around her hips and bolted down the track, her pulse skipping. She could almost see the Surface, the fresh storm of colors spreading before her in a bouquet of drifts and hills.

At the exit, a limestone path forked east and west. Lileala headed west, took a lift to the nearest Sweep Station and hurried. Passengers were in line on a platform facing a vast span of airspace and were already preparing to board. She panted and ran. But just as she stepped onto the ramp of the platform, a cloud of energy funneled upwards and sped off. She had missed the Point Two Sweep.

"No, no!" she shouted, despite knowing that no one was there to hear her or care. She sulked and continued up the sixteen-meter ramp to the boarding area. The station was more of an atrium, open-roofed with iridescent floors and high walls shrouded in green ivy. In contrast, a fusion of cranberry and yellow stones brightened the ramp and all four platforms.

Rather than take a seat, Lileala stood near the edge and leaned against a steel railing. Out of habit, she yanked a palm-sized mirror from her satchel and toyed with the tight coils of her hair, watching as each strand pooled into a teeny loop and bounced back in place. She loved her hair's buoyancy, though it was her complexion that was most celebrated. It was the height of Indigo: a shimmering blue-blackness that Indigo Host, Mama Xhosi, described as coal kissed by the sun.

Lileala looked skyward, wondering how long she'd have to wait. She inched away from the railing and paced, hands on her hips. A family of locals joined her, but the man, woman and minor-child were so busy fussing over an infant curled in the woman's arm, it took a few minutes for them to glance at Lileala and gasp. She heard the woman whisper, "Is that her? Is it really her?"

Mirror in hand, Lileala checked her appearance again and flashed the family a smile. Their adoration reminded her that before long she'd be an actual showpiece. At her Eclipse Ceremony, set to happen in just three months, she would be ushered into The Nobility's palatial headquarters, The Grand Rising, and declared the first Rare Indigo in four decades. She would be the only woman in Boundary Circle's cloistered society allowed to escort visiting dignitaries on guided tours, and she would stand beside The Nobility during their bi-annual speeches or when they attended interplanetary functions within The Outer Rings. She would be the ultimate idol. One of Swazembi's main attractions.

While Lileala was still doting on herself, The Sweep barreled into the station. Raising both arms, she surrendered to the suction of the cloud, letting it pull her inside. The family followed and along with Lileala settled in a short distance from three female passengers who were already on board. One was local, swaddled in a body wrap of gold fabric. The others were dressed tourist-style in body-hugging trousers that no local woman would ever consider wearing.

Lileala always considered their undignified attire strange, but deep down she admired it, just because it was disrespectful. She wondered what it would feel like to be as free of oaths and codes as they were. The two tourists floated upright, wobbling and giggling, and she tried to guess where they originated – from Jemti? No. Not with faces the color of clouds and chins that narrowed to a sharp point. Lileala figured them to be residents of Toth, Swazembi's ally world.

Positioning herself flat on her belly, she allowed The Sweep's magnetic winds to propel her forward. Sweep energy was like a friendly storm swooshing through an invisible tunnel, just below the upper circumference of the underground. Lileala swam through the moving currents until she was adjacent to the Swazembian woman who lay flat just like her while the force transported them to the next station. They arrived at an atrium and The Sweep dipped without jerking and deposited all of the passengers on a platform ramp just above The Outer Ring.

At the end of the ramp, everyone but Lileala boarded a moving skywalk and rode it down to Ring Two, Concourse

B30. Lileala stopped at the entrance to the concourse and tried to unlock her stubborn lips. The best she could do was a half-smile. She was still aggravated about Baba Malik's peculiar device and had to fight to stomp it out of her mind. That was the only way she'd be able to summon a hint of Shimmer.

She pushed air through one nostril, releasing gently. After the second breath, she wore wisps of pale light, almost imperceptible. The very first stage of Shimmer. A tourist was loitering and staring at her. She was obliged to act cheerful and demonstrate a shine, however frail. "Waves of joy," she said, letting a full smile replace the half one.

"My stars, you're lovely," the man answered. He was stout, dressed in rumpled trousers and a crude, rubbery jacket made of animal skin, probably a relic from Earth.

"Thank you," she said and gave him a gracious nod. The man continued, "Are all the women of Swazembi like you?"

"All of us are dark, if that's what you mean?"

He gawked and extended a hand. "Dalton, from West Neptune. My first time here. It took a while for me to finally get acceptance stamps." He bared both wrists to reveal two glowing green lines, then he gazed over her head and down a busy aisle of pedestrians. "I just love it here."

"Grace to you," Lileala said, fake smile still in place. She wished he would hurry up and be on his way.

"And, bless the stars, you have the best music chips here too. I understand all of it's from Earth," he went on. "Too bad, don't you think, that those people were so reckless."

"Yes, too bad," Lileala shrugged. She wasn't nearly as intrigued by Earth history as the tourists were. She always wondered why some locals believed that Earth was part of Swazembian history. She found the idea ridiculous.

Dalton kept rambling: "It's been thousands of years, and no one's been able to figure out how they destroyed themselves. Sometimes, I think there might be clues in the music. What do you think?"

"I don't know," Lileala said. "Maybe you should visit the tourist knowledge haven. It has information about the whole galaxy." She took a slow sidestep toward the concourse.

"But listen," Dalton stood in place. "I hear your people are planning more visits to Earth's ruins and are digging up more music. Do you get to go?"

"No. Never been." Lileala answered in a tone that no longer hid her lack of interest. She was fighting the urge to reach for her compact and check the tidiness of the scarlet paint she had smeared onto her lips.

Dalton's eyes were a blizzard of questions. Lileala could see them examining her and she noted that at least he was careful not to intrude her personal space.

"I think I saw a report on the viewerstream about ladies who glitter like you," he said. "You're one of those Indigo Aspirants, aren't you?"

"I'm no longer an Aspirant. I'm the Rare Indigo."

He stared.

"But, well, I guess I misunderstood. Doesn't the Rare One have to be at least fifty?"

"I am. We live till we're nearly five hundred here."

For a moment, Dalton didn't react.

"Um, you look n-nineteen, miss," he stuttered. He walked away wagging his head.

The Outer Ring was a jumble of chatter and the wails of reconstructed Earth horns. Lileala flowed with the melody and waded into the crowd nearly unnoticed. Most of the tourists were distracted by the gliding crystal floors they were riding on and by gift havens that hung from the ceiling in ten-foot glass globes. The globes were stationary boutiques among a banquet of jewels that shimmied, flickered and opened and closed like hundreds of sparkling eyes. Gusts of pink sugar swarmed from the windows of confection stores. Rock songs blasted from octagon dance havens.

Oval hotels, encrusted with amber and opal, spun in place like stranded planets. Tourists looked up, then down, their heads twisting, their senses competing to take it all in.

Lileala scuttled past them all and entered one of the smaller, slower-moving orbs for a twist of sweet cassava and a few chunks of hard molasses. Right away, she flinched. The interior of the confection haven wasn't misted with colored sugar like most and, judging from the empty shelves, the majority of the inventory had been cleared out long ago. She approached the counter that was being tended by a man with a bewildered stare. He might have been handsome, she thought, if not for the confusion on his face.

"You are the rare girl, no?" the merchant said. It sounded more like an accusation than a question.

"Yes, I am," she said. She looked around and nodded. The haven was plain, but one showcase near the counter was packed with cocoa-sprinkled pine nuts. She stepped beside it and peeked inside.

"I recognized you soon as you walked in," the merchant continued. "But I don't understand. Rare One, why are you here?"

"For this," Lileala pointed to a square of molasses next to the pine nuts. "And for…"

He spoke over her. "That is not for sale. Not to you."

"What? Did you say…?"

"I said no sale," he said. "The sweets cannot go to you."

"Pardon me?" Her voice shook.

"I know who you are, and I have made my decision," he said.

In defiance, Lileala showed him a sheer marble the width of a thumbnail. The marbles in her allotment were larger than most, fashioned from pure, sand-blown glass and laced with colors from the Surface, colors that were fresh and still in motion.

"There's no need to offer payment," he said. He flattened the palms of his hands on the glass countertop.

To calm herself, Lileala bit down on her lip and glared. He watched her with an equal amount of indignation.

"I'm told that as the Rare Indigo you are not to have sweets," he said after a pause. "Be on your way."

"No," Lileala said. She held up her marble and waited. "I would like four chunks of molasses, please. I'm not leaving without them."

The merchant scowled. Reaching for a gauze sack from beneath the counter, he filled it so fast a couple of pieces toppled onto the floor.

"Here, take it." He thrust the sack in front of her. "And keep your payment."

She fiddled with the marble and shoved it at him. "You can't tell me what to do."

"Young one, you are not yet official," he said. "I suggest humility."

"I suggest you leave me alone," Lileala said in between breaths. She was trying to maintain her glow and add more firmness to her voice. "I'll complete my Eclipse ceremony three months from now. Until then, I don't have to stick to restrictions. And I don't have to listen to you."

A group of tourists wandered into the haven and the man fell silent while Lileala dropped the marble on the counter and moved back, her smile gone.

The merchant looked her directly in the eye. "I meant no harm, but you must be mindful. You are the first Rare One in a long while. That means you…"

"That means I listen only to The Nobility and to The Uluri," Lileala said, then breathed deep. Dim twinkles seeped from the pores of her skin then flit across her forehead. She pulled in her ribcage and the twinkles became a soft blue spritz.

"I'm the Rare Indigo, yes," she added. "But I'm still a person."

The merchant said nothing, and she knew she had made her point. She snatched her sweets and hurried off.

Outside the haven, his insults clung like tar. Was he

suggesting that she had dishonored The Grace of the Ancestors? With what? A sack of molasses? Lileala bristled. She knew it was unorthodox for a Rare Indigo to yield to useless desire, particularly for a thing so common among the villagers. But The Nobility had not granted merchants the right to chastise her. Had they?

While the merchant gawked through the window, Lileala tucked a music chip in her ear and poured herself back into the highway of pedestrians. They swept around then past her, moving like a single organism. She shuffled through them, again unnoticed. Onlookers were drawn by the noisy aroma of spiced chickpeas, the knit caps with "The Sweep" emblazoned on the front, and stretchy shirts labeled "EarthWear".

Content, she moved on, undisturbed, and took an automated walkway to a spot that offered a panoramic view of the grounds below. At a drop of one hundred and twenty meters was Mamadou Park, the only region in The Outer Ring with enough gum trees to make up a small forest. Lulled by the view, Lileala lingered. The guard rails around the area were sturdy, easy to prop her back against while she peeked at her dial. She'd wasted too much time in the confection haven, she knew she needed to get moving. She didn't care. At the moment, she wanted to do what she felt like doing. And she felt like lounging in the park overlook before visiting Otto.

ANGRY ROBOT

We are Angry Robot

angryrobotbooks.com